Stolen in Paradise

A Lei Crime Companion Novel

Stolen in Paradise

A Lei Crime Companion Novel

Toby Neal

Stolen in Paradise

ISBN 978-0-9891489-1-7

Photo credit: Mike Neal © Nealstudios.net
Cover Design: © JULIE METZ LTD.

Book design by Mythic Island Press LLC

Ecclesiastes 3:1
There is a time for everything,
and a season for every activity under heaven:
a time to be born, and a time to die.

Chapter 1

The smell—seaweed with overnotes of decomp—hit Special Agent Marcella Scott as she ducked under the crime-scene tape roping off a rocky corner of Waikiki Beach. A woman's body was wedged between slippery boulders, waves rocking her in a parody of a lullaby.

Marcella squatted between the boulders for a better look at the bullet hole set between the woman's brows like a misplaced Indian *bindi*. The expression on her face was one of astonishment—mouth ajar, eyes wide and opaque. Iron-gray hair tangled over utilitarian clothing split in unsightly places.

The body still wore a plastic ID tag on a lanyard, and it was the name on it—Dr. Trudy Pettigrew—that had the Honolulu Police Department calling in the FBI. Pettigrew was on a short list of researchers who worked for the University of Hawaii on security-sensitive projects.

Marcella glanced up at Matt Rogers, her partner. "Looks like an execution."

"Yep. I'm wondering if this lady scientist was working on something that got her killed." Rogers, an ex-military man, was from the Texas Panhandle and clung to a drawl even after five years in the islands.

"She was a biologist. Maybe her project was involved." Marcella straightened up, catching the uniformed patrol officer with his eyes on her ass. Not without reason—it was the best Italian heritage and Tae Kwon Do could brew up. She tucked the tail of her plain white blouse back into light gray trousers. "Maybe it was a crime of passion."

Rogers just snorted, folding his muscled arms. The substantial body before them seemed the antithesis of passion. "I don't think we can find much else here. No sign that this is the original crime scene."

The medical examiner, Dr. Fukushima, a prim-looking Japanese woman in a wide sun hat, had been fussing with the body bag and her supplies, waiting for them to finish. Marcella shot the scene and a few more photos with her point-and-shoot, including a pano spread of the high-rise hotels fronted by calm turquoise water, the gleaming beach, and colorful carved dragon boats and canoes pulled onto the sand nearby.

Just beyond the site was the Waikiki Yacht Harbor, sunshine sparkling off the boats—and the mouth of the Ala Wai Canal, a water conduit that ran through downtown Honolulu. She shot that too. Context was important.

She turned to the ME. "Thanks so much, Dr. Fukushima, for waiting on us."

"No problem," the doctor said. "I'll let you know what I find when I've completed my report." The medical examiner picked her way carefully among the slippery rocks to squat beside the body, opening a black old-fashioned doctor's bag. She covered the woman's hands, slipping rubber bands over clear plastic bags. She then got out a pair of scissors and gestured to her assistant. "Let's roll the body."

"Want some help?" Rogers asked when the assistant, a young

woman, and Dr. Fukushima failed to turn the heavy corpse. With the three of them putting some heave into it, what was left of Dr. Trudy Pettigrew flopped with a splash facedown. Dr. Fukushima wielded her scissors and added a coup de grace of indignity by inserting a thermometer deep into the rectum.

Marcella looked away—she wasn't squeamish, but she sensed how much this particular woman would have hated being this kind of spectacle. "I'm thinking she was shot somewhere else and washed up here."

"You heard me say it first." Rogers gestured toward the ocean. "Could've been anywhere out there." Marcella looked back as Dr. Fukushima wiped off the thermometer and stowed it in a plastic sleeve.

"She's warming up again with decomp starting. Rigor's come and gone, so it's been at least twenty-hour hours since she went into the water." Fukushima looked up at them, must have read Marcella's expression. "I don't like doing liver temps." The ME referred to making a small incision in the sternum and inserting the thermometer there. "Rectum is just as accurate, and later on in the post, I haven't damaged the liver."

It took Rogers, a uniformed police officer, the assistant, and Dr. Fukushima to roll and heave the slippery, waterlogged corpse into the body bag. Marcella winced at the spectacle and strode over to the pair of detectives originally assigned to the case, who'd been standing in the thin shade of a palm tree. She let her dimpled smile and shiny teeth wreak some havoc as she snapped off a latex glove and shook Detective Ching's hand and that of his partner, Detective Kamuela.

"Thanks again for calling us, guys. I'm sure we're going to be able to work well together on this. What do you know so far?"

"Uniforms called us in, said there was a body. We came down, secured the site, radioed in the ID from the tag, and that's when the captain called you. Not much to it." Kamuela, a tall, muscular

Hawaiian, was doing the Tiki-god face thing and resisting her dimple. Marcella flicked her eyes to his left hand. No wedding ring.

"The University of Hawaii has some scientists working on sensitive projects. Dr. Pettigrew is one of them." Marcella unbuttoned the top button of her blouse, fanned herself with the file she'd quickly printed off on Dr. Pettigrew. "Hot down here on the beach."

When she looked up, Ching appeared hypnotized. That was how she liked them—easily controlled. Kamuela cut narrowed eyes to her, apparently unimpressed.

"So what did you learn from the scene?" Marcella asked.

"Not much. Seems like the lady was shot, pushed into the ocean somewhere, maybe off a boat or something. Nothing on her, so maybe it was robbery, but a head shot seems extreme for that. Shoes still on. We were thinking she washed up here," Kamuela replied.

"Good summary." Rogers reappeared behind Marcella. He was spattered with seawater, rings of sweat marking his arms. "Let's go somewhere more comfortable, get a plan."

They moved to a nearby hotel umbrella/table combo and eventually sent the detectives to canvass along the hot Waikiki beach. The two agents got back into the air-conditioning of the Bureau's Acura SUV to head to the University of Hawaii to find out what Dr. Pettigrew had been working on. Rogers got behind the wheel.

"Damn, Marcella. Thought you were going to give Ching a hemorrhage with those shirt buttons."

"Just spicing up their day a bit." Marcella unbuttoned a few more buttons, leaned in to the blasting AC with her eyes closed in bliss. "Sucks to be in FBI uniform when everyone else is running around in chinos and golf shirts."

"They let us stop wearing ties, and the sleeves are short. Don't know what else we could get away with in the Bureau."

Marcella wiggled a brow and dusted sand off her low-heeled Manolo T-straps—regulations called for closed-toe shoes, and the delicate leather sandals barely qualified. She worked the computer on its drop-down panel/glove box as Rogers drove toward the University of Hawaii. "Pettigrew was one of their most respected professors," Marcella read off the university website. "Taught biotechnology and biochemistry. Her specialty was bioengineering with agriculture. Doesn't sound too dangerous."

"Lotta people feel strongly about genetically modified organisms around here. Maybe she had a hater."

University of Hawaii Manoa wasn't far from Waikiki, but it might as well have been another world. They left the hot, busy streets bordered by high-rises and drove into a lush green valley. Low-key buildings spread along both sides of the road, separated by pockets of trees and verdant courtyards. Lawns rolled away from the road, and spreading monkeypod trees made cool oases of shade speckled with students.

"Maybe, but that's a pretty serious hater. Says here she did contract work for AgroCon Ltd. Gonna have to look into what they were working on." Marcella brushed her long, curling brown hair and repinned it into what she called the FBI Twist, a smooth roll at the back of her head. She rebuttoned her blouse into professional as Rogers pulled into one of the stalls in front of the dignified Agricultural Science Building. They got out, each carrying an investigation kit in black leather, and headed up the cement steps.

That's when they were ambushed.

"Marcella!" A screech somewhere between operatic and fishwife rent the air. "*Bambina*, darling! What you doing here?"

Marcella barely had time to brace herself before ninety-five pounds of energetic Italian mother catapulted out of nowhere and enfolded her in a hug. Anna Scatalina, formerly a fashion plate in New Jersey, had taken on the muumuu-and-slippers look of

Hawaii with a vengeance. Today's muumuu was a fitted sheath in bright yellow spattered with plumeria print, and the sandals were heeled, glittering with rhinestones. She and Marcella shared a shoe fetish fed by the flow of her father Egidio Scatalina's shoe-import business.

"Mama! Good God! What are you doing here?"

"'Cella! You know I'm a culinary student. I've told you a hundred times. What *you* doing here?"

"Ma, it's a case. Can't talk about it." Marcella straightened her shirt, detaching herself.

"Oh, Mattie, good to see you!" Anna Scatalina reached up and patted Rogers's granitelike jaw, making him blush. "We making nice chicken coq au vin at the student cafeteria for lunch. You come? I serve you."

"Mrs. Scatalina, I would love some of anything you're making. I'm sure we can fit it in."

Marcella glared at her partner as she tucked loose hair bits back in. Her mother patted Rogers's arm, wide, dark eyes sparkling. "Oh good. I see you then. Both of you." She shook her finger at Marcella. "You come. You never eat my cooking."

"It's fattening, Ma," Marcella said, and sighed as her mother flitted, canarylike, in her lurid yellow muumuu toward the adjacent building. "I don't know how she never gains weight. Guess I know where we're eating lunch."

"I like her." Rogers turned back toward the entrance of the building. "You must take after your dad."

"Gee, thanks. And no, not really." Marcella pushed the stiff glass door open. "I'm something of an abomination, if you ask either of my grandmothers."

"Something I've been meaning to ask you. Why did you change your last name?" His question echoed off the tiled floor of the foyer as Marcella scanned a wall-mounted directory for the biotechnology department. "Scatalina has a nice ring to it."

"Scott sounds better." She'd spotted the listing. "Two floors up."

"I beg to differ. The Bureau would love to identify yet another agent as not only female, but ethnic, any kind of ethnic."

"Scott sounds better—people don't ask questions about it. And there's this: Scatalina means 'little shit' in Italian."

They got into the elevator.

"You're kidding me, right?" Rogers didn't bother to suppress a huge grin. "I know what I'm calling you from now on."

"Don't even try it."

The elevator doors opened and Marcella stepped out into a beige hallway shining with state-funded janitorial effort—which was to say, drab, dingy, and deserted. They strode past locked, windowless doors marked with keypads to the biotech lab.

The door was marked with a Far Side cartoon and a small whiteboard that pronounced in bold capitals, Dr. Pettigrew is not in.

"Ya think?" said Rogers, pointing to the note.

Marcella knocked.

Chapter 2

The door opened and a tall young man looked at them through floppy black hair. His Adam's apple bobbed.

"Help you?"

"We're here about Dr. Pettigrew," Marcella said. She and Rogers held up their cred wallets. The man's dark eyes flashed back and forth between them, and Marcella could swear she saw him memorizing every jot on the IDs.

"Come in." He backed up and they stepped inside. Once again the smell hit her first, an ammonia cleaner and something dark, like burnt plastic. Marcella put her hands on her hips, did a slow survey of a large room laid out with long steel tables topped by shelves.

That was where the resemblance to anything familiar ended—boxy contraptions sprouting wires, racks of tubes, jumbled logbooks, pipettes, and glassware crowded the counters. Round, humming white freezers squatted in a row. A venting system dangled elephantine flexible piping over each workstation.

A woman and two men communed with microscopes as harp music massaged the atmosphere. Marcella was about to shatter the focused, peaceful work environment, and she felt a twinge of regret. Breaking bad news was one of her least-favorite parts of the job.

"I'm Jarod Fernandez," the young man said. He flapped a white-gloved hand at them. "Sterile. Can't shake."

He made a sound with his throat, almost a cough. His white lab coat confirmed his identity with a small block-printed patch that proclaimed FERNANDEZ. Marcella no longer found men in lab coats attractive and almost forcibly suppressed a memory of a time when that had been far from the case.

"That's fine. Can you gather your colleagues? We're hoping to get some information regarding an investigation involving Dr. Pettigrew," Rogers said.

Fernandez went to the sound system and punched the Off button on an iPod.

"These FBI agents have some questions," he announced to the room at large.

Three heads swiveled their way, eyes blinking in what was clearly an adjustment to intrusion from the outside world. The woman, a rounded brunette, turned off her mysterious equipment and rolled her stool over in front of the agents.

"Cindy Moku," she said. "What's this about?" She had thick, lustrous long hair in a braid and a classically beautiful Hawaiian face with dark, long-lashed eyes and a mouth with a curl to it, even though she wasn't smiling.

The other two men had joined them.

"I'm wondering, too," the short, dark one said, almost vibrating with energy. "I'm Zosar Abed. Something up with Dr. Pettigrew? She didn't come in yesterday—is something wrong?"

"Let them ask the questions," the square-built Korean one said, adjusting black-framed glasses over his nose. "My name's Peter Kim."

"Well, we're here with some bad news," Marcella said, her eyes taking in reactions on each of their faces. "Dr. Pettigrew is dead."

Gasps all round. Moku clapped her hand to her mouth, eyes spontaneously filling. "Oh no."

The men had gone wooden-faced, and it was Fernandez, the young man who'd let them in, who finally spoke.

"How?"

"She was murdered." Marcella kept her eyes moving. The Korean guy had his hands in his lab coat pockets, was jiggling something in there. "What were you working on? Anything that might get her killed?"

"No. No." The Indian guy now looked on the verge of a meltdown, chocolate eyes overflowing as he patted around for a tissue and ended up wiping his eyes with a square of wax paper. "This is terrible. We all loved her. We need her for our program, our research. She was a great woman. Murdered?"

He burst into the harsh kind of sobbing that made male grief painful to watch.

Moku put her arms around him and the Korean guy patted his back. Only Fernandez kept his arms at his sides, but his Adam's apple fluctuated like a bobber on a fishing line, as he uttered a series of froglike grunts. Marcella punched their names into her multipurpose phone to run background, wondering if he had Tourette's.

"What were you working on?" Rogers had located a box of tissues and presented them to the distraught intern, who tore out handfuls and covered his face with them.

"We're doing an important project," Moku said. "Biotech chemistry involving the formulation of an enzyme that binds protein in photosynthesis."

"Doesn't sound very controversial." Marcella typed "biotech enzyme" into her notes on her phone, but didn't catch the rest.

"It's important research. It would revolutionize the time it takes for algae to grow. We have our first cell stock of what we've nicknamed BioGreen. It's got the potential to be the answer to world hunger and the key to biofuels becoming a viable oil alternative." Peter Kim fussed with his glasses again.

"Now we're talking," Marcella said with a hint of her dimple as a reward. "Can you explain it in layman's terms?"

The Indian guy seemed to be pulling himself together. "There's an enzyme involved in photosynthesis called RuBisCO. People have been trying for years to get it to bind faster in the photosynthesis process so that growth in plants can be accelerated. BioGreen takes just days to grow to harvestable volume."

"Shee-it!" Rogers said. "I grew up on a farm, so I'm trying to picture that."

"Here." Cindy Moku, not to be outdone, turned to a nearby monitor and woke it up. "Check this out."

She activated a video icon, and Marcella watched a time-lapse video of a small patch of algae seemingly exploding in size to fill the pond area. "This is time lapse of two days." Cindy pointed to the counter in the corner of the video. "We just developed this video before we harvested a batch of cell stock."

"Where is that?" Marcella asked.

"We keep the data, the lab books, and the cell stock formula locked up, and only Ron Truman, our lead researcher, has the key besides Dr. Pettigrew."

"Where's Mr. Truman?"

"Dr. Truman. Don't know. He was supposed to be in," Abed said. They all glanced at one another.

"Let's take a look at the back room," Marcella said.

Kim led the way to a door in the corner of the lab, and his abrupt stop caused them to pile up.

The door had been jimmied. Splintered wood and pry marks gave testament to an illegal entrance. Inside, papers were scattered everywhere in the small windowless space, boxes of materials upended.

"Oh my God," Moku breathed. "We had the results on a laptop

on the desk and our lab books piled next to it with the cell stock in a sealed canister. It's all gone!"

Rogers took a camera out of his bag and photographed the scene as Marcella oversaw Kim making calls to all the numbers they had for Ron Truman, and he eventually answered his cell phone.

"Come down to the lab," Kim barked. "Dr. Pettigrew's dead and the formula and cell stock are gone." He closed his phone on the head researcher's hysterical squawks. "Do you think Dr. Truman did it?"

"We'll proceed with our investigation and pursue every lead," Marcella said evenly. She herded the interns out of the back room and turned to Rogers. "Impressions?"

"Moku told me nothing else seems to be missing. This mess could be a red herring, trying to make it look like some outsider broke in," Rogers said. "Let's keep them here, get initial statements before they have time to figure out their stories."

"I'll get some background checks in on these lab rats." Marcella stepped outside into the hallway and called the central Bureau office for a full workup on each of the interns, starting with Dr. Ron Truman. She was still on the phone when a man approached her at a run, white coat flapping.

The ID badge bouncing just above his crotch declared him the missing Dr. Truman. He pulled up in front of her, fisting bulky arms on his hips. Bold green eyes lit a face better suited to magazine covers than a laboratory as he flexed square jaws in a good imitation of outrage. He was definitely hot, and she felt a tingle.

"What the hell's going on in my lab?"

"Dr. Pettigrew's been murdered and your research is missing."

"Holy shit," Truman replied, and punched a code into the pad by the steel door, pushing it open with Marcella close behind. "What happened?" he bellowed to the interns clustered around Rogers.

"Someone stole the cell stock, our lab books, and the formula laptop!" Moku said.

"And Dr. Pettigrew's dead!" Abed wailed.

To Marcella's surprise, Truman opened his arms as he walked toward them, and each of the PhD candidates dropped what they were doing and crowded in for a group hug, Abed and Moku giving in to renewed tears and Fernandez croaking like a jungle's worth of tree frogs.

"It's probably one of them, given the restricted access to the main door," Marcella whispered to Rogers, unimpressed by the emotional display. "Let's isolate them, take fingerprints and DNA, do alibi statements, and seal the lab."

"Copy that." Rogers picked up the portable crime case he'd brought in and moved in on Peter Kim while Marcella pulled Ron Truman aside.

"Come with me, please." She led him into the back room, took up a power position behind a counter. The handsome Dr. Truman propped one ass cheek on a stool and folded his arms.

"I heard you tell the other agent you were going to seal the lab. That's out of the question. There are a plethora of time-sensitive projects in the works."

"This lab is part of a crime scene. Who knows; Dr. Pettigrew may have been killed here. In any case, this lab is now officially closed."

"Can we at least put some of our work on thumb drives?"

"Out of the question. Until cleared, these computers are a key element in the investigation."

Truman pushed away from the tall steel stool, paced. His eyes fell on the pry marks around the open door, and he spun to pace the other direction, pushing a hand though blond Ken-doll locks. "This is bad," he muttered.

"I need you to give a brief statement, which I will record. We'll follow up with longer interviews later." Marcella set her phone on the counter, turning the video feature on, and Truman sat, frowning into the blinking red light. "Where were you yesterday evening?"

"With someone."

"Name and address?"

"It's complicated."

"Murder is complicated. This is your alibi; I suggest you provide the information." Marcella softened her voice and gave a dimpled smile.

"Well. It's like this. I'm married. But…I met someone. We were together."

Marcella felt the tingle he'd aroused drown in a wash of contempt. "Name. Address."

"I told my wife I was working late at the lab. I'd appreciate it if you didn't bother her about this."

"I can't promise that she won't find something out, but I don't see at this time that your alibi need concern her."

"Well, then, I'm not going to say—and anyway, it's nothing to do with Dr. Pettigrew."

"Let me be the judge of that."

"I'm sorry. Right now I'm not going to tell you."

Brown eyes clashed with green. Marcella shook her head. "Doesn't matter. I'll find out where you were. It's just going to take longer and be more embarrassing—your choice. DNA sample now, to rule you out, and fingerprints." He submitted to the fingerprinting and DNA swab with ill grace. "Send in Moku. We'll talk more."

He straightened up, jaw squared, and strode out.

Marcella's phone rang, a blare of "We Are the Champions," the ringtone she used for the Honolulu Police Department. She sat on the metal stool and picked up.

"Special Agent Scott here."

"This is Detective Kamuela. We wanted to check in with you

before we went and did death notification—next of kin is one Natalie Pettigrew, niece. Dr. Pettigrew wasn't married and had no other relatives in the area." Kamuela had a voice like dark chocolate—husky, with the underlying rhythmic cadence of the islands.

"We'll do the notification," Marcella said, thinking fast. "Dr. Pettigrew's research project is gone—stolen—and we've got some interesting possible suspects in the lab crew. Looks like it could be an inside job dressed up to look like a burglary."

"Want me to send in a sweeper crew?"

"We've got our own lab, but thanks."

"So much for interagency cooperation." The chocolate had some bite to it.

"This *is* us cooperating. Trust me. You want our people working the lab stuff. We're much less backed up."

"So why do you want to do the death notification?" He still sounded pissy.

"Next of kin is always an important interview. We need to get eyes on this girl." Marcella was already pulling Natalie Pettigrew up on her phone's connection to the local law enforcement database. "Looks like Miss Pettigrew has some priors—marijuana possession and two assaults that look like bar fights."

"Yeah. Girl's got some psychiatric history, too," Kamuela said. "Rumor has it she's bipolar, no meds."

"Who's your source on that?"

"I've got a confidential informant—no need for more detail at this time."

Marcella winced. He was paying her back for taking over so much of the investigation. Well, screw him and his tender male ego, she thought irritably. "We're sealing the place and doing initial statements with the microscope jockeys in here. We'll do follow-up interviews with them back at HQ. You can be present for those."

"Gee, thanks."

"We need your assistance. I didn't mean to sound..." She tapped her toe against the metal rung of the stool, annoyed with the standoff. "Dammit. Don't be like that. We need to work together."

A long pause. He seemed to relent, because he said, "Well, we didn't turn anything up in the canvassing of the beach."

"Not surprised. I'm guessing she went into the Ala Wai Canal and washed up on Waikiki later. I'll check in with you guys after the death notification. Thanks for calling." Marcella punched off, hoping her next contact would go better. Keeping things moving with local PD always had its challenges.

Truman had closed the door behind him, and Cindy Moku looked through the little glass pane in the door. Marcella got up to let her in, gesturing to the steel stool.

She activated the phone's record feature. "Please state your name, address, and where you were last night."

Moku's shiny brown complexion had gone gray around the lips and nostrils. Her eyes were puffy from crying.

"Dr. Cindy Moku. Or almost. I'm finishing my doctorate on this project. I live in Honolulu." She gave an address. "I was home. Studying."

"Anyone able to verify your whereabouts?"

"You don't think one of us did it? We all loved Dr. Pettigrew. Or at least, we respected her. We needed her. She was our PI."

This was the first glimmer of a side to Pettigrew that was less than ideal. "You didn't love her? And what's a PI?"

"I...I respected her. She wasn't the warm, fuzzy type. And she was our PI, which is a primary investigator, the head of a project. Without her and the research...I don't know. The last two years of our work could be gone. The last two years of our lives. My doctorate." Moku's voice wobbled.

Marcella pushed a roll of paper towels over, and Moku blew her nose with a honk that vibrated the camera phone.

"Anyway, there's no one. Oh wait. I had an online chat window open. I was talking online to Abed and Fernandez." A rosy blush marbled up Moku's neck.

"Good. We'll check that. Something going on between you?" Marcella kept her voice neutral, her eyes on the young scientist's betraying skin.

"No, it's nothing. We're all friends. We were comparing notes, that's all." The blush darkened to mulberry.

She was lying.

Rogers stuck his head in. "Almost done? I got the rest."

"Yes. Thanks, Cindy. We'll talk more." She punched off the phone and collected a swab and Moku's prints. The young woman left, wiping the ink off her fingers with a bunched-up wad of paper towel.

"It's late, but let's go to lunch. I'm hungry for some of your mama's cooking." Rogers sealed the door with crime tape and contacted the university to change the touch pad at the door to a new code. Marcella called the Bureau to send out the evidence-collection team.

Marcella was a little light-headed with hunger by the time they hiked across the lush grass toward the building that housed the Culinary Arts Cafeteria, where students studying to be chefs cooked for the rest of the campus at reasonable rates. She trailed Rogers, who pushed open the door to a pleasant café-style setting, where hairnetted students served choices from behind a gleaming glass counter. Little tables dotted the room.

"Marcella! Mattie! You sit. I serve you!" Anna, swathed in a white apron with a chef's hat dwarfing her head, waved at the tables. "Sit. I bring the food!"

Marcella picked a table in the corner and sat facing out.

"Everything your mother says seems to have an exclamation point to it," Rogers observed as Anna loaded two plates, chattering in Italian to another student.

"You should see my parents together," Marcella said. "Can't get a word in edgewise."

"That why you never had me and the family over? You live with them, right?" Rogers poked her with a grin.

"Hells, no. I've got my own place," Marcella growled as Anna set loaded plates, redolent with garlic and spices, in front of them.

"Eat. Eat!" she exclaimed. "Or as my husband would say, *Mange! Mange!*"

"Where's yours, Ma?" Marcella asked, forking up the delicious chicken dish. "Sit down with us."

"I ate already." Anna Scatalina perched on a chair. "So, Mattie. You have a family, don't you?"

"I do, Mrs. Scatalina." He cut his eyes at Marcella with a slight emphasis on the full form of her last name. "I have a wife, Bettina, and two little girls."

"So you *can* have a family and be in the Federal Bureau of Investigation." Anna pronounced it "infestigation." "I asking Marcella who she dating, when I get some grandchildren, she always saying she have no time. Always working."

Marcella rolled her eyes.

"It's not easy, Mrs. Scatalina. I found the right woman, and she works part time to be home with the children. I think it would be very hard to have two working parents with the hours I put in. Besides, Marcella is picky. She's waiting for just the right guy." Rogers addressed his chicken, keeping a straight face.

"You got that right." Marcella bolted down the glass of water Anna had brought with the meal and stood up, gripping her chair back. "I'm waiting for the right guy, Ma. We're not even going to think about babies until that's settled. If ever."

"Well, of course not, darling. No good, that single-mother thing. Though if it happened, we would help you with the baby." She patted Marcella's white-knuckled hand. "We just want you to have the happy of a family."

"I have the happy of family—you and Dad. Matt, you ready?" Marcella picked up her tray. "Thanks for the great lunch, Mama. We really need to get going."

"Yes, it was delicious, Mrs. Scatalina. Thanks so much for the invite. Where do we pay?"

"Your money no good here," Anna said, standing and straightening her chef's cap as she addressed Marcella. "I see you Sunday?"

"I told you I would come." Marcella hugged her petite mother hard. "I'm sorry, Mama. Just please leave this alone, will you? I love what I do. It's enough for me right now."

"I know. I no understand, but I know. Okay then. Don't get shot." She blew Marcella a kiss.

Marcella tightened the FBI Twist and made sure her buttons were all the way up as they parked in front of a run-down apartment building a few blocks off the hotel district—Dr. Pettigrew's next of kin's address. Whiffs of the Ala Wai Canal, redolent of ripe algae and unpleasantness, tickled Marcella's nostrils as she slammed the door of the Acura and faced the building. Tired bougainvillea struggled to brighten a moth-eaten scrap of lawn in front of the entrance. Inside a linoleum-floored lobby lined with aluminum mailboxes, the elevators were out of service.

"Dammit," Marcella said, looking down at her beloved impractical shoes. It was all her dad's fault—he'd given her the Manolos the last time she'd had dinner at the parents' condo. Maybe it was time he gave her something more orthopedic…

"Getting my cardio on. The apartment's on the fifth floor." Rogers pushed through the glass doors and headed up the metal-and-cement stairs on the outside of the building at a brisk military trot.

Marcella followed, and by the fifth floor she'd developed a blister and had to redo her hair yet again. Fanning herself with the folder on Dr. Pettigrew, she gave an irritated squint to Rogers's grin as she rang the bell on the sun-bleached door.

A long moment passed. Marcella took in the view off the banister (nondescript) and the decor she could see through the blinds (early 1980s, well worn) before she leaned on the bell again.

The door flew open so abruptly that Marcella's hand landed on her weapon. A tall, whippet-thin young woman glared out of violet-blue eyes raccooned in mascara. Jet hair capped a shapely skull, and tattoos banded wiry, pale arms. Natalie Pettigrew was an attenuated Goth cartoon.

"Yeah?" The girl sported an attitude evident in her cocked hip and narrowed eyes.

"FBI. May we come in and speak to you a moment?" Marcella and Rogers flipped open their creds.

"No." Automatic, decisive. The girl took the cred wallets and studied them, handed them back. "What's going on?"

"Some bad news. It would be better shared in privacy." Rogers tried a friendly smile.

"No thanks. I take my bad news standing up."

"All right then. We're here about your aunt—Dr. Trudy Pettigrew. She's—dead." Rogers's voice had gone appropriately somber. Marcella waited for a reaction—surprise, grief, anger, denial—nothing.

Finally the girl said, "I bet you want to ask me questions about it. That I'd prefer to do inside." She retreated, leaving the door open.

"We're sorry for your loss." Rogers followed her, Marcella bringing up the rear. "We hear she was a great scientist."

"She was a prize bitch, is what she was." Natalie walked into the kitchenette—roughly the size of a double bed—and poured herself a glass of unfiltered cranberry juice, sipping it. She didn't offer them any.

Marcella still hadn't spoken. She did a three-sixty in the narrow living room, taking in furnishings that hadn't improved on closer inspection. "Mind if we sit?"

"Yes. But sit anyway."

Marcella parked on the battered pistachio microfiber couch. Rogers was still trying to engage.

"So you and your aunt weren't close?"

"I didn't say that."

"You said she was a bitch." Marcella locked eyes with the girl. "Cut the shit. Talk to us here, or we can take it back to the Bureau office."

Natalie took a leisurely sip of cranberry juice, a stray sunbeam catching in the red liquid and dropping a reflection on the girl's white skin like a drop of blood. She strode on black-jeaned pip-estem legs to sit on the love seat across from them. She set the glass down and crossed bare feet on the coffee table.

"Ask away."

Marcella set the phone on the coffee table and activated Record. "What kind of relationship did you have with your aunt?"

"We…" For the first time, the girl bit her lower lip. "We fought a lot."

"What about?"

"The usual. She wanted me to make something of myself." Natalie made quotation marks with her fingers. "She was always on my case."

"So what is it that you do?"

"I'm an artist."

"I don't see any art." Marcella gestured to the bare, dingy walls.

"I don't keep it out here." A long pause, then: "I have a day job. I work at Hot Topic, the clothing store."

"So where were you two nights ago?"

"I don't remember."

"Do you use drugs? Is that why?"

The girl stood abruptly. "You know what? I don't need this shit right now. You haven't even told me why you're here—I'm assuming there's been foul play, since it's the FBI telling me my aunt's dead and interrogating me." Natalie's lips trembled, and she pressed a hand against her mouth. Yellow paint marked bitten nails, lending credence to her claim to be an artist.

"My partner gets a little direct, sorry," Rogers said. "And, yes. Your aunt was murdered."

Natalie sat down, this time abruptly—as if her legs couldn't hold her anymore. The hand was still pressed against her mouth.

"We do need to know where you were. Just routine. We're asking everyone who was close to Dr. Pettigrew." Rogers was gentle, leaning toward the girl, with his elbows propped on his knees and big hands cupped. His posture seemed entreating—a practiced ease and sincerity to it. Marcella still admired his interviewing skills.

"All right. Well." Natalie leaned forward, picked up the glass of juice from the coffee table, took a sip. "I was with someone."

"Who?"

"I'm seeing someone, so I have an alibi. But I'm not saying who it is unless I have to."

"Why not?"

"It's complicated."

That reminded Marcella of another evasion she'd heard that day. She made a mental note before asking, "Do you own a handgun?"

"No. Hate those things. So...she was shot?" Again a little vibration in the voice, a hum like the sound of rain moving in.

"Yes. She was."

"So she...Did she suffer?"

"It was quick. She couldn't have felt a thing," Rogers said. Marcella was silent, picturing the openmouthed expression of surprise frozen on Dr. Pettigrew's face. She'd felt something all right—she'd been betrayed. Marcella was willing to bet money on it.

"I think we're going to need that alibi," Marcella said.

"I'm—not making the right impression." Natalie's eyes filled, but she widened them, blinking rapidly to keep the tears at bay—and the blue of them was definitely purple, Marcella decided. "I loved my aunt. We just didn't—get each other. She wanted me to...I guess, be living another kind of life. But I can't. I want to show you something."

She got up, and the two agents followed her down a tattily carpeted hallway to a bedroom, flicked on the light. Color assaulted them from huge artworks lining the walls to the ceiling. The backing material appeared to be plywood, and the girl's abstract style filled the room with a vibrating energy that left an impression—Marcella knew because she closed her eyes for a second, still seeing the vivid triptych of slashing contrasts on the wall across from her.

"These are good," she said. "You have a distinctive style."

"Thanks. But this isn't what sells in Hawaii. This is." Natalie reached behind a stack of paintings and held up an innocuous illustration of a turtle sunning itself on the beach.

"That's a nice one," Rogers said, admiring.

Both women gave him a glare, and he raised his hands. "Hey. I'm no art critic."

"Thanks for showing us these," Marcella said. "Mind if I take a photo?"

"If you must."

Marcella photographed the room, ending with a shot of Natalie Pettigrew holding the turtle painting. "Appreciate that."

"No problem. Since I didn't do it, I have nothing to hide." Natalie led them back into the living room.

"Did you know of anyone who would wish your aunt harm?"

"No. Those students of hers have—had—her on a pedestal.

But I think she was working on something pretty high-powered. Maybe whoever shot her was after that. Are we done?"

"For now." Marcella handed Natalie her card. "We are still going to need your alibi."

"I can't tell you right now." The girl set her mouth in a stubborn line. "I will when I have to, but not a minute before. People could be hurt."

"Oh please." Marcella did a tiny eye roll. "Wish I had a nickel for every time I've heard that. I'll find out anyway; you can bet on it. In any case, call if you hear or remember anything that could help with the investigation."

The girl gave a brief nod, looking down at the card, and the sun-blistered door closed firmly behind them. They heard the light patter of Natalie's feet running away to the back of the apartment.

"She's going to her bedroom to cry," Marcella said as they clunked down the stairs. "And she's got a bladder infection. Probably from boffing whoever's name she won't give up."

"How do you know?"

"Cranberry juice."

"I'll remember that," Rogers said as he beeped open the Acura. "You're scary."

Chapter 3

Marcella locked the door of her apartment with a couple of dead bolts and a heavy brass chain and turned back into her apartment, tossing the stack of reports onto a sleek glass coffee table already buried in background reading from other cases. She shed the light jacket she always put on in the Bureau office, taking time to put it on a hanger and put it away in the bedroom closet, unbuckling her weapon harness with a sigh and a scratch, yanking the now-dingy white shirt out of the gray trousers.

She leaned in close to a round clear glass bowl of water beside her bed, tapped on the glass.

"Hey, Loverboy." The purple-blue betta fish flashed his fins at her, made a little charge at the glass. "I'm happy to see you too."

Marcella stripped on her way to the bathroom, tossing soiled clothes into a wicker basket and getting into the shower. She let the massaging shower head work on her shoulders for a while, but she still couldn't uncoil inside. She stepped out of the shower, toweling long brown hair. The red light on her old-fashioned answering machine was flashing. She punched On and listened.

"Marcella, hey. It's Lei. Call me back when you can."

Lei Texeira, the detective friend she'd recruited for the Bureau, was currently at the Academy. Lei was a local Hawaii girl with a dark past, an attitude, and great instincts as an investigator. She hooked the phone out of its cradle, called Lei's phone back, but it went to voice mail.

"Hope you're doing all right, girl. Let's catch up soon. Try my cell."

Marcella hung up, looked at the report pile. *Ugh.*

What she needed was to get laid—she advocated for recreational, no-strings sex as a right. Yet here she sat, single, lonely, and in the mood. Not even a decent booty call on the speed dial. She scrolled through her contacts to make sure, pausing over Detective Kamuela's number and moving on. Maybe it was time to try out the Club—but she didn't feel up to it.

Nope. Guess it was going to be another night in, with Loverboy the betta fish to talk to and battery-operated company in bed.

Chapter 4

Marcella sipped her first extra-strength cup of black coffee of the day at four a.m., dressed in a black bra and panties, her elbows on her knees as she hunched forward off the couch. Insomnia had plagued her, and she'd finally started reading the reports to pass the time. She glanced up at the vista of sparkling lights her tenth-floor apartment yielded, the ocean a black smudge somewhere out there she'd paid extra to glimpse. This early, morning hadn't even begun to lighten the Honolulu sky.

The field office background techs had worked up preliminary reports on each of Dr. Pettigrew's grad students yesterday, and Marcella scanned the manila folder filled with printouts on Cindy Moku. The oldest of four in a Hawaiian family, Cindy had attended Kamehameha schools and graduated with honors. She'd done her undergrad in biotechnology at UH and gone straight into a PhD program under Dr. Pettigrew. Several of her family had police records, mostly related to drug use and trafficking, but Cindy appeared to be a shining example of someone with focus and drive maximizing her opportunities.

Marcella went on to Jarod Fernandez, the tall, young man

who'd greeted them at the door the day before. Somehow he'd managed to avoid looking into the camera in his state ID photo, his eyes cast to the side, long hair obscuring what could have been a good-looking face. No driver's license. He was the son of a doctor and a pharmacist and had gone to Punahou, another exclusive private school, and was diagnosed with Tourette's syndrome. No criminal record, though according to his school records, he was implicated in several suspicious fire-setting incidents.

Marcella sat back thoughtfully, took a long draft of the cooling coffee. The faintest hint of rose lightening the sky drew her out onto the minuscule balcony, barely big enough for a sun-bleached aluminum table and chairs. She leaned on the railing, looked out at the promise of ocean, navy with new dawn. Sighed. Took another sip of coffee.

The photo of Fernandez's parents in the file, resplendent in white coats, made her stomach clench. That early love, her first year in college—so desperate and so twisted—had left her more jaded than she liked to admit.

She only had relationships she could control now. She'd heard about the Club from a friend and joined a few months after moving to Honolulu, but had never actually gone. The Club touted itself as a no-strings, safe alternative to random pickups in bars: "Ideal for the Busy Professional Who Doesn't Have Time for Games" was the slogan on their website. That described her. She was a busy professional with no time for games—games that could lead to heartbreak, to vulnerability, to losing focus.

With the Club, if she used anyone, it was going to be mutual. You chose possible partners online, met to see if there was a fit, and if you were so inclined, rooms were available at the back. No one would get hurt, and she'd be in charge. She turned away, striding back to the coffeepot for a refill. It was time to try it out—another night of insomnia with work to liven it up didn't appeal.

The smell of coffee, the taste of it, was tied to home and family—

Marcella thought she remembered tasting her first milky, sugary sip of what would become her favorite beverage while sitting on her papa's lap. It was great to be so loved, to be the apple of her parents' eye—and it was smothering too. She had her ways of rebelling—joining the FBI after graduation from college was her main one, instead of following her father into the shoe business or marrying a nice Catholic boy and having babies.

Joining the FBI—and the Club. Those choices were Marcella's defiant nature in action—but sometimes she wondered if Trevor wasn't responsible for it all. She shut down that thought—it would be giving that abusive asshole too much credit.

She still had several more bios to get through before the day really got started. Marcella sat back down and opened the file on Dr. Ron Truman, second in command of the project. Nice résumé and list of colleges, but apparently he'd washed out of Stanford med school, taken a step down to researcher, and finished his PhD at the University of Hawaii.

Those bold green eyes stared up at her from his driver's license photo. Six foot two. One hundred ninety pounds. Address in Kahala, the ritzy suburb of Honolulu. Married to Dr. Julie Truman, formerly Beecham, for three years. No children.

At least there were no children, since he was likely having an affair.

The photo of Julie Beecham Truman showed a preppy-looking brunette, smiling big. Marcella didn't let herself feel sorry for Dr. Julie Truman with her orthodontic smile and shining bob. People chose a road and paid the toll. Maybe it was growing up in New Jersey that taught her that—Hawaii didn't have toll roads.

She stuck a Post-it on Dr. Truman's picture so it would hang out the side of the file, made a note in her bold block writing: ALIBI? WHO'S THE WOMAN HE WAS WITH?

She opened the file on Zosar Abed. Born in Calcutta, the only child of a wealthy family, Zosar appeared to have had a passion for science and agrobiology from early on. According to his entrance visa essay, he "wanted to be a part of bringing solutions to the world that would help his country's people." He made annual trips home to India to visit his mother. Father was deceased.

Zosar's over-the-top grief could fit with his attachment to his mother. Marcella studied the big chocolate eyes and waifish build of the Indian intern with a frown.

India had a huge need for something like BioGreen, and Zosar might have financial or other pressures on him pushing him to steal the formula. His explosion of weeping at the news of Dr. Pettigrew's demise could also be a discharge of tension and stress as much as his mommy issues. Marcella wrote WORK UP CONNECTIONS: INDIA AND FINANCIALS on another Post-it, stuck it on his photo.

She opened the last folder, on Peter Kim. Glanced at the open sliding door, where a cool breath of wind had stolen inside, brushing goose bumps across her skin.

Trevor used to touch her that way: at first with a feather, then with a wet Japanese sumi paintbrush, and later with the edge of a razor. Gently, so lightly, raising a line of "chicken skin" as they called it in the islands.

Then not so gently. And he'd made her love it and cry for more. Her hand stole up to touch her breast, threaded with tiny, almost invisible silver scars hidden under black lace. She wished she didn't have scars on her soul too—it wasn't just what he'd made her do sexually; it was how he'd tried to get into her head.

She stood abruptly, walked over and closed the glass slider. Dawn was ruffling high feathery clouds with a blush of vivid salmon, gilding the high-rises across from hers, sparkling diamonds in the windows. It was going to be another glorious Hawaii day—such a departure from the gray skies and gritty streets of New Jersey, and just the change she'd been seeking. When an opening had come up in the Honolulu office, she'd competed fiercely for it. She hadn't bargained on her parents following her over just six months later, but there was no stopping them once they made up their minds.

Marcella sat back down, scanned the report. Kim was also in Hawaii on a student visa, from Korea. Now, there was a nation aggressively pursuing various kinds of genetic engineering, and ethics had always been in short supply. Peter Kim was another only child, from a poor family this time, but one that had Korean connections in Honolulu—specifically an aunt married to a local councilman.

She made the same note as for the Abed file, though it didn't appear Kim had returned to Korea since he arrived five years ago. That didn't mean he didn't have some sort of information pipeline back to a lab there, though the local political connection meant they'd have to be careful how they proceeded.

She closed the files, stacked them neatly, poured a refill of coffee, and headed to the back bedroom to get dressed. She chose a black poplin button-down with short sleeves this time, a chunky steel diver's watch, gray striped trousers in the lightest fabric regulations would allow. She strapped on her shoulder holster, loaded up the Glock 19 she preferred to the bulkier police-issue .40. Wound her hair up into the FBI Twist, speared it with a few bobby pins, clipped the shiny Federal badge to her waistband.

Loverboy charged the glass of his bowl a couple of times to catch her eye.

"Hey, buddy." She gave him a few pellets, watched as he attacked them vigorously. "Don't get into trouble while I'm gone."

She slid her feet into a pair of pointy-toed slingbacks and buckled the delicate straps around her ankles. Took a quick look at her face in a nearby mirror and decided that, as usual, she looked better without makeup. Anything more than ChapStick tended to make her full lips, wide brown eyes under arched brows, and bold cheekbones look cartoonish.

The slingbacks had tiny round kitten heels and made a sound like castanets as she went into the kitchen, turned off the coffeemaker, verified there was indeed nothing to eat in the fridge, scooped up the files and slid them into a leather portfolio, and banged out the door, locking it behind her.

It was already 6:27 a.m.—and she had a lot to do before the meeting with the medical examiner about Pettigrew's body at eight.

Marcella pulled on latex gloves and rubbed a bit of Vicks under her nose. She extended the little vial to Rogers, who snorted and made a flicking motion.

"Don't know why you need all that," he said. "You seem okay at the crime scenes."

"Gotta smell everything at the scene. Don't need to do anything but look in the morgue."

She followed her partner through the sally port where the vans pulled up into the main autopsy area. Four tables and autopsy stations filled the big room, but only the ME, Dr. Fukushima, was working. She was hunched over Pettigrew's large, fish-belly white, naked body, sewing up the Y-incision with coarse black thread. Marcella was grateful for the Vicks under her nose as a waft of nastiness blew up from the last of the cavity as it closed. She cut her eyes to Rogers, who'd gone a little paler under his tan.

"Hey, Doctor. How's it coming along?" Rogers's voice had the nasality of someone mouth breathing.

The doctor looked up. "Fine. Just finishing. I came in early to have preliminary results for you."

"And we appreciate it," Marcella said. "Though cause of death seems pretty obvious." She pointed to the black hole in the broad white forehead, just above Pettigrew's mannish brows. The woman's iron-gray hair straggled off the table, except where the top of the skull had been neatly removed along with the glutinous pile of brains in a steel bowl on the scale.

"Yes, that's correct. COD is gunshot wound to the head. What's interesting is the caliber of the weapon. I noticed this at the scene—there was no exit wound." Fukushima held up a small lead bullet for them to see. "It's a twenty-two caliber. Small, easily concealed handgun with enough velocity to penetrate the skull at close range. The bullet ricochets around inside and destroys the brain tissue." She indicated the mound of gray, pulpy brain matter on the scale. "I had to use an instrument to clean out her skull cavity."

Marcella suppressed a shudder at the sight of the steel utensil resembling an ice cream scooper resting on the edge of the table.

"Do you think that caliber shot was intentional? This was a woman whose brain was everything. Could be part of the MO." Rogers was still mouth breathing.

"That's for you to determine," Fukushima said, dropping gore-covered instruments into a tray in the sink. "I also found some trace on her."

"Oh yeah?"

"Grass blades caught in her shoes consistent with walking along the canal. Her stomach contents are here." The doctor held up a screw-top plastic container that swished with a thin brown liquid filled with bits of pale, threadlike particles. "Top Ramen. Dinner of the busy single scientist."

Marcella really noticed Fukushima's soft round face for the first time, crow's feet just beginning to show around fine brown eyes magnified by goggles. The doctor gestured to a stack of her own Cup Noodles next to the sink. The thought of eating in this room made Marcella's stomach lurch, and suddenly the Vicks wasn't doing enough.

"Anything else, Doc?"

"Yes. She had some hairs on her body indicating she was up close to someone." Fukushima held up a small plastic evidence bag. The hairs looked black and short. "Good guess is that whoever these hairs belong to had something to do with her death. Did you collect DNA and hair samples from the interns?"

"DNA and fingerprint. Not hair," Rogers said. Hair wasn't required by protocol, but Marcella pushed herself away from the table in irritation that she hadn't thought to collect that in the initial pass with the interns.

"Let's hope there's some viable DNA on these hairs; that would make things easier."

"Unfortunately, the hairs all look naturally shed. There are three of them, and I didn't see any root bulbs. You're out of luck there." Fukushima continued to tidy her autopsy area, covering the body with a green paper drape. "The transcription service will have my report available for download tomorrow or the next day."

"Anything under her fingernails, anything other than the grass?"

"No. And we were lucky to have any of that after at least twenty-four hours in the Ala Wai," Fukushima said, dropping the brain scooper into the pot with a clang. "Only way I got the grass was that it was caught in her shoe. What that informs us is that she walked there and was probably shot by the canal. In other words, the canal is most likely the crime scene."

Marcella keyed the last of her notes into her phone. "Unfortunately, the canal is a big area."

"Well, the grass in her shoe was a blue fescue. Perhaps that will help narrow things down."

"Hope so," Rogers said. "Thanks, Doc."

Marcella dialed the County of Honolulu park service to ask about grass plantings as they hit the double doors to the exit.

Chapter 5

Marcella looked down at the notes on her phone as they pulled out of the parking lot, Rogers behind the wheel of the SUV. "Had us down for a meeting with the UH brass at ten a.m. to talk about Pettigrew's work, but finding the crime scene takes precedence."

"Let's get whoever's available at the Bureau and those HPD detectives out to help."

Marcella worked the phone as Rogers pulled up at the first of a series of mini parks that ran along the canal. He looked out at the lawn, shook his head. "Like looking for a fescue in a haystack."

"Not that bad. County says only three of the parklets still have that blue fescue. They're trying to gradually replace it with some more drought-tolerant strains. This is one of them."

Marcella opened the door, stepped out. Snapped on a pair of latex gloves, took her kit out from behind the seat. Rogers came around with his just as her phone rang. She pulled it out of the pocket of the light jacket, looked at it. PAPA GIO shone up at her as the Italian National Anthem burbled.

"Papa? What's up? I'm working."

"Can't a papa phone his girl? You have lunch with your mama. Now I want you to meet me for coffee. Only fair."

Another black SUV pulled up, disgorging their office's special agent in charge, Ben Waxman. Marcella turned away, the phone to her ear, as Rogers headed over to brief their boss.

"I'm so busy, Papa. Maybe later. I'll call you."

"Only fair!" he bellowed. She pictured his handsome square face purpling. He really needed to watch his blood pressure, and his ongoing competition with Mama for Marcella's attention was wearing her out. The six months since her parents had moved to Waikiki had begun to feel like years.

"I'll call you if I can make it for coffee. Maybe this afternoon. I'll call you," she said firmly, and punched Off, slipping the phone into her jacket pocket and pasting on a smile for Waxman and his sidekick, Special Agent Gundersohn—both of whom she was surprised to see outside the office.

SAC Waxman was the latest branch chief sent over from Washington. Six months in Hawaii hadn't served to unbend him, though she fancied his tie was knotted just a hair looser than normal and he'd stopped coloring his hair. He'd had a recent short buzz cut, Marcella assumed to get rid of the dye, and his scalp shone pink through the silver stubble. Gundersohn, also a veteran agent, had the thick neck and cauliflower ears of a boxer matched with the slow-moving thoroughness of a Swedish farmer. Marcella hadn't been able to charm either of them, which she chalked up to Waxman's apparent asexuality and Gundersohn's lack of imagination.

"Good morning. This is one of three plots of a blue fescue associated with the trace on Pettigrew's shoes," Marcella said.

"Your partner briefed us." Waxman addressed the Ala Wai Canal. No eye contact, frosty. Marcella mentally shrugged and turned away—she tried not to let him get to her.

"Thought we'd start with the landing area, work our way back," Rogers said. "We can pace off a grid."

They did so, fanning out to peruse the remains of a worn wooden deck, a relic from a time when boats had tied up there. Most of the wide, calm canal was bordered in concrete or decorative stone—this brief section might have caught something, but even with the spray bottles of luminol, they found nothing.

Marcella let the GPS guide them to the next pocket of blue fescue, and that's where Gundersohn, moving slowly, lit up some blood trace near the edge of the concrete lip. They moved in, took samples, photographed the area. Marcella put her hands on her hips, swiveled to take in the surrounding park, a narrow strip of grass, trees, and bench between the canal and a busy street.

A beige Forerunner pulled up to the curb. Detectives Kamuela and Ching got out, carrying their kits.

"Just missed the action, Detectives," she said. "Looks like we found the primary scene. Blood trace on the coping. Pending verification, looks like she went in here."

"Kind of expected somewhere along the canal to be the scene," Ching said. Kamuela wasn't looking at her, eyes on the cluster of agents around the spot on the cement working their cameras and chemistry kits.

"Why did she come down there, still wearing her ID badge? It must have been an urgent call from someone." Kamuela's straight black brows had drawn together over mirrored Oakleys as he swiveled to take in the whole area.

"And where's her car? She couldn't have walked this far." Marcella continued the thought. She pointed to the park bench facing the canal. "Maybe she was in the lab, eating her lonely Top Ramen dinner, and gets a call to meet someone down here. Someone who wants to meet in public. Someone who wants her out of the lab so the research can be stolen."

"But why kill her? It's like killing the goose that laid the golden egg." Kamuela turned to look at the bench. The idea of a phone call reminded Marcella of something.

"We still haven't located the woman's phone or purse, and we still need to search her home." All items on the ever-lengthening list of to-dos for the investigation. She frowned, looking at the bench, and approached, ran the light over it slowly. No blood, but the magnifying lens attached to the light gleamed on a long, iron-gray hair caught in a splintery board.

Marcella lifted the hair carefully, slid it into a small evidence bag. "She must have sat here, talked to whoever called her."

Kamuela and Ching continued the slow perusal of the bench.

Rogers walked over. "Gundersohn thinks she was shot and fell backward into the water." They glanced back at the wide, calm surface of the canal. "Small vestiges of GSR on the coping. Seems plausible."

"At some point she sat here." Marcella held up the little bag with its coiled hair. "I wish I could find some other trace on the bench, because she was probably talking to someone."

"Well, we still have to verify all this, but it's looking strong that this is the primary site."

Waxman approached. "These detectives the liaison with HPD?"

"Yes, sir," Rogers said. "Meet Detectives Ching and Kamuela. Detectives, this is Special Agent in Charge Waxman."

"Thanks for your help, Detectives." Handshakes all round.

"Agent Scott found a hair that looks a lot like Pettigrew's caught in the bench here." Rogers, always trying to give her a boost with Waxman. "Looks like Pettigrew sat on the bench. We're thinking she was called to meet someone here. Did anyone tell the detectives about the COD?"

"No," Ching said, and Marcella filled them in on the visit to the morgue that morning.

"We still have a lot to do, and Matt and I have to meet with the University of Hawaii senior faculty to find out more about the project and closure of the lab," she finished.

"Good thing we're all here. Detectives, why don't you go to Pettigrew's apartment, see what you can find there. We're especially interested in her phone, datebook, contacts. Anything that could tell us who might have called her to meet here," Waxman said.

"Sir, are you sure we can't put off the meeting with the university people until after the search? Seems like more of a priority," Marcella said. She was curious about the brilliant scientist and eager to explore Pettigrew's home herself, gather first impressions. "We should keep the primary role here."

"No. You and Rogers need to go to that meeting. The university has been calling because the lab is shut down. They want to get back to work on the project, and our regional director is on the Board of Regents, so he's assured them we'll give them every professional courtesy and keep things moving," Waxman said.

"Local politics." Kamuela smirked. "Nice to know we aren't the only ones who have to deal with that."

"I'll be coming to Pettigrew's with you," Gundersohn rumbled. "You got scene collection kits? We can go to the residence now."

Marcella smirked back at Kamuela as Gundersohn headed toward the beige police SUV to ride with the HPD detectives. "Guaranteed to be a thorough search now," she said, surrendering her evidence kit to Waxman.

"Gundersohn finds things others miss," the SAC said. He never forgot or forgave careless mistakes, and she'd made a few in her time.

Marcella set her jaw and strode toward the Acura. She found her eyes wandering down Kamuela's tall, burly physique as she followed the detective—he was definitely well put together, and eyeing him helped her deal with the irritation she was feeling between rivalry over the case and Waxman's subtle put-downs. Kamuela headed to the Forerunner and got behind the wheel of the police vehicle as she climbed into the Acura.

"I know you don't want to miss anything, but with Gunder-sohn on the job with them, the Bureau's represented." Rogers got in and fired up the engine, echoing her thoughts as he often did.

"You're right. I don't like to miss anything." Marcella stared out the window as they pulled away from the canal.

Marcella and Rogers sat in front of a blond wood desk with the Hawaiian flag and university flag draped in limp folds on either side. The university president looked them over with sharp brown eyes from behind the desk. She was an imposing Hawaiian woman, with a pile of thick silver hair speared by chopsticks adding to her height. The graceful folds of a formal, subtly patterned muumuu with an oval scoop neck and velvet trim created a frame for her face.

"What's the progress on your investigation?" Dr. Kaiulani Moniz had a deep voice with a vibrating timbre and was known for her *kumu hula* background. Marcella could well imagine that voice calling ancient chants in a firelit darkness filled with drums and dancers.

"I'm sorry. We can't comment on an open murder investigation," Marcella said. "We're just getting started."

"The work the Pettigrew lab is doing is of utmost importance. To the university, to the students working there, and to the world that's waiting for the results."

"We know it's important work, and we also know it's even more important to bring the person who killed Dr. Pettigrew to justice. We're still processing the lab for evidence."

"When do you anticipate being able to release the lab premises back to Dr. Truman and his team?"

"We don't think she was killed in the lab, so that should speed things up. We're working as fast as we can, but there are a lot of computers to check—we have our IT specialists working on it. We're looking for anyone who wanted that research enough to kill and steal for it. Do you have any ideas about that?"

"I was briefed by Dr. Pettigrew just a few days ago on the status of the project and her plans for it." Dr. Moniz looked down at a folder in front of her. "AgroCon had given a grant for her project, and so had a conglomerate affiliated with Chevron, so they are interested parties. But she had plans for BioGreen other than selling it to the highest bidder."

Rogers sat forward, exchanging a glance with Marcella. "What other plans? I thought researchers published and the world read the journal articles."

"That's what happens with most research. But the BioGreen project was—is—a project that's not only theoretical, it's already applied. That algae stock was ready to go, and the Pettigrew lab stood to net our school some much-needed revenue." Dr. Moniz looked down at the folder. "I have offers for the rights to BioGreen here from three major companies. But that's not what Dr. Pettigrew wanted to do. She came to me to argue for something else."

A long moment stretched out, and Marcella realized Dr. Moniz was waiting for the "And what did she want to do with the research?" that finally came from Rogers.

"Trudy Pettigrew wanted to give away BioGreen. She didn't just publish research articles that could be read by anyone—she wanted to create a biofuel lab, produce algae stock to give away to developing nations. Give it away to anyone who wanted it. She wanted to feed and fuel the world." Dr. Moniz was a showman as well as an administrator, and her ringing voice delivered words that echoed through the room.

Marcella sat back in the hard plastic chair. "Huh. Wow." It was beginning to seem more and more tragic that Dr. Pettigrew now lay on a table in the morgue. "We're going to need information on who made offers on BioGreen. Oh, and a list of who knew the research was completed and people who knew she wanted to give the formula away. Anything else you think might be relevant."

"I anticipated that." Dr. Moniz closed the manila folder, handed it to Marcella. "Dr. Pettigrew's death is more than just a loss to us—it's a loss to the whole world."

Marcella narrowed her eyes at the older woman. "Are you telling us you were going to approve her giving it away? Let her do the biofuel farm?"

Dr. Moniz shrugged, and sadness gleamed in the depths of her rich brown eyes. "I hadn't decided. If we did give the formula away, I had a nomination for the Nobel Prize already prepared."

That was big and spoke to the impact of the research. Marcella stood. "A Nobel beats cash any day for a university."

"Maybe, maybe not. Please just make every effort to move things along and recover the research." The older woman turned away to her computer, dismissing them with a nod.

Chapter 6

*P*apa Gio's favorite coffee shop was more of a greasy spoon, a corner diner called Rosie's several blocks off Kalakaua Avenue. It could have been any linoleum-floored, vinyl-boothed food joint, its only concession to Hawaii a plastic napkin holder shaped like a pineapple on each Formica table. Maybe that's why her father liked it. Marcella blew on the tarry surface of black coffee in a thick china mug, eyeing her father over the rim.

"What's up, Papa? You know I'm coming to dinner on Sunday."

Egidio Scatalina brushed an imaginary crumb off his immaculately pressed sleeve. "Nothing up. But I want to see my daughter, see what she doing."

"Working. It's what I do, Papa." Her eyes strayed out the window to the curb where Rogers sat in the Acura, working his phone and the laptop that folded out from under the glove box.

"I know what you do, Marcella." He rolled the syllables of her name the way they were meant to be spoken. "I worried about your mother."

"What do you mean? Mama's fine. I saw her yesterday. She's having so much fun with that culinary school, she can hardly stand it."

"That's what I thinking is bad thing. That culinary school."
He looked down at his inky coffee, stirred it with a clinking
sound. He still liked to add too much sugar, as if it were an
espresso in the Old Country. His full mouth was set in something very like a pout. Egidio Scatalina was not in favor of
women's liberation.

"So that's what this is about. You don't like it that she's not at
home, at your beck and call." Marcella reached over, patted his
hand. "She's having fun, and you're not in on it. You need to get
out, find some interests."

"I thinking we go back to New Jersey." Papa Gio had retired
from his successful shoe-import business, though he maintained
an interest in the company and a steady stream of free samples he
passed on to Marcella and her mother. A continent and an ocean
hadn't been enough to get Marcella much distance. Her parents
had followed her to Waikiki recently, and the six months they'd
been in Hawaii had been a big adjustment for all involved.

When Papa was upset, his accent thickened, and Marcella had
to lean closer to make out his words. "I no like the heat here."

"Oh, Papa. Give it a chance. You could also wear fewer clothes,
you know." She gestured to his long-sleeved shirt, slacks, and
wing-tip shoes with socks. "You know what? There's a men's
clothing store nearby. Let me take you over there, pick out a
few things. I'll tell Rogers I'll take a cab back to HQ." Before
he could protest, she speed-dialed Rogers, and as they paid the
check, the Acura pulled away from the curb.

Marcella took her father's arm, and as they walked down the
sidewalk, the sun beating on their heads, she could feel him relax.
Palm trees swayed above them, and the canal was far enough
away that the air felt fresh with moisture and a warm breeze.

"How is my angel?" he asked in Italian.

"Great, Papa. You know, working. But I love what I do." She
replied in the same language.

"I have never understood you. But I love you. I try to accept you are a modern woman."

"That's good, because that's what I am. I love you too."

"So when we going to meet a young man?"

"You never give up, Papa."

"Your mama, she never going to give up on grandbabies."

"Don't blame this on her. You two need to get a dog. Maybe a small yappy one that needs a lot of professional grooming."

"We have to keep an eye on you. That *cazzo* you were with. He hurt you. We come, we make sure you okay," he said, switching back to English.

"Papa. For godsake, that's ancient history. I was a freshman in college." Marcella shook her head. "Now I finally know why you followed me over here, and it wasn't for the weather. You don't have anything to worry about. Seriously."

She steered him into the air-conditioned depths of the Tommy Bahama store. "Excuse me; we need some help here." She waved a saleswoman over.

Half an hour later they came out. Papa Gio wore knee-length Bermudas, huaraches, a lightweight cotton aloha shirt, and a Panama hat. He finally looked like a retired Mainland transplant, not a tourist.

Her father drove her back to the Federal building in the boatlike Cadillac he'd driven the last twenty years and had shipped over.

"You look good, Papa," Marcella said. She leaned over and kissed both his cheeks.

"I can get used to this clothes." He adjusted the hat to a rakish angle. "Not so hot."

Marcella opened the heavy car door. "Don't get lost going home."

She didn't look back. She knew he watched her walk into the building and out of sight before he drove away.

———————

Marcella's phone rang as she rose in the elevator to the tenth floor of the Prince Kuhio Federal Building, the Bureau's headquarters. She dug it out of her jacket pocket as the doors swished open on to the marble-floored lobby that did a good imitation of a regular office, complete with couches, a fan of magazines, and a shiny-faced New Agent Trainee behind a bulletproof window.

"Scott here." She headed to the interior door—reinforced steel disguised as wood—and swiped her ID badge. The door swished open.

"Agent Scott." Gundersohn's voice, each word rendered hypnotically pedantic by some internal metronome. "We have found some items at the residence."

"What, exactly?" Marcella's kitten heels clicked on the smooth hall tile. She turned into the Spartan little office she shared with Rogers, flung herself into her office chair. She hoisted her feet to the corner of the desk, unbuckled the shoes, wiggled her toes.

"You could always wear sensible shoes," Rogers said from behind his computer. She held her finger up to her lips.

"The woman's car is in the university parking. No purse or phone at her home. We have her home computer though. Bringing it in for IT to go over. Encrypted."

"Good. Want any help down there?"

"We have it under control. Will let you know if we find more contacts." He cut the connection.

"They don't want us at Pettigrew's apartment," Marcella said, turning on her computer. "That makes me think we should go. Just let me rest my feet a minute—had to walk a couple blocks to a clothing store with the paterfamilias."

Rogers tossed her a bottle of water from a box beside his desk. A former military man, he was fanatical about health and fitness and believed drinking enough water was the secret to eternal youth. Given his ripped muscles, high energy, and shiny hair, it seemed to be working.

"Waxman stopped in and wants us to drag the canal where she went in for her purse. You're the only one of us who scubas, so you have fun with that. I'll supervise from shore."

"Great," Marcella muttered, sipping the water as she scrolled through her e-mail. "I get to catch some biological disease in pursuit of a biologist's murderer. Perfect."

"Yeah, the bacteria count in the Ala Wai is pretty high." The broad pathway of water flowing through downtown was used for flood control and sewage disposal, though supposedly the waste was treated. During annual flooding, bacteria multiplied, and there were always surfers who insisted on riding the break near the canal mouth who came down with various infections—some of them lethal.

Marcella checked her messages. "AgroCon got back to me. We have an appointment tomorrow to talk with the vice president. Let's swing by Pettigrew's. I'll see if I can get anyone else to help with the scuba."

Chapter 7

Marcella ducked under the crime-scene tape crossed over the doorway of Dr. Pettigrew's corner-unit condo in the prestigious Kahala area. Rogers brought up the rear as she opened the door with gloved hands.

Gundersohn had his head buried in the cushions of the couch. He straightened and frowned as he turned to face Marcella, a high-powered flashlight in his hand. Kamuela and Ching appeared in the doorway of the bedroom.

"What are you guys doing here? We have it handled." Kamuela's husky voice had an edge.

"Just wanted to pop in, have a look around. We know you've got it handled, and in fact, we're on our way to drag the canal, look for the murder weapon. We just wanted to get a sense of the victim—I always like to have a look at the residence." Marcella kept her voice conciliatory but firm—she wasn't about to be excluded from any part of the investigation, and she was there to prove it.

She turned to look around the sparely furnished apartment. Furniture was typical rattan-and-tropical print on beige shag, a plastic palm and artificial fern decorating the corners—decor of the seldom home. The only real individual touch in the place was a great blazing canvas hung above the couch. Three dark shadowy outlines low to the left huddled in front of what appeared to be a nuclear explosion threaded with rainbows and touched with gold leaf.

"Must be the niece's work. She's a painter." Marcella leaned close and could make out the initials "NP" in the corner. The detectives went back into the second bedroom.

"Weird painting. Don't think I could look at that every day," Rogers said.

"It's a metaphor, Texas Boy. This is a great painting." Marcella shook her head. "That girl's got talent."

"We're mostly done," Gundersohn said. "Since you're here, let me orient you." He led them to the first bedroom. "She slept here. Doesn't appear she spent much time here." He opened the closet. Matched sets of plain elastic-waisted slacks hung with polyester shirts, a row of plain orthopedic-soled shoes on the floor below.

"A fashion plate she was not," Marcella said. "Pettigrew was all about her work."

"No signs of company, male or female," Gundersohn said.

"Not even a vibrator?" Rogers pulled open the side drawer. "Aha. The Kangaroo 3000. Guaranteed to replace ninety-five percent of husbands." He slammed the drawer shut. "The picture we're getting is pretty consistent."

"It worries me that you recognized the brand of her vibrator," Marcella said.

"I've got eyes. It's writ big and bold on the—oh, never mind." Rogers's ears turned red.

"The other bedroom is where she did spend some time." Gundersohn ignored the byplay and led them into the other room. Once again, one of Natalie's dynamic paintings lit the wall. The room had been made into an office, with computer desk, floor-to-ceiling books, and facing a TV in the corner, an exercise bike.

Kamuela had unplugged the computer and lifted it off the desk, heading for the door. "Understand you want to take this in for the techies to have a look at."

"Yes," Gundersohn said.

Marcella felt the hairs rise along her arms as Kamuela brushed by her, a ripple of awareness, and she had to wrench her eyes away from the corded muscles wrapped around the bulky stack of equipment he carried.

"Well, you're sure there's no sign of her purse or phone?" she asked Gundersohn for form's sake. "Or a personal calendar. Anything like that."

"Nothing."

"Okay. Well, I'm thinking maybe the killer just tossed them in the Ala Wai. Maybe we'll get lucky and even find the gun when we go in and search."

"Sounds like SAC Waxman's idea," Gundersohn said, reaching up to rub the back of his ear. "I don't scuba. I will take everything in to inventory."

"Good. We should try to get into the water today, not let any more time go by. I could use a dive buddy—any of you scuba?"

"I do," Kamuela said. None of the rest of the team were certified. They arranged to meet in an hour at the primary crime scene with scuba gear. Marcella tried not to think about the unsanitary waters of the Ala Wai by imagining Kamuela in a wet suit.

Marcella's phone toned as she struggled to drag the wet suit over her curvy hips, clad in a sensible black tank suit. "Get that, will you?" she barked at Rogers, who was kneeling on the cement beside the canal, screwing the regulator onto the scuba tank.

Her partner picked up the phone, glanced at it. "It's an unknown number."

"Answer it! Please." She hauled the claustrophobic rubber suit up over her arms. As usual, the zipper went up the back, and the long tape to pull it up was gone. Damn rental equipment.

"It's Cindy Moku," Rogers said. "She wants to talk to us."

"Gimme that." Marcella strode over on bare feet, took the phone. "This is Agent Scott."

"Hi, Agent Scott. I was wondering…if I could come in and talk to you. I'm worried about a situation."

"Of course. We're in the middle of something, but we could meet you in a couple of hours."

"No, tonight's not good. How about tomorrow morning?"

"That's fine. Are you sure you can't just tell me now?" Marcella felt sweat spring up on her spine as the black rubber suit heated up. Her eyes scanned the road for the tan Forerunner Ching and Kamuela drove. If he didn't show up soon, she was going to have to jump in without him or expire of heat prostration. On that thought, the Forerunner drove up.

"No, I can't talk about it on the phone, and I feel bad…I might be wrong. I have to check something out first before I say anything more."

"Well, we'll call you first thing tomorrow morning," Marcella said, her eyes on Kamuela getting out of the Toyota SUV, his wet suit already halfway on, the rubber torso and arms dangling around his waist. Her breath hitched at the sight. *Damn.*

"Okay." Moku's voice sounded wobbly and uncertain. She hung up.

Marcella handed the phone back to Rogers. "I gotta get into the water ASAP before I die of heatstroke. Where's my BC?"

"Right here. And here are some beacon markers and a high-powered flashlight for your head and a handheld. You're going to need both."

The rented Buoyancy Compensator Device, or BC, was an unfortunate hot pink. Marcella curled her lip but clamped the strap around the air tank. The BC, an inflatable vest, was the secret to being able to descend and ascend in the water, compensating for a weight belt worn to create negative flotation. Marcella bent over, slung the weight belt across her lower back, and straightened up, slipping the plastic buckle into its cradle with a click.

"You're forgetting something." She heard the rasp of the long zipper running from her ass to her neck ascending, felt the tightness and restriction of the rubber suit molding itself to her body.

"Thanks." She turned, but it wasn't Rogers who'd zipped her up—it was Kamuela. He was packed into his suit as tightly as she, and it wasn't the heat that made her cheeks flush.

"Scuba would be a great sport if it weren't for all the equipment." He already had his weight belt on. "Let me hold your gear for you, dive buddy." His voice was carefully neutral.

"Sure."

He hoisted the BC, tank, and regulator up and held them out to her, the vest arms open for her to slip into. A moment later she did the same for him. They turned on each other's oxygen, checked their dive computers, and compared their compass readings.

Marcella took a look at the murky water before them. "Can't believe it's looking good to me, but I'm hot enough to be ready to get in there."

"You got that right."

The last touches were mask and fins, which they put on while sitting on the cement edge of the canal. Marcella was the first to slide forward into the murky, briny water, bobbing easily with the BC fully inflated.

Marcella and Kamuela turned on the flashlights and gave each other thumbs-up. Marcella reached up to compress a valve on her vest. A stream of bubbles emitted, and she sank into greenish dim pierced by the yellow lances of their lights and a silver stream of bubbles. She tracked Kamuela beside her, descending at the same rate, and let herself smile a little around the rubber regulator in her mouth.

He looked even better in the wet suit than she'd imagined.

They hit the bottom in seconds—the canal was no more than twelve feet deep. Marcella's fins sank into the muck on the bottom, and as she pushed up, a cloud of mud obscured visibility even further. They were going to have to get very close to the bottom and try not to disturb the silt.

Marcella took a compass reading and set her first tracking beacon, a triangular cone with a flashing light on top of it. Two feet over, per protocol, Kamuela set a second beacon.

Marcella inflated the vest slightly without moving her legs and rose a couple of feet off the bottom, high enough to reach down into the muck with her hands. She experimented with height by manipulating the air in the BC until she was able to hover at just the right depth. Kamuela rose to parallel her, and they waited for the silt to settle.

The deep inhale of her breath followed by the singing stream of bubbles was remarkably soothing; Marcella felt herself relax. Suspended weightless in the dark, no sound but the mysterious song of her own breath, safe with Kamuela beside her, she finally stopped thinking.

When the silt had settled a bit, she pointed her light down into it, and they began systematic passes, looking into the silty mud with the lights and keeping their movements small. As they suspended in the hypnotic environment, time seemed to slow.

Marcella was surprised to see her O2 gauge begin flashing a yellow warning on the dive computer dangling from her BC. She glanced at the built-in clock—they'd been down an hour. Kamuela suddenly kicked forward, engulfing them in a brown cloud. She shone her handheld light on his face, grinning around a stream of bubbles.

He was holding a cell phone.

They still had around fifteen minutes of oxygen, and moments later found a beige purse drifting gently against a cement piling, a few feet away from where Kamuela had found the phone. Marcella photographed both items where they were found.

The purse was weighted with something or it would have washed away even in the slow current. Marcella's heart picked up speed with excitement, but now wasn't the time to investigate its contents. Hopefully the .22 Pettigrew was shot with was weighing down the purse.

Marcella's O2 meter began flashing red. She caught Kamuela's eye and pointed up. He nodded, and they inflated their BCs, rising at the speed of their silvered breath to the surface. They were mere feet from the concrete lip of the canal.

Kamuela held up the purse, streaming water, and Rogers reached for it, grinning. "Yes!"

"This too," Marcella said, holding up the phone. Rogers took the items as the divers reached up for the edge. Kamuela was able to haul himself out with brute strength, his gear still on, but Marcella was rendered too clumsy and heavy without the buoyancy of the water. She took off her weight belt, handed it up to Rogers, then her BC. He hoisted the gear up onto the cement, and Marcella took hold of the edge, pulled herself up. She flopped on her back, panting. The sky had gone dark, streaked with the flame of sunset, and late-evening shadows surrounded them. She sat up.

"I'm hoping the purse was weighted down with a weapon," Kamuela said. He'd stripped out of his gear and squatted beside her.

"Let's see." Rogers turned the purse upside down.

Out poured water, a ballpoint pen, a Nikon digital camera, a metal pill canister, a comb, a ChapStick, a pair of sunglasses, a soaked paper datebook, a roll of Tums exploding out of their wrapper.

No gun.

"Must have been the camera weighing it down," Marcella said. "Maybe we can save the SIM card."

"Same with the phone. Hopefully the water didn't get all the way into it." Kamuela shook his head briskly. "We need to get this water off us—I can feel an itch coming on. Everywhere."

"Yeah. Why don't you guys take off? I'm going to run this stuff back to headquarters and hand the SIM cards and whatever else over to IT. They're going to need some time to process it, so let's call it a day." Rogers glanced at his watch. "My wife's given me an hour, tops, to get home before she and the kids break into the steaks without me."

Marcella's stomach rumbled at the mention, and she glanced over at Kamuela as she heard a similar sound come from his direction. He grinned, the first time she'd seen that blaze of smile without a regulator in the way.

"No such luck for me," Marcella said, pulling off her fins. "I just want to get home to a hot shower. Doesn't seem like you're doing much when you're down there, but you sure feel it when you get out of the water." She stood, hunched her shoulders. "Can someone unzip me? Damn zipper tag is gone."

"No problem." Kamuela pulled the zipper down to her waist. She wriggled her shoulders, and he tugged at one side of the long sleeve so she could pull her arm out. She tugged the other side down, turned with a smile. "Need any help?"

"Sure." His tag was still on, but she pulled the zipper down anyway, enjoying the deep groove of his spine, his supple height, the way his muscles seemed to swell out of the confines of the suit as the zipper moved down. He shrugged; she pulled the shoulder of the suit—and he pulled his right arm out.

On the inside of his biceps was a small gray hammerhead shark tattoo. It made her wonder what else might be tattooed on that big brown body.

Marcella moved over to unscrew her regulator and unclamp

the BC from the oxygen tank. She busied herself with the various tasks of taking off and sorting her gear, hauling it to the Acura, peeling off the wet suit, toweling off her sleek black tank suit. She didn't want to be attracted to Kamuela, someone she worked with. Nothing good could come of it, she told herself sternly.

"See you guys tomorrow," she said to Kamuela. Ching, who'd been napping in the SUV, had woken up to help his partner with the gear. Kamuela lifted a hand as she climbed into the Acura. She didn't wave back.

"Get me home, Matt. I can feel the bacteria multiplying as we speak."

"You got it, babe." The Acura laid down a little rubber as they pulled away, and Marcella thought that expressed her frustration nicely.

Chapter 8

Marcella finally got out of the shower when she felt par-
boiled. She wrapped her long hair in one towel and dried
herself carefully with another, checking for any wounds that
could harbor bacteria. Nothing on her but the mole on her hip and
the bullet scar on the outside of her triceps, where a bank robber
had winged her a year ago. She slipped into her terry-cloth robe,
and with the towel on her head tucked in turban-style, went in
search of food.

She hit the On button of her computer and put a Lean Cuisine
meal in the microwave. The calm the underwater world had
wrought might have been a dream. The e-mail icon was lit up
on her computer, and she opened it to find a message from the
Club.

Funny timing. She'd been going to surf their catalog. She
clicked on the icon.

Kamuela appeared in a photo avatar, under the name "Mano,"
asking her to meet. She knew *mano* meant "shark." He wore a
black mask, a silky unbuttoned aloha shirt, and worn jeans. Part
of the Club's anonymity, and its sexy appeal, was that every-

one wore masks—but he was easily recognizable with his broad chest and muscled arms.

"Oh my God." Marcella clapped her hand over her mouth. "He must have recognized me. Oh my God." She clicked over to her own avatar, where she appeared with the mask on, her lush hair down, looking flirtatiously over a bare shoulder, under the name "Maria." In the photo, she was wearing a bustier that laced up the back, showcasing her curves.

She was probably as recognizable to him as he was to her.

Marcella got up and went to the fridge. There still wasn't much in there—a withered apple, some dubious leftovers—but there was a bottle of Pinot Grigio. She grabbed it, splashed a glassful, took a swig.

He had to know it was her. He was a detective, for godsake, used to assessing people, memorizing them, mask or no mask. She remembered his arm brushing hers in Pettigrew's apartment—his nearness had activated something subliminal, a sizzle they must both be feeling. But why approach her through the Club? Why not just ask her out?

But maybe he hadn't recognized her. Maybe he was just looking for someone to hook up with.

No. The timing couldn't be coincidental, she told herself. He'd been trolling profiles and he'd seen hers. He could even blackmail her with it, ruin her reputation. The Club wasn't illegal, but it was definitely inappropriate—too much vulnerability for the agent and the Bureau.

She went into the bedroom, picked up Loverboy's bowl. "This is what other women have girlfriends for," she told the betta fish, carrying him into the kitchen as she sat at her little table with the Lean Cuisine. "They call each other. Talk over men. Take a vote and decide what to do. My only girlfriend is Lei Texeira, who's as messed up about men as me—maybe more so. She'd shoot herself in the head before she'd sleep with a stranger, like I have so many times. She'd never understand this weird situation. No. I need to figure it out myself."

Loverboy had little to add to this monologue.

Marcella shoveled in the woefully small portion of food in minutes, then tore into a loaf of bread sitting on the shelf and ate a couple of slices. Sipped the wine. Loverboy fanned his fins at her, and she dropped a few bread crumbs into the bowl. Rogers and his family had given her the fish for Christmas, and she was surprised at how attached to him she'd become.

"Who says fish aren't good companions? Okay. I know. I wanted to check out Natalie's place, see if I can get a look at whoever she's sleeping with. I'll go do that for a while, see what that kinky artist is up to, then just drive by the Club. Have a look. I don't have to decide now."

Loverboy did a few laps, gobbled at the floating crumbs.

"Okay. It's a plan. I can do this." Marcella went back into the bathroom and blew out her hair with the hair dryer, reveling in the sensation of hot air blowing over her squeaky-clean skin. When it was thick and straight, brushing her waist, she touched up her full mouth with fire-engine red. She whisked mascara over thick, curly lashes and slid into thin black silk pants. A loose velvet tank top completed the ensemble.

She put on the heavy gold Scatalina family cross her parents had given her for First Communion. It felt a little superstitious as she did so—as if warding off some sort of spell. She decided not to overthink it. She might be promiscuous, but she was no slut. There was a difference—and the difference was, she was in charge of whom she slept with.

Marcella slid her cred wallet and the small .19 caliber into her soft black leather purse. On her way out, she picked up the fish bowl and planted a kiss on it. A bright red lip print remained. Loverboy attacked it, bumping the glass.

"Love you too, baby." She locked the door behind her.

Marcella took the elevator for once, feeling a very real physical tiredness masked by nervous energy—scuba diving really did have a sneaky physical effect. In the building garage, she got into her car, a black Honda Accord two-door.

She whipped the light canvas cover off, tossed it to the front of her parking stall. The dim lights of the garage gleamed off the chrome of custom rims, and Lei's humorous gift of a pair of fuzzy purple dice dangled from the mirror.

She rolled out and, ten minutes later, drew up in front of Natalie's dilapidated building, parking across the street in the shadow of a tree just enough to be hidden but not so deep in shadow she couldn't see out. Seeing the dice reminded her to call her friend Lei, and she speed-dialed Texeira. It went to voice mail again.

"Damn, girl! Call me back. I need to talk to you." What the hell. She doubted Lei would have any idea what to do, but the impulse to tell someone her ridiculous situation was strong—and this situation reminded her how few people she had to really talk to.

Marcella looked up the building to Natalie's windows. The lights were on in the tenth-floor apartment, but no movement appeared. Marcella reclined the seat, turned the radio to a Latin guitar station.

It didn't take long before she began to have trouble keeping her eyes open, and she checked her watch. Only nine o'clock. The time frame for partners to meet each other at the Club was between nine and eleven. If she waited here long enough, she'd be making her decision.

A pang somewhere south of her navel informed her that some parts of her body were casting a vote for going.

The lights went out abruptly in Natalie's apartment.

Marcella waited. Five minutes more, and she'd leave, Natalie no doubt tucked up for the night.

She put her hand on the key to turn on the car and spotted

Natalie. The girl was all in black, coming out the glass front door of the apartment building. Natalie walked rapidly along the sidewalk to the corner, head down, then stopped. Raised her head, looked around. Marcella scooted down in her seat.

Natalie's hair was spiked in tufts, and a metal-studded collar gleamed around her slender throat. Her hands were buried in the pockets of narrow black jeans, and the pale skin of her arms gleamed under the streetlight like poured cream.

A car rolled up—navy blue Toyota RAV4. Light-colored hair gleamed in the driver's seat, height consistent with a man. Natalie hopped into the vehicle, and the little SUV pulled away on the opposite side of the road. Marcella spotted the plate as they passed, memorized the number, and did a U-turn out of her spot to follow the Toyota. She speed-dialed HQ as she cranked the U-turn.

"Federal Bureau of Investigation, Honolulu Branch. How may I help you?"

"This is Agent Scott, Angie." Marcella rattled off her ID number. Angie was the graveyard-shift dispatcher, a veteran operator recruited from HPD emergency 911 when she got "too stressed out" by years on the job. The Bureau maintained its own twenty-four-hour dispatch. Though technically closed during nonbusiness hours, the dispatch kept the communication loop humming within the agency.

"I need you to run a plate on a Toyota RAV4." Marcella rattled off the number, keeping the Toyota in sight and half a block away.

"Just a minute, Agent Scott."

Marcella took a turn a little too quickly, nervous as the Toyota headed into heavier traffic. They were headed farther downtown. Dinner out?

"That Toyota is registered to a Dr. Ron and Julie Truman. Need the address?"

"No. I have it." Marcella punched off.

She wasn't terribly surprised, given how cagey they'd both been about their alibis—Dr. Handsome Truman was meeting Natalie Pettigrew. A more unlikely pairing she had yet to see. She kept her eyes on the Toyota until it turned in to an underground garage. She circled the block and then entered, rolling up and down the rows until she spotted Natalie and Truman walking toward the stairs.

She pulled the Honda into the nearest stall, grabbed her purse, and hurried after them. She was glad she'd worn pants and low-heeled sandals this time, because she was able to hurry up the metal stairs and poke her head out the exit in time to see them walk down the block.

Ron Truman looked great, not that that had ever been a problem. His blond hair shone gold under the streetlights and he was all in black—and suddenly the pairing didn't look that odd. They turned into the entrance of a building. Marcella hurried to catch up, pulling up short in front of a pair of double doors.

Techno music thumped from inside. A blue neon scripted sign above the black doors spelled out BATCAVE.

Marcella pushed it open. A chain-covered bouncer eyed her. "Welcome to the Cave."

"What kind of club is this?"

"First time? Well, the bar's over there." He gestured into a darkness lit by glowing orbs set in the walls. The music, all synthetic and percussion, thrummed through a packed dance floor. "We're a Goth club. You know, vampires, bondage. Dark shit like that. I can show you around." His incisors had been sharpened, and he showed them in a feral grin.

"No thanks. I'll check it out myself." Marcella pushed past him. At least her dark clothes would help her blend. She elbowed her way through ghouls of various sorts to the bar.

She had no idea the Goth scene was so alive in Honolulu,

a city better known for surf, sun, and bikinis. Natalie was one of a handful of Goths she'd come across in a year of working the city, and here she was in a club jam-packed with the freaks. She appropriated a stool and ordered a cosmopolitan. Once the drink was in her hand, Marcella swiveled to survey the dance floor.

As she'd suspected, the couple was already out dancing. She wouldn't have been able to spot them if it weren't for bloodred spangles from a mirror ball hitting Truman's tall blond head. Natalie—in black with black hair—was all but invisible.

Marcella spent the next hour fending off passes from various men and a few women and keeping an eye on the couple on the dance floor. Finally they headed for the bar, and on that cue, Marcella glided off her stool and onto the floor, quickly joined by a fledgling vampire who kept trying to bite her on the neck.

She kept the couple in visual. Quick consumption of drinks, then back out to the dance floor. They twined around each other in endless variations of foreplay.

Marcella checked the glowing dial of her dive watch—ten thirty. She'd seen enough and got some valuable intel. She brushed off the vampire and headed for the exit.

More than likely, Truman and Natalie would go back to Natalie's place, and she didn't need to see it to predict it. Interviewing them was going to be interesting—and she felt an unexpected tenderness for the clumsy way they'd tried to protect each other. They really seemed, if not in love, seriously into each other.

Marcella found herself trotting down the sidewalk, galvanized. Her mind was made up, and that ache south of the belt buckle was getting the final vote. She could put her mask on, pretend she didn't know who he was, see where it all went. She roared out of the garage and the mere half mile to the Club. But as she turned on to the block, she felt her heart speed up with something other than anticipation.

She parked the car across from the red door of the Club, a move strictly against their policy—members were supposed to park in a nearby garage. She did some breathing. Clenched and unclenched her hands on the steering wheel. Looked at the door. Realized the unfamiliar feeling she had was terror.

She hated being afraid.

As if on cue, Kamuela came out through the red door. He wore the silky shirt, the worn jeans. Her palms itched to touch him as he looked up and down the empty street. Then he spotted her car. He looked at it, hands on his hips—the silly mask dangling from his fingers.

Her heart raced.

He couldn't know it was her inside. She had tinting on the windows. Her plates were unlisted, a precaution agents had as a security measure, but if he ran them, he'd know the car was owned by someone in law enforcement.

He looked away. Paced a bit. Looked at his watch.

She slid down in the seat. He could still come over, and if he did, he'd see her.

She imagined opening the door, walking over to meet him, going inside. Dancing. And what came next. She broke out in sweat and couldn't tell if it was terror or lust. Maybe a little of both.

She'd brought her mask, and her hands shook as she slipped it on. She peeked over the edge of the window—only to see the flutter of the back of his shirt as he disappeared into the parking garage.

It was only 10:55. He hadn't waited until eleven! He'd left early. Dammit! She might have worked up the nerve to get out of the car in the next five minutes.

Disappointment was sour in her mouth.

Marcella turned the key, and the Honda roared to life. She didn't want to be sitting there when he drove out of the garage and maybe got a look at her plates. She peeled out and blazed home.

Ever since Trevor, she'd told herself whatever she was afraid of, that was the thing she was going to do. And for the most part, she'd been true to that resolve. Until now.

It was a long time before she fell sleep.

Chapter 9

Marcella scrolled through her departmental e-mail the next morning, a third cup of inky coffee cooling at her elbow. Rogers hung his jacket on the back of the door, frowned at the sight of her.

"What you doing here so early? You look like you could have used a little more shut-eye."

Marcella rubbed her eyes, sat back, took another sip of coffee. "You have no idea. How was the steak?"

"Excellent, thanks for asking." He got behind his computer. "What did I miss?"

"A lot, in fact." She swiveled her chair a bit. She'd worn her hot-pink heels today, hoping they'd give her a little energy boost. Sure enough, looking at them on her feet helped. "You first."

"Not much to tell. Dropped off the camera and purse at the lab last night. Only Andy was on; we just inventoried the items. We should go down later, see how they're doing with the computers from the lab, Dr. Pettigrew's desktop, and if they're going to be able to read the cards off the camera and phone."

"Okay. Let's do that." Marcella yawned, shook her head. Her loosely pinned hair fell down. She scooped it up, wound it into a ball, and stuck a pencil through it. "I staked out Natalie last night. Guess who her mystery alibi is?"

"Hm. I'm betting on Dr. Truman, since he wouldn't give up his alibi either."

"Shoot." She took another sip of coffee. It was bound to work, anytime now. "I was hoping to surprise you. Yup, around nine p.m., Natalie left her apartment and was picked up at the corner by Dr. Handsome in his blue Toyota RAV-4. They went dancing. Can you guess where?"

"No idea."

"That Goth club on the corner of Kalakaua and Ellis—the Bat-Cave. I had no idea there were enough Goths in Honolulu to have a club. Well, it was very much the dungeon-scene meat market. I watched until about ten forty-five, then called it a night. Got tired of fending off people who wanted a taste of my neck."

"Did you see her leave with him? Did they go back to her place?"

"No. I didn't stay to see the inevitable, but Julie Beecham Truman she's not. Talk about an odd couple—and yet they seemed really into each other." Marcella felt something like envy, remembering the way the couple's arms had twined around each other, their passionate kissing.

"I liked Natalie. I don't get her art, but hell—if you say she's got talent, I'm sure she does. Maybe she and Truman brought something out in each other. Something more than the obvious."

"Thanks, Dr. Phil." Marcella yawned again. "Okay. Let's line up the day. At eight a.m., I'm going to call Cindy Moku and set up a time to talk. Then we have to check in with Waxman, bring him up to speed. After that, we've got the AgroCon interview at ten. How about we check in with the lab on the tech stuff when we get back from that?"

"Sounds like a plan. 'Course, you know things seldom go according to plan."

"I know. But I like to have one anyway. We also need to go through Pettigrew's financials. We should check with her lawyer and see what's in her will, if there are any financial motives hanging around out there."

Rogers lifted the thirty-pound barbell next to his desk, did ten pumps while his computer booted up. He did stuff like that—and she'd decided not to find it annoying.

SAC Waxman stuck his head in the door. "Briefing in my office at eight."

Rogers looked at Marcella as the branch chief disappeared. "And so it begins. Don't know why you think having a plan is a good idea."

"It comforts me," Marcella said. She shrugged into her FBI-gray jacket. "Let's go."

Marcella headed out of the building, her cell phone ringing with the third attempt so far to contact Cindy Moku. She left another voice mail as Rogers opened the Acura.

"Are you thinking what I'm thinking?" she asked her partner as they got in.

"What? That Cindy got cold feet about talking to us? Yeah."

"Let's go by her place on the way to the AgroCon meeting. Just swing by."

"We don't really have time." The "briefing" in Waxman's office had been slowed by Gundersohn, who insisted on a step-by-step review on the progress of the investigation.

"Okay. The way back then."

Her phone rang again.

"Agent Scott."

"This is Dr. Zosar Abed." Mellifluous voice with an Indian accent. "I am calling with a concern."

"Hi, Dr. Abed. How can I help you?" She glanced at Rogers. They were all coming out of the woodwork now.

"I have some information for the investigation."

"Yes? What would that be?"

"I think some people were having a relationship. And maybe Dr. Pettigrew didn't approve."

"Is that so? What people would be having a relationship?" Marcella asked for Rogers's benefit.

"Cindy and Fernandez. But he wasn't good to her." This last spoken in a rush. "He didn't appreciate her. He took advantage."

This wasn't the pairing Marcella had anticipated—she'd been expecting something about Dr. Handsome and the Goth.

"Cindy and Fernandez had a relationship? And how does this connect to Dr. Pettigrew's murder?"

"She didn't want anyone having the relations in her lab." From what Marcella could tell, the lab was a regular soap opera. "So maybe one of them killed her. But not Cindy. Cindy would never do that."

"If it wasn't Cindy, then you're accusing Fernandez of murder. Do you have anything more to go on than this?" She frowned over at Rogers, who glanced at her, sandy brows lifted in question as they left downtown. They were heading into the foothills where AgroCon owned a complex of low-key buildings.

"Fernandez, he didn't agree with Dr. P on a lot of things. And he came up with one of the main concepts of the research, and I don't think he agreed with what she was planning to do with it. He wanted to get rich."

"So you guys knew what she was planning to do with the research."

"She had a lot of interest from funding sources. We know BioGreen is important—critical even. We know there were offers. And we also know Dr. P wanted to help the world." The note of hero-worship was back in his voice. "But she hadn't told us directly, no."

"So Fernandez didn't agree with Dr. P, whom you look up to. Sounds like you didn't like him very much."

A long pause.

"Jarod Fernandez took advantage of Cindy. And he didn't understand Dr. P. That's all I'm saying. If you don't believe me, well, I've done what I can." He hung up, an abrupt click.

"Hm. Could be sour grapes," Marcella said, looking at her phone. "Or it could be a good tip. Either way, we need to schedule those longer interviews with the interns ASAP."

Rogers slowed down as they approached the AgroCon complex. Protesters lined either side of the street, holding signs saying LABEL GMOS and STOP POISONING OUR `AINA.

"What's all this about?" Marcella frowned.

"Been following it in the news. AgroCon grows a lot of test crops and tries their experimental products, including pesticides, here in Hawaii because of its geographic isolation. People aren't happy."

"Whoa. Wonder what AgroCon will have to say."

"This should be revealing," Rogers agreed, as they pulled up to a discreet gatehouse beside a mechanical metal gate that didn't identify AgroCon Ltd. anywhere—but clearly the address had been identified by the protesters. He held up his cred wallet for the armed security guard in the booth. "Special Agents Scott and Rogers to see your vice president."

Chapter 10

*T*he director's office was more like a fancy lawyer's than an agriculture company's, with deep carpets, Swedish modern furnishings, and a huge view of Honolulu spread out below them. Vice President of Operations Lance Smith came out from behind his minimalist desk to shake their hands and inspect their creds with equal thoroughness.

"Please, sit," he said, indicating a seating arrangement around a beautiful ikebana arrangement of bird-of-paradise. They sat. Smith had the beefy, sunblasted look of a golfer and the lavender polo shirt to go with it. He showed them a lot of veneered teeth. "I'm wondering how we can possibly be of interest to the FBI."

Rogers took the lead. "We're investigating the murder of a prominent scientist, Dr. Trudy Pettigrew. She was working on a project AgroCon is reported to be interested in, and her research was stolen. We're following up on anyone who had an interest in the research."

"What!" The man's shock appeared genuine. "I did hear about Dr. Pettigrew on the news, but I didn't know the research was stolen! I thought the rights to her work reverted to the University of Hawaii."

"No. Her research was stolen and the sample stock as well."

Smith's face reddened and a vein pulsed in his forehead, indicating a possible problem with his blood pressure. "This is news to me."

"Be that as it may." Rogers forged on. "What was AgroCon's interest in Dr. Pettigrew's research?"

"We helped fund it. We owned an interest in it. This is a terrible loss." He stood up, paced.

"What exactly was your understanding about ownership of the rights to BioGreen?" Rogers asked.

"We gave Dr. Pettigrew a five-hundred-thousand-dollar grant. We had a handshake agreement that she would entertain our offer for the rights first, over other competitors, if the project was successful. Which we had heard it was."

"Hm. We were given to understand by the university that grants are given no strings attached; unless it's a privately funded lab, all work product is jointly owned by the researchers and the university. No one can unilaterally 'buy' a project; nor does the research automatically belong to anyone who contributes to the project," Marcella said.

The AgroCon VP flapped his hand in a dismissive gesture. "Grants are the lifeblood of research and we all know that, as do the researchers. Dr. Pettigrew knew which side her bread was buttered on, and now that I'm aware of this, I'll be having our legal department draw up a claim."

Rogers and Marcella exchanged a glance. Marcella finally spoke. "We are in the middle of an active murder investigation. Perhaps Dr. Pettigrew didn't see it the way you did—perhaps she had other plans for BioGreen. And you killed her for it."

Smith's high color faded, leaving him the same mushroom shade as the seating arrangement.

"That's ridiculous. No one would be that stupid. Dr. Pettigrew was worth way more alive."

"How deeply caring," Marcella said.

"What I mean to say is, AgroCon Ltd. would never stoop to such tactics. We are a worldwide conglomerate with no need to compromise ourselves in this way."

"Oh. In what way do you compromise yourselves?"

"No comment. Now, if you have nothing further to ask me, I have a company to run."

"We'd like copies of all the paperwork between your firm and Dr. Pettigrew."

"There wasn't much. Just her grant application and our letter approving the grant. Anything further was a verbal agreement, which we will still consider binding."

"Not when the woman is dead, leaving no paper trail. We'd also like any internal memos, etcetera."

The VP depressed a button on his desk and spoke into it. "Janice, can you notify legal that these agents are asking for internal paperwork and copies of correspondence relevant to Dr. Pettigrew? Thank you." He released the button, showed his veneers again. "I'm sure you have a subpoena for that information."

"By the time you collect it, we'll have it," Rogers said. "Your lack of helpfulness is duly noted."

They left the office, Marcella working her phone to get subpoenas for the AgroCon correspondence. Back at the Acura, Rogers loosened the collar of his pressed white shirt, yanked out his tie, turned the key with a roar.

"Corporate ass."

"Did you expect anything different? Types like that, all they do is make phone calls and generate memos. I've got no problem with AgroCon having a motive—but finding out who in a giant organization actually pulled the trigger, or hired someone to pull it, is going to take time. I, for one, want it to be one of the students—much easier to track them."

Rogers pulled the vehicle out of the parking lot. "I just hate that faceless corporation shit. Someone somewhere in that big-ass building is making decisions, and one of them might have been to kill Dr. P and steal the research."

"You'll get no argument from me." Marcella copied Cindy Moku's address off her phone and plugged it into the GPS. "Let's see what Cindy's up to that she isn't answering her phone."

Cindy Moku lived in a small add-on ohana, or in-law unit, attached to a bigger family home near the university. They pulled the Acura up outside the small building. Marcella stepped out onto the concrete driveway, dodging a skateboard. She and Rogers walked up three rickety wooden steps to the peeling front door, knocking softly—then louder.

A dark-haired toddler on a Big Wheel rolled out of the nearby garage, eyed them. "You know where Aunty Cindy stay?" Marcella tried a little pidgin, which she was bad at. The child appeared to think so too and shook her head, pedaling back into the garage.

"I'll go around the back of the house," Rogers said. Marcella tried to peer in the window, but the blinds were down, and with the inquisitive child nearby, she couldn't blame Cindy for keeping everything shut up tight.

"Agent Scott!" Rogers called from the back of the house. Marcella left the porch and swished through untrimmed grass dotted with the fallen pinwheels of plumeria blossoms to a small back deck with a sliding door. Rogers had it open, and one look at his face told her bad things waited inside.

She pushed the door wider and stepped inside, the shadowed interior throwing her off so she almost walked right into the figure that hung from the ceiling fan in the living room.

She took a step back as Rogers reached up to apply two fingers to the empurpled throat of the young scientist.

"Gone."

"No. Dammit." Marcella covered her mouth with her hand, her eyes filling. They took in the scene a minute longer: the tipped-over chair. The rope wrapped around the fan base, which must have been screwed into a beam to take that kind of weight. That sweet-faced scientist, so full of promise, scion of her family—motionless but for a gentle spin of the still-rotating fan, long black hair hanging down to conceal the cruel means of her death.

Marcella tasted bile—not from horror, but from a sudden and profound grief. Fucking waste of promise. Homicide or suicide, this death was a damn shame. Marcella wondered—if she'd just taken the time to talk to Cindy yesterday, maybe the young woman would still be alive.

There was no way to know.

Sometimes she hated her job. On the other hand, better for them to have found the remains than the child playing in the driveway.

"I'll call it in." Rogers called Dispatch as Marcella shook herself back into her role and did a slow cruise around the room. She found the note on the cheap little side table. She used a tissue from a nearby box to pick it up.

Rogers hung up. "They're notifying HPD. The ME and our crime lab team are on the way."

"Good. Lemme read this to you." Marcella cleared her throat around an unexpected blockage. "'I can't take it anymore. I killed Dr. Pettigrew because she was going to give the formula away—she had no right. And now it's just a matter of time before my life is over. I just can't hurt like this anymore.' It's not signed." Marcella set the note back where she found it.

"Looks like plain computer paper and typed," Rogers said.

"I'm not buying it," Marcella said.

"What doesn't sit right for you?"

"Cindy doesn't seem the type. If anything, she's practical. Her biggest concern, from what I could tell, was that Dr. Pettigrew wasn't around to sign off on her research. Not only that, her call to me yesterday. She was 'checking something out.' She tipped her hand somehow, made herself a target, and now she makes a handy scapegoat."

They went back outside onto the tiny deck. Marcella drew in a sweet, sweet breath of fresh air, pushing her fists into her lower back, arching her head to look up at the sky, indifferently blue and depthless. She sighed the breath back out again, thinking terrible thoughts of how Cindy's last moments must have been.

"I hate this," she said. "I hate this a lot."

"Me too." Rogers avoided her eyes, reached out to give her shoulder an awkward pat. They walked out to meet the blare and scream of sirens filling the street.

Kamuela and Ching were in the wave of third responders to the hanging. Marcella noticed Kamuela out of the corner of her eye. He moved quickly toward Rogers, who was standing outside the front door, and her partner brought the two HPD detectives up to speed. Marcella turned a bit farther away so she wouldn't be distracted. She continued her questioning of Cindy's weeping cousin, who owned the main house. The woman's arms were wrapped around the toddler as tears flowed freely.

"Did Cindy have any history of depression? Was she on any medications?"

"No and no!" The other woman sobbed, hunched on the back steps in her muumuu and rubber slippers, a dish towel to her face as she held the child.

"Was she acting any differently lately?"

"She was so upset about Dr. Pettigrew. She was worried about not getting her doctorate now that the doctor died."

"Was she upset enough to kill herself? Could she have had anything to do with Dr. Pettigrew's death?"

"No!" The cousin recoiled. "No talk crap like that. No disrespect her name!"

"I'm sorry. I meant no disrespect." Marcella floundered a bit, not wanting to reveal anything further and not sure how she'd gone wrong. The woman stood up, scooped up the toddler. She drew herself up proudly and gave Marcella a contemptuous glare, or "stink eye"—as Marcella had heard it called.

"Cindy, she was a good person. She loved God. She would never kill herself. You find who wen' kill her, you'll find who killed Dr. Pettigrew too." She spun on her heel and stomped back into the house, slamming the door so hard, the windows rattled.

Marcella sighed, looking down at her phone. She'd have to come back later and reinterview the woman. She'd mishandled that somehow.

"Problem?" Kamuela's voice. She looked sideways at him, a quick glance, and felt her heart speed up.

"No problem." She made her voice as cold as possible. "The witness was understandably upset."

"Hawaiians don't take kindly to insults to their families. Implying Cindy was unstable won't go over well—besides, Rogers says you don't think Cindy hung herself."

"I don't." Marcella watched Dr. Fukushima and her assistant, pushing a gurney, hurry up the little driveway. "I think Cindy knew something and was about to tell us." She filled him in on her theory. "This really points to someone on the inside."

"Or, she was calling to confess yesterday and chickened out. Went home and killed herself." Rogers joined them. Ching had followed Fukushima into the cottage along with the lab crew to assist in cutting down the body.

"I'm with Marcella. I think someone on the inside killed her because she knew something. They cover their tracks and point the finger for Dr. Pettigrew by making it look like suicide," Kamuela said.

"Well, we're not any closer to a main suspect with those interns," Marcella said. "All the lab people have motive. Natalie, I suspect, is Pettigrew's heir and has money problems. AgroCon thinks they own that formula already and might kill to get it. Too many suspects is what we have, and too many things to follow up on."

"We have Gundersohn, the tech team, and the lab team, and of course two of HPD's finest. I think we can do this, Marcella." Rogers gave her a narrow blue stare. "Buck up and let's get busy."

"We shouldn't be having this conversation in a witness's garage. Let's go see how they're doing in there and talk in private."

Just then Dr. Fukushima and her assistant rolled by with the black-bagged, strapped-down body on a gurney. Wails of grief rose at the sight from the crowd of friends and relatives gathered on the other side of the crime-scene tape at the end of the driveway. Marcella blinked hard. She turned her back, squared her shoulders, and led the way back into Cindy's little place.

"Okay. We need to search in here. Take her computer in. Let's go over the place now. I don't want to wait for Fukushima to pronounce; I think we have enough motive to move ahead as if this is another murder. After we're done with that, we'll pool ideas and divide up the leads that are left."

"Sounds like a plan," said Kamuela. The agents and detectives gloved up and went to work along with two lab techs from the FBI office.

Cindy's life had been simple. A life that had revolved around her studies, marked by a few relics of her childhood: a pennant from a Kamehameha football game, a teddy bear. Her bedroom was cluttered and small, used just for sleeping. Her fridge was full of food, though—the antithesis of Marcella's—and everything looked homegrown and local. Who went to the farmer's market for fresh produce, then hung herself? Marcella wondered.

In the end, they packed up the suicide note and yet another computer to take into the IT department. Not a lot left to mark a life. Darkness stained the sky indigo when Marcella's phone rang.

"Marcella!" It was Papa Gio. "You forget Sunday dinner? Your mama, she upset."

"Oh crap, Papa. We have another murder. I can't come." Marcella ripped a glove off to rub her burning eyes.

"You always have another murder. Your mama, she cooked for you!" His volume climbed. Kamuela lifted his head from sorting through Cindy's desk, a flash of his white teeth lighting his face.

"Marcella's in trouble," he singsonged. Kamuela had a nice smile, Marcella noticed. She realized she didn't know his first name. Never had heard it.

"I'm on my way," she barked into the phone. She punched off. "You obviously don't know what it's like to deal with an Italian papa."

"It's my Hawaiian mama that cracks the whip. It's much the same with Sunday dinner—only they live on Maui, so I don't have to go too often. And my mama's laulau makes it worth it."

"Well." She looked around. "Things are pretty much done here. How about we all meet at HQ tomorrow morning and go over all the leads we have?"

They agreed, and Marcella and Rogers left the lab techs and the detectives going through the last few areas of the apartment.

On her third glass of a nice Chianti, Marcella finally began to feel a little more relaxed. Her parents' condo was right on the Waikiki Marina, and the ocean blew cool refreshment over her. She'd shed her jacket, weapon harness, belt, and shoes at the door, and now she forked up the last of a huge bowl of seafood linguine.

"Wonderful, Mama. This is the best yet of your recipes."

"Thank you, 'Cella. I'm experimenting." Her mother, resplendent in an electric-blue fitted muumuu, gestured to the corner, where an elaborate hanging contraption sported clusters of ripening Roma tomatoes. "For good Italian food, you must have fresh tomatoes. The salt air is hard on them, but they growing."

"She make me bring it in every night," Papa Gio grumbled from his side of the little square table on the deck. "I keep inside under the grow light. Those tomatoes, they cost about fifteen dollars each."

"So. Mama. What did you think of Papa's outfit we bought the other day?" Marcella had already run through her four safe topics: the New Jersey Spartans football season, the weather, family gossip about other relatives, Mama's cooking. "He looked mighty spiffy, if I do say so myself."

"I like it. I buy him some more shirts online, more the shorts. He more comfortable now."

"I living the island life with shorts ever'day," Papa Gio said. He swirled his wine in the balloon glass. "I found some fellas to play cards with."

"Cards? Really? Where?" Anna Scatalina didn't sound as thrilled at her father's social activity as Marcella would have wished. She sneaked a glance at her watch. By eight thirty she could make a getaway. Cindy's murder felt nearby and raw, making her current setting feel surreal as emotional and physical exhaustion set in.

"They have a club at the marina. They call it the Yacht Club. I go for lunch; they invite me for cards."

"What kind of cards?" Mama's voice was sharp. Alarm bells rang somewhere in Marcella's mind. Her father had had a problem with gambling on the horses in Jersey, another (and private) reason for the couple's exodus to Waikiki.

"You always telling me, get a socialization." Papa Gio swirled his wine.

"You never tell me what kind of cards!" Anna's shrill voice brought Marcella to her feet.

"Let me clean up." They ignored her, already off and running in Italian on what was clearly a well-worn argument. Marcella cleared the table, loaded the dishwasher. This was beginning to feel way too much like when she was a kid and they'd get going. She returned to the deck.

"I'm going now, you guys." She went to her father, kissed the top of his head. "Wear that hat, Papa. And don't gamble too much. Mama, cut him some slack. He might need to play a few hands of poker to make new friends."

They exploded into more voluble argument as she slipped outside and drove home. Once there, she spent a long time in the shower, letting the water, as hot as she could stand, pour down her body as she tried to ignore the restless wired hunger that continued to gnaw at her.

She wanted to cry for Cindy, for so much promise cut short, but her eyes felt hot and burning, the tears locked behind them. There was only one thing that would help her relax. Life was short, and she needed what she needed.

"Fuck it," she said aloud, and got out of the shower. She toweled off, slid into her terry-cloth robe, and went to her computer.

She wasn't surprised to see a message from the Club in her in-box, and this time she clicked the Accept icon next to Kamuela's picture.

If he hadn't already wanted to meet her, she would have looked for him on the site. The tragedy of Cindy Moku's death, followed by the angst-ridden evening at her parents' had left her aching for release, and it really didn't matter who with.

At least, that's what she told herself.

The Club was quieter at nine p.m. on a Sunday night than on other nights, according to the bouncer who screened her membership and showed her around the bar/lounge area and dance floor. Dim lighting and cushy seating in clusters lent an intimate feel, and the dance floor, dark and lit with spangles of colored light, beckoned Marcella as Latin music, her favorite, played. There was no sign of her partner, so Marcella had a quick drink and stepped out onto the dance floor alone, her mask in place.

She'd left her long hair down, wearing a suede halter top and miniskirt that left a wide band of tanned, toned midsection visible, and tall heeled boots that laced to the knees. Other dancers joined her, and the floor filled, couples moving and changing into every possible constellation. The samba was almost enough to unwind her knots, and she danced alone, rocking it until sweat gleamed on her golden skin.

Kamuela seemed to appear beside her, coalescing out of the darkness with the stealth of a djinn—but the hand he set on her hip as he drew her into the dance was pure flesh and blood. He wore a silky shirt, tight enough that she could appreciate what it emphasized as much as concealed. Her eyes met his in their mask, and her breath quickened as he matched her steps.

Of course he knew how to dance samba, she thought. What local guy knew how to dance? What did he do with himself in his spare time? Study Latin? Fold paper cranes?

These thoughts were driven from her mind as he spun her out, reeled her in, dipped her, and planted a possessive kiss in the center of her cleavage as she bent backward. Marcella felt every fiber in her body light up at his touch.

She moved with the grace of a natural athlete, stomping, shimmying, swirling—belly dancing and martial arts in her past informing movement now. Her long hair flew like a matador's cape around her shining body. His tall shadow fell across her, pierced by arrows of light from the mirror ball. She glimpsed his corded arms, bronzed brown skin. The unbuttoned silky shirt and broken-in Levi's were the same he'd worn in the photo.

Not an exhibitionist or a pretty boy, he was a real man with a solid body—the kind that felt as good to touch as to see. His mask hid everything but the glitter of his eyes as they matched rhythms. She moved in, ran her fingers down his chest, brushing his belt buckle. She heard his quick intake of breath, felt his hands move up her back and down, pulling her in to move against him, leaving no doubt as to his intention.

She moved away and he pursued; she stalked and he retreated.

No one else existed in the crowded darkness. Words were unnecessary—and dangerous.

Finally she took his hand—a big hand, square, calloused between the thumb and forefinger—and led him off the floor, through the lounge where more sedate clubbers chose each other, and down a hall to one of the "Unoccupied" rooms.

The cubicle was simply furnished—a mirrored ceiling and a king-sized bed, a side table stocked with every imaginable unguent and sex enhancer, a narrow cabinet stocked with fresh sheets. All the necessities were there—and the partners were anonymous—except when they weren't.

Marcella let him peel her clothing off, tasting and teasing her, his fingers tracing the outlines of her neck, her arms, her breasts. She unbuttoned the last of his shirt, enjoying the splendor of his muscular body—what she'd only imagined when he wore his wet suit. She tugged him by the belt until she sat on the edge of the bed and pulled him between her legs, stroking his muscular buttocks. She made short work of the belt, the buttons, and finally the jeans, and in a moment she had him in her mouth. His hands fisted in her hair as he watched, a growl rumbling in his chest.

When he pushed her away and went to dive in, she shook her head. "Now you."

He moved in on her with the confidence she'd sensed, working her with his tongue and fingers until she felt the first wave roar up from her toes, heaving through her body, heels drumming on his back.

That's when he surprised her, flipping her around and drap-
ing her boneless body over the end of the bed, her ass in the air
and boots still on. He entered her from behind, and she slid back
and forth across the white sheets, the surface abrading sensitive
nipples, relentlessly exquisite. He reached down in front of himself and found the kernel of her pleasure. She reared back with a
cry as he bore down on her again and again.

Their passionate explosion was wordless but far from silent.

Marcella collapsed facedown, his bulk draped over her as they
cooled.

"Wow," she muttered.

"Amen," he said. Both their masks were still on; that was the
rule. She turned her head and glimpsed the hammerhead tattoo
on his inner biceps. She rolled away and stood up, pulling wipes
out of the canister by the bed, tossing him some as she rubbed
herself down while he discarded the condom he'd somehow put
on without a hitch.

A discreet plaque hung on the wall declared, "Leave it the way
you want to find it."

She and Kamuela stripped the bed, tossed the sheets into the
hamper in the corner, and remade it with extras from the cabinet.

As they headed for the door, he smacked her rear lightly. "I'll
look for you again."

Her head turned sharply, not liking his presumption, but he
was already disappearing into the swirling darkness of the dance
floor.

She caught a cab back to her apartment. In the cool dark of the
backseat, wrapped in the cover of the silk trench she'd worn over
her outfit, Marcella took inventory.

She felt wonderfully relaxed. A little loose in the knees, even.
She'd be able to sleep tonight after the horrors of the day. She'd
called the shots; she'd gotten what she ordered, like getting a
good workout. She wished she could lose the last bit of Catholic

guilt and the even larger bit that wondered how the hell she'd ever look Kamuela in the eye again.

At home she took a shower and had the best sleep she'd had in days.

"All right, let's review." Waxman sat at the head of the FBI's gleaming conference table asserting dominance. The rest of the investigative team lined the table, and Marcella braced herself internally for the inevitable. He liked to make her write notes for the group on the whiteboard-lined walls. She was convinced that he liked to have her ass as visual entertainment for the rest of the group.

She was sick of it, but cooperating with his little humiliations kept her off his radar. She'd seen what he did when he really had an agent on his shit list—and doing secretary duty was the least of it. Besides, maybe this time he'd ask someone else…Marcella thought of her defiant friend Lei and wondered how she'd handle this situation. Maybe Lei wasn't right for the Bureau after all— she might be too much of a loose cannon to fit into the hierarchical structure of the FBI, where massaging male egos was a full-time job.

"Agent Scott, will you keep us organized?"

Dammit. "Yes, sir."

She stood up, picked out several colored markers. She'd chosen her baggiest black pants and a plain white blouse that morning when she heard there was a briefing. Worried she'd see Kamuela again, she'd wanted to feel very covered up. There was still some hope he didn't know who she was, though she was probably fooling herself. The guy was a detective, after all. But as long as they pretended…maybe they could meet again.

The thought brought a rush of blood to her cheeks.

Marcella turned to the whiteboard, uncapping a marker, spotting Kamuela enter the boardroom out of the corner of her eye.

Too weird, she thought. This couldn't end well. There was just no way it could. Her stomach tightened with a cramp.

"In case you haven't met her—this is Agent Sophie Ang, from Information Technology," Waxman said. Marcella turned to face the doorway—good, she wasn't the only female after all. The striking brown-skinned woman, with her cap of short-cropped hair, nodded to the room at large. Rumor had it Ang was one of Waxman's pets. "Sophie's going to be primary on the tech aspects of this case, which are considerable, and has pulled together some reports for us. Let's start with the Pettigrew murder. Agent Scott, let's keep that on one wall, and begin with the Moku murder on the other."

"Oh, was she pronounced?" Marcella asked. "At the scene we didn't think it was a suicide, but I didn't know Dr. Fukushima had had time to make a ruling."

"Dr. Fukushima pronounced Cindy Moku a homicide this morning," Waxman said. "She was strangled with the rope, then hung from the fan. The note wasn't signed, so we think the killer composed it afterward. Keyboard was wiped clean, something Cindy wouldn't have done."

Marcella started a heading, *Moku Murder:* and noted both details. Sorrow about Cindy's death made it an effort to push the squeaky marker across the board to form the letters. She kept her eyes away from where Kamuela sat, directly across from her.

"So we have a lot of reports here from various departments." Waxman gestured to a folder in front of each seat. "Let's take a look at Pettigrew's legal and financial report first."

Everyone obediently opened their folders. Marcella didn't have one. As one of the primaries on the case, it was a ridiculous oversight and another of Waxman's little games. Rogers shot her a glance and slid his report over in her direction so she could look on.

"The niece is the heir. No big surprise there. What is a surprise is Pettigrew's net worth. Apparently, she had some inherited wealth and some business savvy. She's a multimillionaire and even owns the building Natalie lives in."

"She sure didn't show it in her apartment," Marcella said, frowning. The woman's closet of utilitarian outfits came to mind.

"Any unusual payouts?" Rogers was scanning Pettigrew's bank statements along with Marcella. "Anything that could be traced back to AgroCon or another grant funder?"

"Doesn't look like it," Gundersohn rumbled.

"That would have been too easy," Marcella said. "From everything we can tell, she seems to have been straight as an arrow—and with her own fortune, why would she take a payoff?"

"Moving on." Waxman flipped a page. "Each of the staff at the lab had motive, too, in some way. Perhaps they didn't agree with how she ran the project, what she was going to do with BioGreen, with her policy of no relationships in the lab. One person we're all pretty certain wasn't her killer was Cindy Moku. No history of any aggression in her past, a recent call to share information that was cut short, and a staged suicide. So that's one down."

Marcella had listed each name under *Pettigrew Murder: Fernandez, Kim, Moku, Truman, N. Pettigrew, Abed.* She crossed off *Moku* with a big red X. Damn, she hated that girl's death.

A little distance away, she wrote, *AgroCon LTD.,* and jotted what they knew under the heading: *million-dollar grant, sense of ownership, opposed to other uses of the research.*

"Take a look at the next report. Dr. Fukushima faxed this in. Traced the three hairs on Dr. Pettigrew's body to Natalie Pettigrew. Agent Scott, when did Natalie say she saw Dr. Pettigrew prior to her death?"

"She didn't say. She wouldn't give up her alibi, which I'm pretty sure is Truman." Marcella enjoyed seeing Waxman's eyes widen in surprise. "I staked out Natalie's apartment the other night and witnessed her meeting Truman. They went dancing at a Goth club."

"Did you see them going home together?"

"No. I stayed until almost eleven p.m., watching them," Marcella said, keeping her eyes off Kamuela, who was staring at her from across the expanse of mock burled wood. "I'm pretty sure they ended up back at her place. I can stake her out again. It seems like a real attachment, as neither of them would give the other up in the initial interviews."

"Natalie Pettigrew is looking as good for this murder as any of the rest of them. Maybe Aunt Trudy was going to cut off funds or something if she didn't stop seeing Truman." Waxman tapped the folder. "Take a look at the workup on Natalie. Girl's got twenty-seven dollars in her checking account. A couple million will come in handy launching her as an artist."

"I'm willing to bet she doesn't know she's the heir or how much Pettigrew was worth," Rogers said. "She seemed genuinely grieving when we interviewed her. She didn't mention any expectation of anything but disapproval from her aunt."

"Right now our suspect pool is too large—we're looking at Pettigrew, Truman, Abed, Kim, and Fernandez and possibly a contractor for AgroCon Ltd. The only one we're fairly sure isn't the killer is the one who left a note saying she was," Marcella said. "I think we need to reinterview them all, shake the trees, and see what falls."

"Just what I was going to suggest. Along that line, Agent Ang here brought in some interesting evidence," Waxman said. "She's spent some time on Dr. Pettigrew's home computer and discovered Pettigrew was watching Kim—she had some questionable e-mails highlighted and a keystroke clone program activated on his computer. It looks like Kim has a connection with a lab in Korea."

"Excuse me. I haven't met all of you—I'm Marcus Kamuela

with the Honolulu Police Department," Kamuela said from his side of the table. *Marcus—that was his first name*. Marcella kept her eyes on the board, feeling a prickling flush making its way across her chest. "I went by the banks and pulled the suspects' financials. Nothing interesting on the other three, but Kim has some suspicious deposits. Check the next report."

Marcella and Rogers flipped to that page. Halfway down the sheet, two recent cash deposits for $9,999 were reflected in Kim's account.

"Just under the amount that requires the bank to send a form to the IRS," Marcella commented. "Let's set up the interviews, see what pops."

"Just what I was thinking," Waxman said in rare approval, inclining his head in her direction. "Also good work to you and Detective Kamuela for retrieving the wallet and phone out of the canal yesterday."

Marcella capped her pen. Maybe she wasn't in the doghouse after all—that unfortunate takedown of a Honolulu city council-man a few cases ago was going to be forgiven any day now.

"Any progress, Agent Ang?" Waxman went on.

"We're still working on them, but we should have some-thing soon," Sophie Ang said. "We've got warrants to monitor all the Internet activity on the suspects, so hopefully more will be revealed soon. I still have several of the lab computers to go through."

"That's good, because maybe one of the lab people is work-ing for AgroCon. After all, they knew the project was a success before anyone else did," Marcella said. "Kim could be the one—maybe he's double-dipping to both Korea and AgroCon."

"That's an angle worth pursuing," Waxman said. "Every-one keep an eye out for that when you schedule the interviews and keep me posted. I want to monitor them. Well, people, get to it."

Marcella was working her phone before she got out of the room.

"Natalie? Hi. It's Special Agent Marcella Scott with the FBI. Can you come down to our office for an interview?"

Marcella and Rogers stood waiting as Natalie Pettigrew stepped out of the elevator into the reception area outside the FBI headquarters. Natalie's hand was wound in the tanned, square one of Dr. Ron Truman. The young artist wore black boots that elevated her height, a plain tunic of some silvery reflective material, and narrow black jeans. Her purple-blue eyes were outlined in kohl in a Cleopatra style, but there was no color to her delicate, finely cut lips. Her black hair was brushed straight down in an ear-length bob.

"We're here for Natalie's interview." Truman's square jaw was set belligerently. Dark shadows under his green eyes and the roughness of a day or two of beard just made him more handsome: Ken doll having an emo day.

"Hi. What's your interest in our interview with Natalie?" Marcella wanted to hear what he said.

"We're together." Truman, once he'd made up his mind to come clean, didn't flinch.

"Interesting. Sorry, but you have to wait in the lobby—you'll have your own interview. Had you heard Cindy died? I heard HPD was going to notify you as head of her project." Rogers gave them down-home charm and Marcella doled out a smile with dimple bonus.

"I did hear. They told me not to tell anyone—but I told Natalie. I don't have any secrets from her." Truman just shook his head, exuding distress. "They said it was a suicide. I can't believe she'd take her own life."

"I hardly knew Cindy," Natalie volunteered.

"Let's talk inside," Rogers said, swiping his card. Truman

and Natalie hugged one last time, and she followed the agents down the hall and turned right into tactfully labeled Conference Room A.

Some FBI interview settings employed a different philosophy than police interview ones. The rooms contained all the same high-tech recording and visual-surveillance equipment, but attempted to use psychology rather than intimidation to support the interview process.

A love seat, too small for two and too large for one, took up one side of the room. Corner table with artificial plant. Several armchairs, set at angles that kept people seated in them from looking at one another. A coffee table in the center created the illusion of hospitality. The table was bolted to the floor, as was the rest of the furniture, to preserve the psychologically designed layout.

A carafe and Styrofoam cups on the coffee table awaited them. Just a cozy visit, the room seemed to say. Nothing scary or intimidating here. Let your hair down, trust the nice agents—and tell them everything. Marcella chose the love seat. "Coffee?"

"Okay," Natalie said.

Marcella poured two cups, handed one to Natalie and sipped her own. "Mm. Delicious. The elixir of life."

"So what did you want to talk to me about?" Natalie sat on the edge of her armchair, clearly uncomfortable, as the chair was designed to throw the sitter back at a reclining angle—the better to suggest relaxation. The innocently papered wall piped a live video feed into several monitors in the room next door.

"Why don't you start by telling us about your relationship?" Marcella took another sip. The coffee really was good—the New Agent Trainee minding the reception desk took his duties seriously. She'd heard he actually ground the beans each morning.

"Don't see how that's relevant," Natalie said. "And you should know I've called a lawyer."

"Well, of course that's your right, but you aren't being charged with anything. This is simply a routine interview of all Dr. Pettigrew's lab and close connections. Would you mind telling us where you were the night Dr. Pettigrew was shot?"

Natalie tried to move her chair closer to the coffee table, discovered it was bolted to the floor. She wriggled it. Hard. It should have been funny, but Marcella felt a twinge of something like embarrassment instead. She'd always thought the room didn't do what it was supposed to—it often just pissed people off.

"We were together that night. You happy?" Natalie wriggled the chair again, to no avail.

"This isn't about what makes me happy," Marcella said. "It's about who had means, motive, and opportunity to kill Dr. Pettigrew. So you were with Truman when he was supposedly working late at the lab. Was Dr. Pettigrew aware of your relationship?"

"Yes. And in answer to what you're going to ask next, she didn't approve."

"How did you two meet?" Rogers asked.

"I came to the lab to visit Aunt Trudy, drop off a painting she was buying from me. I met Ron and…" Marcella was surprised to see Natalie's smile, a transcendent expression that made her look like a fallen Goth angel. "I just thought he was the most beautiful man I'd ever seen."

"So going back to the night Dr. Pettigrew was shot. Where were you?"

"We were at my place," Natalie said. So far no real surprises, other than Truman showing up with Natalie.

"Natalie, were you aware you're your aunt's heir?" Marcella kept her voice neutral.

"Uh. No. But I guess I might be, since she didn't have anyone else." Natalie blinked.

"Well, you are. And we found out something else. Your aunt was a very rich woman. She is a millionaire several times over.

She owns the building you live in. She has a three-million-dollar life insurance policy on herself, and you're the beneficiary. All of this wealth goes to you."

Natalie absorbed this, her pale face getting paler. She clenched her fists, stood up. Looked up at the ceiling.

"Bitch!" she said. Stomped her high-heeled boot. "You bitch, Aunt Trudy! How could you do this to me!"

She burst into tears.

Marcella cleared her throat. "I should warn you that anything you say can and will be used in a court of law, should we charge you."

"You reminding me of my rights? I don't care. I didn't do it, and I want you to find the fucker who did." Natalie reached over for one of the coffee napkins, honked her nose. "I had no idea Aunt Trudy had money. She wore those awful polyester pant-suits, lived in that poky little apartment, and all she did was work. I thought she was bitter, and lonely, and hardly made ends meet herself, always saving for some autoclave or something for her precious lab." Natalie fought back more tears with a visible effort. "I loved that old bitch despite everything. I really did. And mean as she could be, I knew she loved me too. I would never do anything to hurt her. In fact, if I could have, I would have tried to make her happy."

Marcella thought of the "poky little apartment" Dr. Pettigrew had lived in, whose only beauty was the life captured in Natalie's riveting paintings.

"I think you did make her happy," Marcella said softly. "I think you did."

Rogers sat forward against the force of his chair. "Well. I'm afraid you'll have to go on record with this alibi, and I'm not sure if that can be kept confidential."

"It's okay. Ron and I want to be together, no matter what."

"All right, then. This is it for now." Marcella stood and led Natalie back down the hall to the waiting area. "Can I speak with you alone for a moment?" she asked Truman, who stood to embrace Natalie upon their return.

"Sure. Natalie, do you want to wait?"

"No. I've got to get to work." The Cleopatra makeup had not been a good choice—most of it was on her cheeks. She pulled another tissue out of the box on the coffee table and dabbed her eyes. "Call me later." She pushed the call button on the elevator. Truman patted her shoulder and whispered in her ear.

Marcella gazed at the girl thoughtfully. She just couldn't see Natalie cold-bloodedly pulling the trigger on her aunt—let alone strangling Cindy Moku and hoisting her up from the ceiling fan with those stick-thin arms. The doors opened and she got on. They closed, and her pinched, smeared face, eyes like bruised violets, disappeared.

"Come on back," Rogers said. In the conference room, Truman took the same chair Natalie had.

"So. Where were you on the night Dr. Pettigrew was shot?" Rogers asked.

"With Natalie. At her place." Truman ran a hand through his Ken-doll locks. Marcella made a note on her pad, more for show than anything. Both their alibis were confirmed. "She was crying. What did you guys say to her?" He frowned.

"Talked with her about her aunt. She got upset. Actually, we have some more bad news that we didn't share with her. I know you must have heard Cindy killed herself—but actually, she was murdered." Marcella kept her gaze on Ron Truman's face. His eyes widened, color drained, and his hands fisted—his shock looked genuine.

"What? How?" he asked, his voice thready.

"Strangled. Hung to look like suicide."

"Oh my God." He covered his face with his hands. "What the hell is going on in our lab?"

"Where were you last night?" Marcella asked.

"We were together—I was with Natalie. We went to dinner at a restaurant downtown. Then—we went back to her place. I went home about one a.m."

A tinny voice came from a speaker on the multiline phone beside the plastic plant.

"Special Agents, there's a woman in the lobby here. She's very upset, says she demands to see her husband."

"What's her name?" Marcella asked.

"Her name's Truman. Dr. Julie Truman."

Truman stood up. He was pale under his tan. "I don't know how she's here. I have to go talk to her."

"Maybe it would be a good time to let her in on what's going on," Marcella said. "She's going to find out about your relationship sometime." Truman nodded, and Rogers escorted him out of the room.

As Marcella gathered the coffee things, a cry rent the air from the direction of the lobby—and even through closed doors, the sound that echoed down the hall had a terrible rage and devastation to it. Dr. Julie Beecham Truman was not taking the news of her husband's infidelity well.

Rogers came back in. He looked shaken, gelled spikes on his military haircut misdirected, as if he'd run his hands through it. "Mrs. Truman was very upset. But the coast is clear now; they're gone. She said she thought he was having an affair and followed his phone's GPS here. Guess you could say she was right."

Marcella looked down the hall to where the NAT was picking up tossed magazines and the upended coffee table. "Looks like Julie Truman is a force of nature. Any woman that pissed is going to get through her divorce just fine."

Marcella's phone toned as she rode the elevator down a few minutes later to meet Mama for lunch at a nearby deli.

"Agent Scott here."

"Hey, it's Lei. Finally got you! I'm trying to get away to come over for a training for
a case—you going to be around in a couple weeks?"

"Of course." Marcella looked unseeing at the potted palm in front of her, wondering whether or not to tell her friend about the situation with Kamuela. In the end, she didn't. Neither of them were good at the chatty girlfriend thing, and in her heart, Marcella knew Lei would never understand her membership in the Club. Lei, a childhood sexual abuse survivor, had finally been able to have a consistent boyfriend in the last couple of years— long-suffering Michael Stevens. That relationship hadn't lasted beyond Marcella's own invitation to Lei to join the FBI.

They arranged a meet in a few weeks. Marcella hung up, feeling conflicted but glad to have heard her friend's voice. She whisked through the front doors and strode down a sidewalk dotted with planters of palms to the corner deli, Lokal Grindz. Anna Scatalina was already inside, chatting volubly with the Guatemalan counter attendant about some arcane spice usage.

"Marcella! I was just telling Eduardo here you are single, you are beautiful, and you speak some Spanish as well as Italian!"

Eduardo turned a plum color and busied himself with a rag behind the counter.

"Mama, for godsake. I'm not going to meet you for lunch anymore if you keep trying to set me up everywhere we go," Marcella hissed. "I only have a few minutes. Did you order for us?"

"Of course. Oh, all right. Well. Your papa, he is not a happy man." Anna, bright in a peacock-blue sundress and strappy sandals, brought a tall glass of iced tea for each of them from the counter to a little table in the corner. "He gambling again, Marcella, and buying him some short pants not going to solve the problem."

"Of course not. He needs to make some friends though, and a few hands of cards can't hurt."

"I wish I believed that." Anna shook her head. "He needs to work, I think. He no liking Waikiki. He need something to do."

Marcella racked her brain. What could a retired Italian shoe importer do for work?

"Why don't you two consider a new business venture? Maybe a shoe boutique where you can have coffee, food, things you make. Maybe there's some way you can do something together."

Anna's busy hands went still on the table for a moment; then she picked up a sugar packet, ripped the corner off, stirred it into the glass with the long metal spoon. The tinkling sound of the stirring went on awhile.

Marcella noticed the shadows under her mother's eyes, the droop to her mouth. It was usually hard to see signs of stress in her mother because she was always in motion, but now they were evident.

"Mama." Marcella put her hand over her mother's. "You aren't that happy here either, are you?"

"I miss my friends. I miss the seasons. The leaves, they almost gone in Jersey," Anna said. She looked up with a bright smile as Eduardo approached. *"Grazie."*

"Two salads," Eduardo muttered, sliding the loaded plates in front of them.

"Gracias, Eduardo. Me llamo Marcella," Marcella said, presenting the dimple as a tip. He retreated, blushing, as she dug into her salad.

"You have a good idea, 'Cella," Anna said, moving salad around on her plate. "I think maybe we need something more for us to do. We thought we see you a lot, but you so busy. I think about this idea of a business. I talk to Egidio."

"Well, it can't hurt," Marcella said. Her phone toned and she slipped it out of her pocket. "Agent Scott here."

"Marcella, IT came back with some info on the phone and camera chip you retrieved from the canal. Meet me in the lab in ten and we can go over it with them." Rogers's voice was charged with excitement.

Marcella stood up, waved. "Mama, I have to run. Eduardo, can I get this to go?"

Chapter 11

The Information Technology Department had their own climate-controlled lab deep in the maze of the Bureau's offices, dimly lit as a subterranean cave. Marcella swiped her card at the steel door and stepped inside.

Rogers turned to greet her. "Marcella, you know Agent Sophie Ang, right?"

"You were at our team meeting." Marcella shook the rangy black woman's hand anyway. "What have you got for us?"

"Take a look." Ang sat back down in front of her workstation, a shallow bay lined with several outsized monitors. "I was able to get the last few days of phone calls off Dr. Pettigrew's SIM card. Some of the older information, like her contacts list, was degraded, but those last few days of recents were still available." The woman hit Print, and a nearby laser spit out a list of numbers, many of them already identified with names.

"Then the real bonus." She activated another monitor and photos came up. "Appears she photographed each page of the missing lab books."

"I know the interns said they were missing, but I don't get the significance," Marcella said, looking at the graph paper sheets filled with handwritten hieroglyphics and hand-lettered charts and numbers.

"Real working labs do every bit of research by hand and hand record it," Ang said. "This is to prove authenticity for replication and publication and to prevent work being stolen or hacked before it's published. Anyone wanting to verify results in a lab should be able to show up at the actual premises, request to see the lab books, and reconstruct the work from what's there. Looks like Dr. Pettigrew was taking her own pre-cautions by photographing the lab books." Ang pointed to a date/time stamp in the corner of each photograph. "Seems like she updated it daily. So since we recovered this, the research isn't really gone."

Marcella felt her spirits lift. "This will be great news for the university and the team," she said. "Let's print some copies of this for Truman at least."

She picked up a nearby phone and updated Waxman on the latest developments.

"Let's use this," Waxman said. "This is the perfect opportunity to see who wants to suppress the information about the lab books. Finish setting up the interviews with the remaining interns and Truman and let them know we've come into possession of the information. Maybe we can set a trap."

Marcella wound the phone cord around her finger. "Yes, sir. I'll keep you posted," she said. She hung up, turned to Rogers. "Waxman's got an idea. A good one, damn him."

She informed Rogers of Waxman's idea as they made their way back to their office, printouts of the many pages of research in a thick file folder.

"That's why he's the boss and we are mere foot soldiers," Rogers said. "I know you think he's an ass, and he is—but he's a pretty good chief for all that."

"He doesn't make you get in front of the whiteboard with a marker," Marcella grumbled. "Okay, how shall we play this?"

"Let's see who we can get in first, go from there."

Peter Kim perched on the edge of the angled seat of an armchair in Conference Room A. Marcella brushed a strand of hair back, adjusting the near-invisible earbud in her ear, which piped to Waxman and Gundersohn in the monitoring room next door.

"Start off slow," Waxman said.

Marcella suppressed irritation. She'd done a few interviews in her time. "Thanks so much, Peter. We so appreciate you coming in on such short notice."

"No problem," the Korean doctoral candidate said, his smile stiff.

"You speak English like a local boy," Marcella said. "How'd you get so fluent?"

"I grew up bilingual—my father had dual citizenship. I made visits to Hawaii ever since I was a kid, to visit my aunt and uncle here—Councilman Kim." Reminding them of his connections, not a bad move.

"That's great. That why you chose the University of Hawaii?" Marcella asked.

"Exactly."

"So what was your relationship with Dr. Pettigrew like?"

"Cordial. She was my principal investigator and my doctoral supervisor. I had enormous respect for her."

"Some people have said she could be a little abrasive. Any of that ever come up for you in the lab?"

"No. She told me what to do, and I did it." Tiny shadow of something in his words. Marcella moved in on it.

"Sounds like she was a bit of a dictator."

"She was. But she was the PI and that was her job."

"Speaking of job. We pulled your financials, and there are some irregularities." She slid a copy of his bank statement over to him. The deposits for $9,999 were highlighted. "That seems like a little more than the usual monthly support you were getting from relatives."

"How did you get this?" Kim's square jaw tightened, his eyes narrowed. "You have no right."

"Actually, we do. Remember that disclosure agreement you signed with the university as part of your immigration application? You agreed to submit your financials to any federal or state agency requesting them. We requested them."

"I don't remember signing that."

"Fine print." She waved a dismissive hand. "I'm sure there's a simple explanation for these cash deposits?"

"You're not being charged with anything," Rogers said, leaning forward. "This is just a little longer follow-up interview of all Dr. Pettigrew's lab crew. We're talking to everyone one more time, especially in light of what happened to Cindy."

"What happened to Cindy?" His angled brows drew together.

"Figured you might have heard she'd died by now. She was murdered," Marcella said. "Strangled and made to look like a hanging. Know anything about that?"

Kim's olive skin went waxy. He stood up, looked around frantically.

"Trash can," Marcella snapped, and Rogers grabbed a nearby plastic-lined rubbish container and shoved it in front of Kim just as the student doubled up and vomited.

Rogers handed over a box of tissues. Kim yanked out a handful, wiped his mouth. "I apologize. Cindy was a good friend. I am—upset."

"I can see that," Marcella said. "Did you have anything to do with it?"

Kim bent and retched again. Nothing much came up. The young man wiped his mouth again, sat back in the armchair. Rogers stood and put the trash can in the hall.

"I'm not sure what I should say," Kim said.

"Okay, that's fine," Marcella said, soothing. "Only we were so hoping to clear you quickly, because as soon as we clear each of you, we can let you back in the lab. And in all this tragedy, there's some good news: We recovered Dr. Pettigrew's photographed records of the missing lab books. So you all can go right back to work when this is over. We've already put the records back in the lab—the university doesn't want us delaying your team even another day when you can get back to work on BioGreen."

The bait was cast.

Kim had taken out his phone and now he put it away. Wiped his mouth again. "Those deposits were a loan from a family member who doesn't want it getting out that they helped me. And I didn't know anything about Cindy dying. It's horrible. But I know who might."

Zosar Abed's big brown eyes filled. "Cindy? Murdered? Surely, no. This is too much!"

Marcella was prepared with not one but two boxes of tissues and a fresh trash can on hand. The Indian student scorned the tissues, letting the tears stream down his cheeks, catching on his full lips, dripping off his chin. "Fernandez. He must have done it!"

"Funny. Someone else pointed the finger at you," Marcella said. She got up, paced a bit near the door, though there was little room what with all the bolted-down furniture. "Apparently, according to this source, you were in love with Cindy."

"I was. I loved her." Fresh sobbing. This could take a while. Marcella rolled her eyes skyward, looked at Rogers.

"I'll be right back." She swiped her card and the door unlocked. Marcella strode down the hall. She could still hear the interview through the multidimensional earbud as she headed to the lounge to get a much-needed cup of coffee—Zosar Abed was an emotional roller coaster.

"What makes you think Fernandez had anything to do with Cindy's death?" Rogers's voice, low and kind, crackled a bit as she got some distance from Conference Room A. She went to the sleek black coffee machine, a dispenser style that kept it warm at a temperature that never burned the delicate brew. She got her favorite mug, the one with the chip in the handle and the FBI logo on it, and dispensed a black stream into it. "They were having a thing. Cindy liked him—more than liked him. I don't know why. He was an ass to her and everyone else." Zosar's voice had an edge of bitterness.

She felt a hand on her shoulder and, startled, she whirled around, splashing hot coffee on her hand. "Shit!" she exclaimed, shaking the hot liquid off.

Marcus Kamuela loomed way too close.

"Oops, sorry," he said. "Looks like it's going well in there." She narrowed her eyes, made a throat-cutting gesture. He looked puzzled, an eyebrow cocked. She reached up and turned the earbud off.

"We have all-way sound comms," she explained. "I was listening in on the interview."

"Seems like you needed a coffee break. Mind if I have some?"

"Help yourself." Marcella shook her head. "Dammit. I can't handle that whiny dude. I don't know why. He gets on my nerves. Anyway, I better get back in there. Didn't know you were here."

"IT needed more help with all those computers. I've got some skills, so I was helping down there. Mind if I observe?"

"Up to Waxman," Marcella said. "Room right next to Conference Room A."

She brushed by him, and damn if her nipples didn't pucker up and send a message that set off an unwelcome throb south of her beltline. The man emitted pheromones or something.

"I'm turning my comm back on." She stomped a bit as she

headed down the hall with her coffee and back into the conference room. There was a time and a place for everything, and now wasn't it for *that*.

Maybe it was time to get her money back from the Club. It had been a bad idea.

"I tried to warn Cindy," Abed was saying. "I told her he didn't seem to respect women. He didn't respect Dr. Pettigrew either."

Marcella sat back on the love seat, crossed her legs, tried to focus, but the thought that Kamuela was in the next room watching was distracting. "How long were Cindy and Fernandez having a relationship?"

"A couple of months. She broke things off with me and started hanging around with him. I don't know what she saw in him. All those tics and noises he made were very distracting in the lab." Abed sniffed fastidiously.

"So it doesn't sound like it was that serious."

"I don't know. I just know I tried to win her back and she said she had 'feelings' for him." Abed blew his nose.

"Let's switch gears a bit here," Marcella said. "We reviewed Dr. Pettigrew's phone records, and she received three calls in the last hour before the phone went into the canal. One of them was from you. Do you remember what you called her for on the evening she was shot?"

Abed rubbed his hands on his thighs, reached up to stroke his shoulder-length hair. He seemed to be soothing himself as one might a pet. "Can't say. I talked with her several times a day."

"Well, we'll be asking you that again, so try to reconstruct the day as best you can. On a positive note, we've recovered the research."

"You're kidding!" The widened eyes, brightened expression appeared to be genuine. "How?"

"Dr. Pettigrew took daily photographs of the pages of the lab books. We recovered the pictures and printed them. As soon as you all are cleared, you can get back to work in the lab." Marcella set the hook. "We've already put the data back, ready and waiting for you."

"That's great news. I hope you consider me cleared?"

"We'll let you know."

"Thanks again for coming in," said Rogers, escorting Abed to the door. Marcella threw back the rest of her coffee in a couple of gulps. Something about that guy—smarmy. Ugh. She got up.

"Way to bag out on the interview, Agent Scott." She'd almost forgotten that Waxman was listening. "Needed a cup of coffee that bad, did you?"

"Sorry, sir. I—just needed a break." She knocked on the adjoining door into the surveillance room. Gundersohn let her in. The narrow space, lit by the glow of monitors, was filled by the Waxman, Gundersohn, and the bulk of Kamuela. "Can I see a replay of the part I missed?"

"Nothing of note." Waxman looked at her. "Your hair is falling down. You might consider cutting it."

Marcella grabbed a Bic pen out of a nearby holder. She twisted her bundled hair tighter and pushed the pen through the wad. "I wonder if you advise our male agents to cut their hair. Sir."

"If it touches their collar, yes, I do, Agent Scott. The FBI has a certain professional appearance to maintain, and I want everyone on my team to maintain it."

Marcella felt her throat close with humiliation, and she withdrew, closing the door with deliberate care. She stomped back to her office, dug in the desk drawer, muttering curse words as she located a handful of bobby pins. Her mouth was filled with a row of them, as she wound her hair into the FBI Twist, when Kamuela appeared at the door.

"Hope you don't mind me saying your boss is a prick," he

said. His eyes wandered over her, and she could swear she saw something warm and appreciative in them. Did he know? Was he thinking about her like she was about him? God. This charade between them couldn't go on.

Yet it did. And she wasn't going to be the one to pull off their masks—at least not yet.

She pushed the bobby pins in, anchoring her hair in the demure roll she hadn't taken time for that morning. "I happen to agree. He's got it in for me."

"Why's that?"

"He's a bit of a misogynist. Also pissed off about a councilman I wrongly accused of embezzlement a few months ago."

"We have asshole chiefs in HPD too, but it's tough to deal with. I thought you set the trap nicely. Only one interview to go, I hear." Kamuela sat in the guest chair. "With Fernandez."

"Yeah. We've got our surveillance unit set up in the lab next door and ready to go if any of the students tries to get the notes."

She noticed his curling hair touched his collar—detectives didn't have quite the restrictions agents did—and she remembered how it felt in her hands, soft and springy. Her palms itched to touch it again. She turned on her computer instead.

"Fernandez is our last interviewee. Unfortunately, he's not answering any of his numbers." Rogers walked in and took a seat at his desk.

"Ching was in his residence area and went by to try and bring him in while you were interviewing. He doesn't seem to be home."

"Wonder where the guy could be, with the lab shut down." Marcella kept her eyes on her e-mail.

"Well. When you finish up, want to grab a bite to eat?" Kamuela asked.

"I can't—I'm going home," Rogers said. "I always try to see

the fam a little each day at least. Yeah, don't know how it happened, but it's already six o'clock."

"Sure." Kamuela cleared his throat. "Ahem. Agent Scott?"

"What?" She glanced up.

"Want to grab something?"

"No thanks. Too much to do." No telling what might happen if she was alone with him—avoidance was the only option. She kept her eyes on her monitor as he left. As soon as he was down the hall, she sat back in the chair. "Damn that man!"

"Little Shit, you are going to die a lonely old maid." Rogers got up, picked up his jacket. "Poor guy likes you. More fool him."

"He does not. Geez." She felt her cheeks heat up. She'd rediscovered blushing—that, or it was really early menopause, God forbid.

"I'm telling you—you two got some chemistry going on. But whatever. I'm off for at least ten minutes of family bliss before the kids go to bed. See you." He left.

"We don't got something going on," Marcella muttered, staring blankly at her monitor. Did Kamuela know? Was he looking for a way to let her know he knew? And if by some miracle, they made it past this bizarre hurdle, how could it possibly go anywhere? And did she want it to?

She wished for a moment she could take her mask off with him at the Club. She pictured his dark eyes widening, the recognition, the flame of hunger between them flaring up, his arms wrapping around her, his lips descending on hers…

"Agent Scott?" Waxman stood in the doorway.

"Chief? What can I do for you?" She pasted a "yessir" look on her face.

"I apologize for my remarks earlier. I should have spoken to you privately about something as personal as your hairstyle." Waxman looked like he was sucking on a penny.

"Thank you, sir. I appreciate that." Marcella didn't have to pretend to be surprised.

"Yes. Well. See you tomorrow." He withdrew his shellacked head and continued down the hall. She heard his steps, each of them. The swish of the door.

The office was empty.

Marcella kept staring at her monitor. She felt something, and it didn't feel good. She searched and came up with what it was—the bad side of alone they called lonely.

She could go down to IT. Someone was always there. Or Evidence Collection. They were still working on all the trace they'd collected from Moku's apartment. She could go get something to eat, but even empty her stomach was too knotted to put anything into it. The worst thing to do would be to sit here and imagine what she could be doing with Kamuela.

In masks. Or not. She was increasingly wishing for not.

Marcella shut down the computer, loaded her weapon into the harness, slipped the creds in her pocket, hooked her jacket off the chair, and headed out.

She'd be fine as long as she never went home and checked her e-mail.

Marcella swiped her ID badge at the door into the Information Technology lab. Low lighting, the better to enhance screen reading, kept the area cavernous. She never spent much time here, but it appeared deserted. She wandered into the various bays where the tech agents worked, each at a U-shaped module ranged with monitors and power strips, veinlike blue Internet cording lining the counters in bundles.

"Agent Scott?" Sophie Ang stood up from a module across the room. "Looking for me?"

"As a matter of fact, but any live body would be nice." Marcella moved toward her. Unlike the rest of the building, IT's floors were padded with a sound-deadening felted carpet, and she seemed to glide over it.

Ang rolled a cushy office chair over to her. "I'm still going through the lab computers. Got one more to go."

Marcella sat. "What are you looking for?"

Ang shrugged. "Anything. I've cloned the hard drive. Now I'm mining it for hidden data, searching the Internet activity, and searching for key words related to the investigation in any capacity."

"Got anything more than you told us about in the meeting?"

"Yeah, a little. I found a cache of e-mail between Kim and a lab in Korea. Appears he was negotiating with them for advance preview of BioGreen. Disappearance of the formula seems to have hung him up." Ang pulled up the correspondence, all in Korean. "I'll print it out in English for the next briefing."

"Good. I can see how maybe he'd off Pettigrew if he thought she was going to give away the research out from under him. But why would he kill Cindy?" Marcella frowned, rubbed her chin.

"I don't know. Maybe she was onto him? I mean, I heard she tried to speak to you." Ang switched on another monitor, a stream of data flowing by as her fingers flew over the keys.

"Yeah. I feel really bad about that. I was in my wet suit, about to dive in the Ala Wai Canal, and I was hot and distracted. I wish I'd taken the time to try to get her to talk to me right then." Marcella felt the lump in her throat that hadn't really gone away since the young scientist's death.

"You couldn't have known." Ang turned on a third monitor. "We have to sift through so much information all the time, and at any given time any bit of it could be irrelevant—or the turning point of the case."

"Yeah. Ain't that a bitch." Marcella noticed the corded muscles of the tech agent's forearms as the woman's blunt fingers flew across the keys. "You work out."

"Mixed martial arts. I'm in a women's fight club. Keeps my combat skills up for the Bureau, too." Ang shot her a sideways glance. "Want to come out sometime?"

"What, to watch or to compete?"

"Either. I'm sure you've got something more going on than just looks or you wouldn't be in the Bureau."

Marcella's arched brows shot up. "Gee, thanks."

A small beep sounded. Ang zeroed back in on the first monitor.

"Looks like we have a suspicious upload to an online site from this computer, Fernandez's usual workstation. Keywords "Dr. P" and "shot." Ang opened another window. "It's a private blog. Let me break in." She drag-and-dropped another window, typed something into it. They watched an hourglass spin; then the blog popped open.

Both women leaned in and their heads bumped. "Sorry," they said at the same time, still looking at the blog.

Ang sucked in her breath. "Let me tag this and print the content. We don't want to lose anything in case he rips the site down."

The poem on the blog seemed to burn Marcella's eyes. "Sick son of a bitch. He blames Cindy for making him kill her."

Ang was preoccupied with her tech tasks. The laser computer spat out pages of the blog's text. Marcella grabbed them. "This is big. Could be some important intel inside."

"I'll say it is. Let's brief the team ASAP tomorrow morning." Ang hit another key. "I'm setting up a trace on the blog. Next time he logs in and posts, I'll be able to trace the computer. I'm running an alert to my computer and my phone, so wherever I am, I'll know."

Marcella gathered the pages of the blog out of the printer.

"I'd like to go study these back in my office. Let me know if anything else pops. I'm not planning to go home tonight. Extension 334."

"Pulling an all-nighter? Me too. I'll call you if anything more surfaces. And give the Fight Club some thought. You might like it."

Marcella nodded and left, the pages tucked under her arm. Outside the womb of the IT lab, her hot-pink heels rang on the echoing floors. She stepped into her office and shut the door. Cleared the crap off her desk with a few sweeps of her arm, then turned on the halogen desk light. Sat down with the cleared surface and the stack of pages.

Blog Entry

I don't like cops. Even ones
That are pretty like
The Fed who stood there all shiny hair and teeth
She's dangerous. Him too, the other one with
A stupid accent, slow as cold honey
But sharp eyes. Smart blue eyes that see more than
they should.
They remind
Me of Dr. P's eyes. Her blue eyes
Were so surprised when
I shot her.
She never expected it of me.
Everyone underestimates me
But I'll show them in the end like
I showed her.
Posted 11:24 p.m.

Blog Entry

Black hair soft hands your beautiful eyes.
Cindy.
Your real name was
Cinderella Kealoha Anuhea Moku
A mouthful of singing that
You cut short because you wanted
To break out.
Conquer the haole world. Be
A big-shot doctor.

And you would have, too.
I could have loved you, if I
Loved like other people do.
I tried.
I wanted to.
But you figured it out and
You had to ask me.
Stupid girl, so stupid. You
Made me do it!
I hate you for that.
I can't forget your eyes
So disbelieving even as the rope
Got tighter until
They bulged and went blank.
This wasn't like Dr. P.
I hated killing you.
You made me do it.
Posted 1:30 a.m.

There weren't many pages. Marcella noted the dates and times, but the clues weren't much more than what they already knew—Pettigrew was shot and fell backward into the canal. Doubtless he lured her there with something important to discuss. And Cindy—Cindy found him out.

This did narrow the search to someone having a relationship with Cindy, though—which narrowed the suspect pool to two, maybe three. Fernandez had to be the main suspect since he was both involved with Cindy and the posts came from his computer.

But could it be a set-up? It seemed almost too easy. Still, as Lei often said, "Usually the obvious is the obvious."

Marcella prepped for the next day's briefing and meeting with the team with a list of what they now knew about the unsub from the blogs and the additional financial intel on Kim. She called over to the unit keeping an eye on the lab at UH—no activity. Reminded them to contact her the minute anything moved.

Her eyes finally grew heavy, and she reached under the desk for a thin, marshmallow-like camping mattress, an inflatable pillow, and one of those silver thermal blankets used for disaster victims—her home away from home. She rolled out the mattress and went to sleep, vaguely comforted by the thought that, a few floors away, Ang was still there too.

She didn't feel so lonely with Ang there.

Chapter 12

Marcella and Rogers stood at Fernandez's door at what Rogers liked to call the "ass-crack of dawn." Marcella had updated him on the blogs on the way, impressing him with the urgency of this interview—they might even be able to make an arrest.

The doctoral candidate lived in an off-campus apartment at the University of Hawaii Manoa, in an older low-rise building, and rosy morning-lit clouds filled the sky. Marcella's third cup of coffee still hadn't started working, and she'd paid for her long night on the office floor with various aches and pains that reminded her she was closing in on thirty way too quickly.

Marcella put some of her bad mood into pounding on the door. "Open up! FBI!"

She stepped back when the door opened. Fernandez stood there in a drooping pair of boxers. "What do you want?"

"We need to ask you some questions." She pushed past him into a dim interior, ripe with the smell of fetid human and leftover pizza. She went into the living room, piled with laundry and empty takeout boxes, and swept some of the debris onto the floor. Sat. Set the camera phone on a cleared edge of the coffee table.

"Please, make yourself at home." Fernandez let some attitude creep into his voice. "I hope you don't mind if I put on some pants."

"That would probably be best," Rogers said as the intern went into his bedroom. "My, aren't we grumpy," he said, eying Marcella. "Is that yesterday's shirt I see?"

"Guy's got some explaining to do," Marcella said. She ignored the question about her shirt.

"How can I help the FBI this morning?" Fernandez walked past her, clad in a T-shirt and sweatpants. He went into the kitchen, turned on the light. "I'm making coffee. Want some?"

"She does," Rogers answered for Marcella.

"Did you hear about your colleague, Cindy Moku?" Marcella carried the phone with her as she went to the kitchen door.

"I did. I'm…very sad and disturbed that she would take her own life." Fernandez busied himself with the coffeepot, keeping his face turned away, a belching sound emerging from his throat. "I apologize. I have trouble with tics, and they get worse when I'm upset."

"Who told you she took her own life?" Marcella asked.

"Dr. Truman called me. He told me. I've been too upset to go out. I took a pill and went to bed yesterday."

Marcella stalked into the kitchen, stood next to him. Tried to get eye contact. "Cindy didn't kill herself. She was murdered—strangled and hung to look like suicide."

Jarod Fernandez became very still, the water flowing into the coffeepot, filling it, overflowing. Marcella reached out, turned him by the shoulder. He kept his head turned away, long hair flopping over his pale face. Another belch ripped from his throat.

"Look at me. She was apparently your girlfriend. What do you have to say about that?"

"Nothing. I can't—I can't imagine that. Not Cindy. No."

"Is that why you didn't answer the door when the officer came by the other day?" Rogers asked. "We held interviews down at the Bureau offices, and everyone else showed up but you."

"I don't know. I didn't hear anything." Abruptly Fernandez's legs folded, and he slid down the side of the sink to sit on the floor, his back against the cabinet. He wrapped his arms around his legs. "I can't believe she's gone. I can't believe she..." He put his head down, the rest of his words lost in a welter of grunts and belches.

Marcella walked through the jumble of food containers to the closed drapes in the living room, threw them open. Rogers reached over and turned off the water. The apartment was exposed in all its bachelor-slob glory.

"Pull yourself together. We need to know all your movements on the day she died. We also have your number as the last one on Dr. Pettigrew's cell phone before it went into the water," Marcella said. She stalked back into the kitchen and was dismayed to see Fernandez was on his cell phone. He held up a hand toward her.

"Uncle Bennie? I have FBI agents here questioning me about my girlfriend's death."

"Shit," Marcella mouthed over her shoulder to Rogers. The intern closed his phone and made eye contact for the first time.

"Uncle Bennie says not to say anything and that he's on his way." Fernandez's eyes and affect were flat. He wasn't easy to read between the tics, floppy hair, and uneven emotional response. Marcella narrowed her eyes at him.

"Your lack of cooperation is duly noted," she said.

Her phone toned and she strode away to answer it when she saw ME OFFICE in the little window.

"I have my report on Cindy Moku ready, if you want to come down," Fukushima said. "Otherwise I'll just fax it to your office."

"Fax is fine. We're in the middle of interviewing a witness," Marcella said. "Anything of note? Any trace on her?"

"Yes, as a matter of fact. She had some epithelials on the rope and a hair caught in it—matching back to Fernandez."

Marcella swiveled to look at Rogers, jerked her head toward the kitchen, where Fernandez was still sitting, silent but for the occasional croak. "Thanks for the heads-up. I'll look for your report back at the office."

She went back into the kitchen. Turned on the overhead light so she could get a good look at him. "Medical examiner says there was a hair of yours caught in the rope around Cindy's neck and skin cells from your hands. Got any explanation for this?"

Fernandez's mouth opened. His eyes still looked flat, vacant. "Bitch," he said.

She reached out to yank him up, but Rogers held her back as Fernandez cried, "I'm sorry. I'm sorry! Sometimes the tics are swear words! Cunt! Whore!"

Pounding on the door penetrated the haze of rage that nearly had Marcella kicking the shit out of an unarmed man. She became aware of Rogers's hand on her arm, and she yanked it away.

"Your lawyer's here," she snarled, and went to the door. Checked through the peephole—it was never a good idea to pull open a door without checking—and opened it to a rotund little man in an aloha shirt covered with parrots.

"Hi. I'm Jarod's uncle Bennie. Bennie Fernandez." He smiled cherubically, a pure white, neatly trimmed beard framing a shiny white grin.

Even new to Hawaii, Marcella had heard of Bennie Fernandez the defense attorney—a man whose Santa appearance had lulled many a prosecutor into losing.

"Come in. Your client's in the kitchen."

"What have you been doing to him?" Bennie rounded on her

and Rogers as he spotted the young man curled in the fetal position on the floor, weeping theatrically.

"He was calling me swear words just a minute ago," Marcella said. "And we haven't laid a hand on him or had time to even ask him anything."

"This man is having a psychiatric emergency. He is under the care of a physician. I'm going to call that professional now and lodge a complaint with your office for harassment of a handicapped witness."

"Hold on a minute, now," Rogers said, letting out his drawl, twinkling with male camaraderie. "The boy just crumbled when we told him his girlfriend was murdered. In fact, he engaged in verbal assault of a federal officer, calling Agent Scott a bitch, cunt, and whore. She's
been a real lady about it, too."

Bennie Fernandez squatted beside his nephew. "Be that as it may, this interview is over."

"We'll be back," Marcella said.

Bennie handed her a card. "All inquiries will be going through me from now on. Now, I suggest you back off before I follow through with that complaint."

Chapter 13

Marcella had taken a moment to brush and retwist her hair, roll on some deodorant she kept in her desk, and make sure all her buttons were up before the briefing. Still, she felt gritty and sticky, and the contretemps at Fernandez's house hadn't done anything good for her temper. She stalked into the conference room and handed Rogers a pair of dry-erase markers.

"You're up, partner. Everyone's bound to notice I'm still wearing yesterday's clothes if he makes me stand up there again."

"You got it, babe." Rogers added bullet point marks to the two lists they'd started the previous day.

Marcella knew the exact moment Kamuela arrived by the prickling of the hairs on the back of her neck. She kept her face turned away but felt him sit beside her.

Waxman took his seat at the head of the table with his anointed, Gundersohn, at his right hand. Ang took the seat to his left. Waxman gestured to Marcella. "You asked for this meeting, Agent Scott. What's the update?"

"Several, in fact. Agent Ang, want to fill the chief in on what you found last night?" Marcella inclined her head toward the other woman.

Ang tapped a pile of papers in front of her. "Last night Agent Scott and I discovered an online blog that was being uploaded from one of the lab computers. This has a lot of implications and narrows our suspect pool, as we were hoping." She stood up, distributed copies of the blog posts. "This is quick reading. You'll see where Agent Scott highlighted the areas that help us narrow down the field."

Marcella gave the other agent a grateful look from under her lashes. Ang could have taken credit for the blog discovery, but she hadn't—instead, taking care to prep for the briefing and give Marcella credit.

"I also uncovered correspondence between Kim and a lab in Korea." She distributed the translated e-mails. "The bad news on this is that when we closed down the lab, the correspondence was disrupted, so we don't know if he was the one to steal the research and sell it—only that he was working on that prior to Dr. Pettigrew's death and that her discovery of it makes for a powerful motive."

"Between the interviews and these e-mails and blog posts, I think we can narrow the field to Kim, Fernandez, and Abed. Natalie Pettigrew, while benefiting financially from Pettigrew's death, doesn't have the means or motive to kill Cindy Moku. Truman doesn't have a relationship with Moku, unless there's a serious love quadrangle going on we aren't aware of. And there's this." Marcella distributed copies of Fukushima's latest report. "Hair and skin cells from Fernandez were found on Moku's body."

"Why didn't you bring him in?" Waxman looked up at her from over his narrow steel reading glasses. She saw him notice her outfit from yesterday by the slight pinch of his nostrils.

"We confronted him at his residence this morning. He reacted emotionally to the news of Moku's murder and called his uncle. Unfortunately, his uncle is Bennie Fernandez," Rogers said.

Ching and Kamuela both groaned. "That man is a menace," Ching said. "Judges and juries can't seem to resist him."

"Yes, and he claimed Fernandez was being forced into a psychiatric emergency by our questions. I'm thinking this Tourette's thing is a put-on. He certainly seemed able to call me a few choice words when it suited him." Marcella filled them in on the aborted interview.

Waxman frowned, set his reading glasses aside. "That still could be Tourette's. Extreme stress can lead to foul language as a part of the disorder. I like where we're going with this overall, but we can't rule out Kim, who has motive with his shady deposits and Korea correspondence, and Abed, who could be after the formula as well as having an attachment to Moku. Not to mention Truman, who as second in command is the next PI at the lab and whose name will be topmost on the research with Pettigrew out of the way.

"We've set the trap at the lab—though I don't know how long we can keep that going. The university is pressuring us to release the lab for actual work. I'd be more interested in the physical evidence on Moku, though Bennie Fernandez will explain that away as circumstantial as his nephew Jarod was known to be having a relationship with her." Waxman put the glasses back on and continued. "So here's what we're going to do—focus on these three interns. Get warrants for their phones and computers—Rogers, you work on that. Round-the-clock surveillance. Everyone takes a shift. Let's gather evidence, build a case on these three, and see what emerges. Keep an eye on Truman for anything unusual, but he doesn't have the flags these others do. Good work, Agents Ang and Scott. But next time—go home, shower, and get some sleep. I need everyone sharp."

Marcella exchanged a glance with Ang. "Yes, sir," they both said.

Waxman assigned shifts. Marcella wasn't on until the next morning. It was time to go home and face her demons.

One of them looked up.

"See you later, Agent Scott." Marcus Kamuela really did have a nice smile.

Marcella woke up at nine p.m. to the insistent toning of her phone. She pushed a handful of heavy, damp hair out of her eyes. "Scott here." She cleared her throat.

"'Cella." Anna Scatalina's fluting voice. "*Cara,* you sounding like you getting sick."

"I'm fine, Mama. Just tired—I went to bed early." Four p.m. was certainly that. She'd taken a shower and fallen into bed, her long hair still wet. It fell rippling around her shoulders as she sat up naked.

"We have news, darling. So exciting. I had to call you first thing."

"What, Mama?" Marcella got up, swaddled herself in her cozy terry-cloth robe, went into the kitchen. Hunger had finally kicked in, and she looked into her empty refrigerator with a frown.

"We doing like you suggest. We getting a business! You know we have some money left over from selling the house and shoe business, so your father, he see a little bistro on the corner. It needs work, but we put in offer."

"Mama, that's wonderful!" Marcella took out two Lean Cuisines—the last of anything edible—and put them in the microwave. Loverboy, still on the table in his lipstick-marked bowl, fluttered his fins to get her attention. She dropped food into the water and he attacked it. "How soon will you know if they took you up on your offer?"

"We hope tomorrow, darling. You must come see." Marcella

took note of the address and agreed to meet her parents to check out the bistro, located near the marina in Waikiki.

The microwave chimed as she ended the call. Marcella took the dinners out.

"Let's look at the lights, Loverboy," she said, and carried the fish bowl and two stacked trays out onto the little deck. She sat down and was just in time to catch a sliver of view between the high-rises of the weekly fireworks display put on by Hilton Hawaiian Village—an explosion of color and light that seemed to only accentuate her loneliness.

She was wide-awake now, and her mind returned to Marcus Kamuela. After Trevor she'd promised herself no relationships she couldn't control—and the attraction she felt for Kamuela had already gone beyond where she was comfortable. But as long as he didn't know who she was—or if he did, he pretended he didn't, and so did she—it was still okay.

She remembered scenes, sensations—the way his big, hard hands felt on her body. The way he handled her on the dance floor. The way he pursued the job, almost as obsessed as she. The way he filled out a wet suit. The way he whispered in her ear. If she wasn't careful, she was going to start liking the guy—and not just because he seemed to know what she liked in bed.

One more time, then she'd stop seeing him. Whatever he knew, he already knew, and one more time wouldn't make a difference. She didn't want to take the chance that revealing herself ruined things—for her, she already knew it would. But damn if she could endure another sleepless night with nothing but Loverboy and work for company.

She turned on her computer, logged into her e-mail. There were requests in her in-box, all right—but nothing from a dark, masked man in a silky shirt and jeans. Disappointment felt like a weight on her chest. She clicked through, declining requests from other potential lovers—and hovered her mouse over his icon.

A moment of truth—she was the one asking to meet—after she'd been so sure he'd try to see her while she was hiding in her office on a camping mattress.

Well, she'd invite him. And if he didn't come, so what. She'd be dancing, and that would feel good regardless. She sent the invitation and shut down her computer before she could chicken out again.

Marcella allowed herself to be led out onto the dance floor by a handsome man—probably Brazilian from his accent and tanned, tight exhibitionism in a pair of gold short-shorts and a suede vest tied shut through nipple rings. Long, Fabio-esque locks brushed his shoulders and his open appreciation of her and confident showmanship as he spun her through a disco routine made her laugh. Her self-reflective mood evaporated as her body got moving, and she thought Fabio would do as well as anyone if she had a few more shots at the bar—provided he wasn't waiting for someone.

She wished she could forget she was waiting for someone too—how much she wanted to see him scared her.

"That's my date, fancy pants." One of those big, hard hands hit the Brazilian in the chest, bouncing him back several feet. The gigolo waggled his tongue at Marcella and took himself off as her masked man reached one hand to the nape of her neck and the other to her waist, pulling her to him.

His mouth descended toward hers slowly, giving her plenty of time to pull away if she wanted to. But she didn't want to, instead stepping into the circle of his arms and reaching up for a kiss that shocked right down to her toes in her favorite pair of lace-up Louboutins.

"I wasn't sure you'd want to see me again," he said. All he didn't say, about who they really were, swirled unspoken between them. They could pretend a little longer; he'd given her an excuse. The dance floor spun and dazzled around them, degrees of erotic foreplay between every possible combination of men and women, and sometimes several of each—and they stood rooted in the center of it.

"No talking," she said, setting her fingertips on his lips, relishing their texture—supple, full, and firm. He drew the tip of her middle finger into his mouth, nibbled and sucked. Tingles shot down her arm.

"Okay then. Let's dance." He pulled her in tight against him, her full breasts crushed against his chest. He spun them both, and the silky wrap skirt she'd worn swirled over his legs.

"Disco," he muttered as the music changed to a Bee Gees song. "I must really want to get laid."

"Tuesday is disco night," she said, laughing. "It's in the schedule."

"So you come here a lot, do you?"

"No talking, I said," she replied, and made a game of unbuttoning a button each time she got close enough to touch him.

"So you do come here a lot."

"I have a membership. And they send a schedule of the themes, if you'd care to look."

"That's not what I'm paying attention to when I come here," he said, reminding her this was still a singles club. Meeting him wasn't anything more than what she'd set out to get—a good time in bed.

"I said, no talking," she said again, and this time she bit him on the lower lip when she kissed him before she spun away. "I think I need another drink."

She stalked to the bar, ordered a shot of Patrón, tossed it down. He followed her. Slid his hand under the heavy drape of her hair. Rubbed the back of her neck.

"Tight," he said. "You need to relax." The deep, gentle pressure of his fingers and the bomb of warmth from the drink hitting her stomach made her sigh, leaning in to him as she rested her head on his shoulder.

"Relax me," she said.

"Your wish is my command." He trailed his hand down her arm, twined his fingers in hers, and led her to a room.

This time was different. She had a sense that every time, if there ever was another, would be. She sat on the bed, and he tenderly, as if unwrapping something infinitely fragile, removed each piece of her clothing.

Tank top peeled off over her head, kisses down her neck and over her shoulders. Hands spreading her hair, fingers combing it, arranging it around her. Silky wrap skirt untied, spread wide like gift paper. She pulled her knees up, suddenly shy, as he revealed black elastic-topped stockings, a wisp of lacy panties and bra, and heels still laced high around her ankles.

He left all that alone—and spent a good deal of time removing the bra. Teasing and suckling. Kissing, licking, plucking, and swirling, exploring the weight, heft, and shape of her breasts, every centimeter worshipped. She writhed and tossed, shuddering with need and reaching for him. He stopped her with kisses, evading.

"Relax. Just feel."

"I want to see you," she finally said, when she had to use words.

"Your wish is my command."

He took hold of one of her heels, untying the lacing, unwinding it from around her calf, lifting it off her foot. Set the shoe aside. Then he slowly rolled the stocking down her leg, kissing and rubbing every inch as he did so, and made a loop with it. He slipped her hands through and tied it to a handy metal ring screwed to the wall. Only when she was securely—if falsely—fastened did he slip out of the unbuttoned shirt. He did a little striptease with the jeans, making her laugh—and making her hungry.

He came back with nothing on but skin. Her eyes ate up the expanse of broad brown body, lightly hairy in all the right places, as big and hard as she remembered. He lay down beside her, licking the tip of his finger and drawing designs on her breasts, moving down her taut belly. She wriggled, impatient, rocking her hips, and he cocked up a corner of his mouth.

"Always in such a hurry." He eventually went to work rolling down the panties.

By the time he was done with that, she couldn't do much more than whimper and beg, and the magic he worked with his fingers and tongue had her arching off the bed, making promises she'd never be able to keep. Yet somehow, in the end, she was the one on top—her hands tied, one shoe and stocking still on—and they both were much more relaxed.

"I can't feel my hands," she muttered, draped over his prone body. She sat back up and he moaned.

"Please, have mercy," he said.

"Thought that was my line." Marcella slipped her hands out of the loop of stocking. She slid down beside him, snuggled in beside his heat. "Think I'll just sleep a minute."

"Don't mind if I do," he mumbled.

Marcella woke when something rumbled beside her. She sat up and realized it was a snore, a deep vibration in the drum of Marcus's chest. He slept on, oblivious—Colossus toppled. She smiled and sat up. A tiny origami crane tumbled out of her hair. She picked it up. It appeared to be folded out of a receipt.

"Ha. You get to make the bed," she whispered, and gathered her clothes, relieved there wouldn't be an awkward reveal. Today, at least. Whatever day of the week today was. She tucked the crane into her bra as she dressed, still smiling.

Who the hell cared what day it was when she felt this good.

———

Marcella sat outside Fernandez's building the next morning, after relieving the HPD officer who'd had the night shift. One of the older campus apartments, it was a stucco low-rise roofed in asphalt tile and painted institutional beige, its only concession to Hawaii a scarred old palm tree in front that listed to the left. His apartment on the second floor was pretty easy to keep an eye on. She'd taken out her Honda and tucked it against the curb in a line of parked cars across the street.

But it was eight a.m. and already hot. She'd rolled down the windows, and no stranger to surveillance, brought a battery-powered mini fan that blew a slight breeze of tepid air across her sweating cleavage. She sucked a measured sip of an icy cup of Diet Coke.

The problem with fluids was, what went in, had to come out… And that was never a good thing on a stakeout. Her cell toned. "Agent Scott here."

"Marcella. What's Fernandez doing?" Rogers, checking in. "So far Kim hasn't got out of bed."

"Fernandez either. There's no shade here and it's damn hot."

"Gonna get hotter before the day is over."

"I know. I'll need to get out and pretend to be a student or something. So have we ruled out Natalie Pettigrew and Truman entirely?" Marcella wondered aloud, fiddling with her straw.

"I think so. I know she has motive, but I think she didn't know how rich Dr. P was. And Truman doesn't have the involvement with Cindy."

"But we don't know that the blogs are true. He could have shot Pettigrew, then framed Fernandez by writing them."

"Stop. I agree we can't rule him out, okay?"

"Well, we aren't watching Truman. So that bothers me."

"And it bothers me that we're assuming there was one killer. What if the deeds weren't done by the same doer?"

"Now *you* just stop." Marcella took another careful sip of Coke as they both considered.

"The truth is, we've made assumptions we maybe shouldn't have—because of the blog posts. They tie the murders to the same unsub," Rogers said.

"I know. But—Dr. P was like a straight-up shoot and steal; Cindy could be an affair gone wrong or to silence her or both—but the methodology on Cindy was different, much more personal. Someone could have written the blog and uploaded the entry about Cindy to point the finger in another direction. Could've planted the evidence from Fernandez to frame him."

"True, but...you know the old saying about the duck." Rogers liked to work in homespun colloquialisms as well as play devil's advocate.

"What about the duck?"

"If it walks, talks, and quacks like a duck...it probably is a duck."

"So you're saying, don't overthink it. Don't read into more at this stage."

"That's exactly what I'm saying. We have three strong candidates here. It could be any one of them, or a combination. We need to just wait and see."

"On that depressing note, I checked in with the team watching the UH lab. No movement toward our bait."

"See? This is at least more interesting than that surveillance detail."

"Speaking of...I've got movement. Checking in later." Marcella hung up and picked up her field glasses.

Fernandez had come out of his apartment with his typical hunched posture, hair over his eyes, baggy clothes. Marcella wondered again what had attracted a vibrant girl like Cindy Moku to the unprepossessing young man. Perhaps his reputed brilliance? He'd certainly seemed able to problem solve in a tight corner yesterday. And he could be handsome with half an effort, which he clearly didn't make.

The young researcher locked the door, fussed with something in the doorway, and walked down the external hallway to the stairs that ran down the center of the building. Marcella got ready to follow him on foot, putting on the black University of Hawaii ball cap with its green-and-white logo. She already wore running shoes, shorts, and a workout tank, hair in a ponytail—carrying her equipment and ID in a light nylon backpack.

Just another co-ed on her way to class.

Fernandez exited the building and strode off down the sidewalk. Marcella got out and followed him at a discreet distance, her head down to avoid him recognizing her. It didn't seem to matter, because Fernandez never turned to look and indeed seemed oblivious of his surroundings.

She tracked him through the campus, and it was only when he got to the Science and Arts building that he slowed down, looked around. As he pushed through the glass doors Marcella remembered from her visit with Rogers, she was suddenly sure he was going to the trap they'd laid in the lab.

She spotted the surveillance van, an innocuous white vehicle with a Hawaiian TelCom logo on it parked under a tree. No time to call. She broke into a jog and, making sure he'd gone into the building, knocked on the back door of the van.

She held up her cred wallet to the detective who opened the door. "Sorry to barge in. I'm one of the agents working this case and I'm tracking one of our suspects. He's just gone in the building and may be approaching the lab."

"Detective Sam Ho," the burly cop said, giving her a quick hand up and into the tight space of the van. Marcella was startled to find Marcus Kamuela wedged in beside Ho, mere inches away. He grinned at her. "Nice of you to drop by, Agent Scott."

Her stomach burst into butterflies that fluttered up to gather in her throat, tightening her voice to a squeak. "Uh. Tracking Fernandez. He came this way."

Several monitors were set up with live feeds of the hallway and the interior of the lab. Marcella's eyes riveted to the figure of Fernandez getting off the elevator and walking down the hall.

"He'd make me for sure if I followed him in there," she said. Ho flipped open a small folding aluminum stool for her and she wedged between them.

"So. What's the plan if he breaks in?" Kamuela asked, his shoulder brushing hers and leaving a trail of fire.

"We wait and watch. If he breaks in, we've got him recorded. I think we can just grab him when he comes out of the building," she said.

Three heads moved in close to track Fernandez as he came off the elevator on the biology lab floor. A new energy seemed to sweep through the young man as he put his shoulders back and strode rapidly down the linoleum hall, brushing his hair out of his eyes—almost a different person. They'd restored the entry code as part of the trap, and he walked straight up to the door. His finger paused over the uncovered keypad.

Marcella found herself holding her breath as Fernandez stood there, finger poised. She was aware of the nearby fan blowing tendrils of her ponytailed hair back, of the steady breathing of Marcus Kamuela beside her, of Detective Ho's intense focus on the other side. The world narrowed to the cramped space, forced intimacy, grainy video, small metal folding stool digging into her bare thighs.

Would he go in? It wasn't definitive, but it was certainly some-thing, and with those hairs on Moku's body…

She let her breath out in a whoosh as Fernandez turned away abruptly and headed back toward the elevator.

"Dammit," she said. On the video, Fernandez dug his phone out of his pocket and said something emphatic into it. He gestured with his hand. He reached the elevator, spun, and marched back. Marcella was again struck by the contrast of this assertive, bold body language as she tapped the monitor. "Where's the damn audio?" she exclaimed. "We need to know who he's talking to!"

"No audio. We're just tapped into the school's video-only surveillance cam." Ho's tone was apologetic.

"Shit! We have equipment. We can wire this up louder than Carnegie Hall. Why didn't you say something?" Marcella snapped at Kamuela.

"Didn't think we'd need it. Thought this was just a trap to see who tried to retrieve the documents," Kamuela said. "You Feds need to spell out what you're asking for."

They watched Fernandez march back and forth, clearly ranting about something. Abruptly, he shut his phone and got on the elevator. The doors closed and he disappeared.

"We still don't have taps on his phone okayed. I'll see where he goes next. I'm ordering audio and more cameras for the hallway and lab," Marcella said, trying not to let the pissed-off tone into her voice. She worked her phone even as she hopped out of the van. Kamuela shut the door behind her with unnecessary force.

Marcella stationed herself in a casual pose on the back side of a tree, ordering a team out to boost the surveillance equipment on the lab as she kept her eyes on the door of the building. Sure enough, right on schedule Fernandez came out. He'd gone back to his hangdog persona, head down, hair flopping, hands in pockets as he walked gracelessly back the way he'd come.

Several hours later, outside his apartment, Marcella was hot, bothered, and had to pee. She alternated watching from the car and a from spot beside a tree. She was beside the tree, pretending to study, when her phone toned.

"We have a court order demanding we release the lab back to the researchers." Waxman's voice was irritated as he delivered unwelcome news.

"Just when we were getting some activity on that! Who initiated it?"

"It's from the university, but the name on all the papers is Bennie Fernandez, the defense lawyer—Jarod Fernandez's uncle."

"So that's who Fernandez was probably ranting to," Marcella said. She'd already briefed her boss on the situation when she called for the additional surveillance equipment. "How long do we have to comply?"

"We can keep the computers we're still working on, but we have to surrender the premises upon delivery of the order. So call the HPD team. We even have to surrender the photographed lab book pages Dr. Pettigrew left—the order claims them as invaluable to time-sensitive work."

"So much for the trap. I'm beginning to wonder if this Fernandez guy is a lot more than he seems." She described the shifts in character Fernandez displayed. "I think we need to find out more about his supposedly indispensable contribution to the project."

"Truman would probably be best to interview on that. Rogers contact you?"

"Not since this morning."

"Well, apparently Kim has been boring to watch." Gundersohn, watching Abed, hadn't had any activity either.

Marcella wondered how long she could last before she had to find a bush to pee in. Her phone beeped with a text message. DET. KAMUELA filled the little screen.

Meet me for coffee Starbucks?

She frowned. She was going to have to tell him the bad news about unsealing the lab. She got back into the car, slid down on the seat. Aimed the fan at herself, took a tiny sip of now-warm Coke. Phoned him.

That voice, smooth and deep, still got her right where it counted—her libido sat up and took notice. "Agent Scott. I wanted to talk to you."

"For godsake, call me Marcella. Yeah, I have news for you too." She blew out a breath, lifting the hairs off her sticky forehead. "Can someone monitor my location? Detective Ho, or someone else? Then I'll meet you at the coffee shop."

"Can do. I have another guy here who can come cover your location. Let's meet in fifteen minutes." He rang off.

Marcella tried to ignore her speeding heart. She had bad news for him, and this wasn't a personal meet from what she could tell. Still, for the first time they were talking with no one else around. She slid the little pointed crane out of her bra, unfolded it. She'd put off unfolding it for some reason. Tiny, cramped writing filled the back of the receipt.

I can't stop thinking about you.

That makes two of us, she thought. Still no hint if he knew who she was, though it was harder and harder to pretend he didn't. She refolded it and put it back into her bra—over her heart.

Like some high school girl with a crush.

Which was exactly how she felt. Not that she'd ever felt that way before. But if she had, it would have been like this—and she didn't want to feel this way about some guy she worked with and banged at a sex club. She was annoyed with all the angst. How had the situation ended up like this? How could it end any way but badly? She wouldn't let herself be hurt again. Period.

Marcella kept the ball cap on. Her bladder was mercifully relieved by a visit to the restroom, and she sat at a corner table with her grande iced coffee, liberally dosed with vanilla sweetener since she deserved a treat. Kamuela still hadn't shown, and she found herself wishing she was the kind of woman who carried a mirror and touched up. She wasn't, so she ran cherry ChapStick over her mouth.

Kamuela came in, eyes moving like any good cop—automatically noticing, registering the other customers, checking for threats. He spotted her, and that white grin made a brief appearance before he ordered. She made busy with her phone until he sat down, angled beside her so they both had eyes on the room. She felt the dimple come out at that.

"What you stay smiling for?" Kamuela did a little pidgin, took a sip of his gigantic Mocha Frappuccino.

"Apparently you deserved a treat too. Girly drink." She gestured to the sweating sides of the Frappuccino.

"I take my poison sweet and dark," he said. "Nothing girly about it."

"And I like mine strong," she answered. Their eyes met, and she felt that prickling rash of heat move across her chest. Dammit. Blushing again. She cleared her throat. "Okay. You asked for the meet. What's up?"

"I…" He seemed to falter. "I could tell you thought I missed something with the surveillance. Your team gave it to HPD to handle, and we just don't have the resources the Feds do. It's all we can do to bring out the van, put a couple guys in there. I was getting ready to go back to your SAC and tell him my chief won't let us do it anymore—we've got some fresh cases, not to mention all my older ones. This thing is taking too many man hours."

"Got it. It's just as well, because we're pulling the plug on that aspect of the op." She laid out the dictum she'd got from Waxman. "Sucks because something had just started there with Fernandez. Dollars to doughnuts it was Bennie the defense lawyer who Jarod Fernandez was ranting to on the phone."

"Dollars to doughnuts?"

"It's a Jersey thing." She took a sip of her coffee. "Anyway, we're going to have to let the rats back into the lab. Which could be okay; we can keep an eye on them in air-conditioning instead of sweating on the side of the road. I've got a team coming to wire the lab and hallway for monitoring and we're taking over a teachers' lounge on the floor above. Compromise with the university on reopening the lab."

"Okay. So—where does that leave us?"

"Working the case, unless you need to bail out." Her heart speeded up at his tone. She looked down, fiddled with her straw.

"No. Us. You and me." The deep chord in his voice made her look up into brown eyes. Brown eyes that were utterly familiar, mask or no mask, and knew her just as well.

She blinked first. "What do you mean?" Marcella felt the idiocy of the words even as she spoke them.

"You know what I mean." Heat swept across her as he reached over, plucked the tiny white crane out of her bra. "This looks familiar."

"Give me that!" She tried to snatch it back, but he held it away. "How did you see that?"

"Little guy was poking out, like he wanted to be found."

"I take trophies sometimes." Mortification and terror made Marcella mean.

She felt the recoil in him. Hurt, then anger right behind, tightening his jaw, the skin around his eyes. He crushed the fragile pointed crane in his considerable fist. "Guess you're one of those women with notches on her bedpost. Or on your tit, as the case may be."

He'd seen her scars. He'd seen all of everything she had. He'd even seen her soul.

"I knew there was no way this could end well. The Club was supposed to be anonymous." Marcella sounded prissy and she knew it.

"Too late, babe. And the shit of it is, I really like you. I don't want it to end."

She took a breath to regroup, battling back claustrophobia. He was moving in on her, exposing her. He was making her vulnerable.

"When did you know it was me?"

"In your photo. How could I not recognize you? No, seriously, you're a distinctive woman. I wondered how I was going to tell you, when you'd figure it out, if you had." He set the coffee drink down. "When did you know?"

"That first time, in your photo." She reached out, rotated his arm so the little hammerhead shark showed. "Then I saw this little guy and knew for sure. Almost like he wanted to be found."

"My *aumakua*, guardian spirit. Always looking out for me." He put his hand over hers on his wrist, trapping it. Warm and strong, just the way she liked a hand to feel. "So. Can we like— go on a date? Or just back to my place? I'm okay with either."

Marcella tossed her head, tapped her toe. She had to do this before he did it to her, and she steeled herself to say the words. "I have no interest in a relationship. That's why I belong to the Club. So no offense, but nothing's changed. Only now I know who you are, so we won't be hooking up again."

Marcella saw him tracking that, absorbing the blow, making a comeback.

"You met me two times when you knew it was me." Kamuela leaned toward her, eyes intense, keeping the grip on her hand. "C'mon. Stop lying to yourself."

Marcella yanked her hand away.

"I never said we weren't sexually compatible. You're a good lay." She shrugged, flippant and hard—a matador delivering the death stroke.

A long moment passed.

"Thanks for that, at least." Marcus Kamuela pushed his chair back and stood. She couldn't look at him. He tossed the crumpled crane onto the table. "I believe I'll be transferring my role on this case to Ho or Ching. I've got fresh cases to work."

She found herself blinking blindly at the crushed note. The bell tinkled over the door.

The long day ended on an ignominious note of boredom as Marcella's shift ended with Fernandez doing his laundry at the nearby Fluff 'n Fold and Detective Ho relieving her in an unmarked Bronco. Back at her apartment, Marcella paced while on hold with the Club.

"Are you the manager? I'd like a refund or something. I ended up sleeping with someone I work with closely. I thought that was supposed to be screened out."

"Is that person listed as an employee in your organization?"

Marcella paused, bit the side of her finger. "No."

"Then there's no way for us to track all the potential combinations of customers. We use an algorithm to set up possible matches based on your survey choices and the workplace you choose to disclose. We can only work with the information we have."

She'd lied on her application. Like she was going to tell them she was an FBI agent—not that the Club was illegal, exactly. It was just not something the FBI would ever find acceptable. She shuddered to think of Waxman finding out.

"You know what? Cancel my membership."

Marcella felt only a little better when she hung up. She'd needed to do that for a while, but now she had nothing to do for the evening and a lot of restless energy. Her old familiar—guilt—hovered, waiting to pounce. She decided to pick the scab a little more and typed "Detective Marcus Kamuela" into her search bar, suppressing a qualm at such behavior.

Her computer was equipped with a sensitive background-checking program. She pulled up his work record with HPD (exemplary), his educational background (Kamehameha schools, football star), BA in criminal justice from the University of Hawaii *(cum laude)* with a minor in art. (Hmm. Maybe that was where the interest in origami came from.) Kept a small debt on his credit card, where his major expense appeared to be his Club membership and payments on a new Toyota Tacoma truck (blue).

No marriages. No children. No criminal activity. Even went to Rotary Club. His smiling face, embedded in the Rotary Club wheel on their website, made her feel shitty—like the spying tramp who'd dumped him that she was.

Marcella knew he'd probably already checked her background, and what he'd have found: Catholic school in New Jersey, BA from NYU *(magna cum laude)* in prelaw. She hadn't gone off the beaten track of predictable until she entered the FBI's training program after graduation, and her obsessive and controlling relationship at nineteen with a professor at the university wasn't in her records anywhere—or at least, she hoped not. She didn't even have a parking ticket in Hawaii for Marcus to hold against her.

She'd hoped that by checking Marcus out, she'd find some dirt, something like a deadbeat-dad conviction that would make her feel better about shutting him down for no good reason but her own paranoia.

Instead, Marcella shut down the computer.

This was definitely not the way to get over the guy. She snatched up her phone when it rang, relieved to be distracted, and brushed off disappointment when she saw it was Sophie Ang.

"Hey. Was getting ready for a little sparring at the Fight Club, wondered if you felt like coming." The other woman's voice was hesitant. "I know you're busy—just thought I'd see."

"Yes," Marcella said decisively. "Perfect. Where do I meet you?"

Marcella felt soft and out of shape in her running bra and nylon shorts, her usual outfit for working out and in this case, fighting—though looking down and thumping her abs, they seemed okay. It had been way too long since she'd really spent time in a gym or done her Tae Kwon Do.

She ducked into the warehouse gym on the corner of Kalakaua Avenue, feeling her pulse pick up at the familiar smells of leather and sweat. Gyms—a home away from home. The gym would have to do now that she wasn't going to the Club anymore.

Ang walked up to her, and Marcella eyed the agent's long,

toned muscles, the tats running down the insides of her arms and down her thighs—kanjis with a tribal look to them. The other woman's triangular face under that sleek cropped cut was perfectly suited for this setting. In this building, as in the cockpit of her tech lab, Ang was a goddess.

"So I'll show you around. Not much to it," Ang said, leading her in. "Lockers. Bags. Weight area. Workout pads. And the ring, as you can see."

Marcella sucked in her gut in response. Just looking at the ring made adrenaline hum through her system. "What do you have in mind for today?"

"Why don't we warm up, do some cardio or whatever; then we can watch a couple of sparring matches and I'll orient you on things. Basically, mixed martial arts is a form of fighting that borrows moves from Muay Thai, Brazilian jiujitsu, boxing, and wrestling."

"I know what it is—I just haven't watched any of it, let alone met any women who do it. I've heard it's popular here in Hawaii, though."

"Yeah, we have quite the scene. Lot of camps, clubs, gyms—and people who follow the sport."

Ang led her over to the bags, and they warmed up cardio with punching and kicking routines. Ang showed her some combinations on the big bag, and Marcella couldn't believe how much better she began to feel with the release of pent-up energy. Eventually they sat stretching. Another pair of women were up in the ring, sparring.

Ang talked her through the moves. "She's trying a takedown. That girl in purple—she's a ground fighter. She'll try to get you down in a submission hold, ground and pound you out down there. The one in green, she's more of a striker. She's going to try to stay out of range and do her beat down with kicking and punching." The fighters wore split-fingered padded gloves, which Ang said helped with gripping in the various different moves while still protecting the hands for striking.

"Ready to try it?" Ang grinned. "One of the practice areas is free."

"Yeah." Marcella followed her new friend into the padded area. They circled each other. Marcella held her arms up and went in for a high kick, reaching for Ang's head. Used to Tae Kwon Do, she wasn't ready when the other agent grabbed her leg and bore her down with her own momentum to thump on the mat, Ang's body tight around hers.

"This isn't Tae Kwon Do. Keep your arms and legs close, and kick only if you know your leg won't be grabbed," Ang said from beside her ear. Hard as Marcella squirmed and wriggled, thumping at the other woman with her free hand, she couldn't move until Ang released her, bouncing back up onto her feet with ease. Marcella staggered back up, shaking her head.

The next hour passed in a blur of getting knocked down, pummeled, thumped and kicked, and grappling gracelessly on the sweaty mats as Ang talked her through the various moves as they occurred. One last bout ended with Marcella hopelessly pinned.

"Uncle," she said, thumping the mat. "Think I've had enough."

Ang bounced back up, hoisting Marcella to her feet. "Good workout?"

"As a matter of fact." Marcella took the thin towel the other woman handed her and rubbed down her flushed, dripping face.

"How do you feel?"

"Great, actually. Just great," Marcella said, feeling a smile move across her face for the first time that day. "This is a blast. When can we do it again?"

Marcella was sore in the morning, a thousand unused muscles complaining as she poured a fourth cup of steaming black coffee from the carafe in Conference Room A into her favorite mug. She poured another one for Dr. Ron Truman. She was glad to be at work—it kept her mind off the debacle with Kamuela.

Dr. Truman's face sported whiskers and dark circles—enough to make him a little rugged and even more handsome. He took the FBI mug she handed him gratefully and sat back in his bolted-down armchair in Conference Room A.

"Thanks."

"You're welcome. How're you holding up?"

"You mean my divorce? Or the project?"

"Both. Regarding the project, we're releasing the lab back to you this morning. My partner, Agent Rogers, is down at the lab unsealing everything and getting it ready for your team."

"Excellent." Truman took a sip of the hot coffee. "My divorce is proceeding, and as to the project, it'll be good to get back to work. With those notes you guys found, we can start rebuilding the research."

"We know it's important—and that's why we're getting your team back into the lab. But we're going to need your help more than ever to find who killed Dr. Pettigrew and Cindy. I have some questions about your remaining interns."

"Of course. Anything I can do to help."

"What was each of the interns responsible for on the project? I heard that Fernandez contributed something major."

"Yes, he did. He was the one to isolate the element that assisted in the RuBisCO bind. We were all stuck on that for months."

"So did he—well, did he get an attitude about it?"

"Jarod's got some—emotional issues, I guess you could call them. We all tried to take him with a grain of salt in the lab."

"So is that your way of saying yes?"

"We all have our idiosyncrasies. Jarod's were a little more obvious than most—his tics, for instance."

"Yeah." She set down her coffee. "How real are those tics?"

"Oh, they're real all right." Truman shrugged. "But the swear words are different. He can control those, in my opinion. I've seen him get really frustrated or upset, which is when they usually come out—and if Dr. P was there, or someone else from the university he was worried about, he'd rein it in."

"Okay. I'm wondering—did he ever show any aggressive or hostile behavior in the lab? Or elsewhere that you know of?"

"He'd say things that were off. Just not appropriate—maybe a little threatening. I chalked that up to the Tourette's."

"Did you know about his reported relationship with Cindy Moku?"

"Yeah. I heard rumors to that effect. I think there was a little triangle going on with her, Fernandez, and Abed."

"What was their relationship like?"

"Honestly, if I hadn't heard about it from Cindy, I wouldn't have known. They kept it very private."

"So no public displays of affection, etcetera?"

"Not that I ever saw. Frankly, I wondered what she saw in him. Abed is a much more engaging fellow, and he moped around when she dumped him."

"What was his relationship like with Dr. Pettigrew?" Marcella rolled her shoulders against stiffness from the workout the night before. Soreness and a few bruises thumped at her from various points on her body, but she was surprised to find that overall she felt good. Relaxed—except for thoughts of Kamuela that kept hitting her at unwelcome moments. She muscled her attention back to the interview.

"Fernandez was rigid in how he liked to do things, and Dr. P was definitely the boss. They butted heads a few times."

"And how about you?" She slid the question in gently between sips of coffee.

"Collegial. She was my director, my principal investigator,

and I applied to be under her after looking for the best. It was her job to develop the research ideas, find the grants, promote the project, gather and vet the team, review the results and get them published. I basically ran the lab and kept all the parts working, troubleshot glitches in the work, served as her gofer when she needed one."

"So how well did you know Peter Kim?"

"He kept to himself. He came in, put in long days, but he didn't interact as much as the others."

"What was his relationship like with Dr. Pettigrew and Cindy?"

"He butted heads with Dr. P too—he wanted the research published in stages, instead of waiting until it was all completed, as she'd decided. Each stage of the research has had several viable articles within it—but Dr. P really wanted to create a sensation with BioGreen by breaking it all at once. He was friendly but nothing more with Cindy. I think Kim is a quiet, but very ambitious man."

This was consistent with Marcella's assessment, and her opinion of Truman went up another notch as well. He was much more than a pretty face—not only articulate, he seemed to have a good sense about people. No wonder he'd been taken with the fey, striking Natalie Pettigrew.

"How about Abed? What was his connection to the others?"

"Well, he's someone who wears his heart on his sleeve. I've thought about it a lot, and I can't see him killing someone in the cold, impersonal way Dr. P was shot. I could see him laying hands on someone who hurt him badly enough—as Cindy did. He took it hard, like I said, when she dumped him. But if he killed Dr. P, I think it would have been something impulsive and personal—hitting her on the head or something like that."

"That's very interesting, but total speculation," Marcella said, privately agreeing. She was beginning to wonder more and more if there had been two killers—but Truman, still a suspect, was not someone to share that with.

"Did any of the interns…write poetry or journals that you were aware of?"

"No, nothing creative like that that I ever saw." He snorted a laugh. "We all hunched over journals, all right, but they were the project lab books, and those follow a strict protocol."

"All right. Are you going to be able to move forward with the staffing you have?"

"No. We have to re-create a lot of the project, and we need some more interns. I've been using the time away from the lab to review grad student applications—but I'm feeling confident we'll be able to rebuild an effective team." He stood. "Speaking of that, you said you'd release the lab to me?"

"Let me check with my partner. He was doing a final walk-through before we turn it over." She speed-dialed Rogers. "Matt. Is the lab ready for the team to come back?"

"I just got done reprogramming a new security code into the door. Write this down."

Marcella scribbled the number Rogers gave her on a notepad and showed it to Truman, who copied it into his phone.

"Thanks. I'll see you later at the office." She cut the call and gestured to the door. "Looks like you're free to pull your people in and get back to work. We left a photocopied pile of Dr. Pettigrew's photos of the lab books for your review in the back office."

"The project's got a foundation to build on, thanks to you," Truman said, shaking her hand with both of his, green eyes shining with something that might have been tears. "It will be great to get back to work, and thank God Dr. P took those photos. Where did you find them?"

"At the bottom of the Ala Wai Canal," Marcella said, ushering him to the door. "Call me if you see or hear any suspicious behavior from your team. Anything at all."

"Oh, I will," he said fervently, and hurried down the hall.

Marcella shut down all the recording equipment and checked her dive watch—it was time to get on the road for an important appointment.

Chapter 14

Marcella pulled the Honda up to the curb, taking one of the pay-by-hour slots near the Ala Wai Yacht Harbor, a picturesque maze of floating docks and crowded slips. The clang of boats and hum of wind against rigging filled the ocean-sparkling air with the song of the marina, the curving yellow arc of the beach just beyond. The whole setting invited leisurely walks in paradise, and the nearby Hilton Hawaiian Village, with its iconic rainbow-tiled high-rise, capitalized on that.

Marcella parked directly opposite the former Cheese Soufflé Bistro—the place her parents had offered on. She got out of the car, did a quick scan as she always did for possible threats, and strode across the narrow street to a dilapidated glass front door decorated with expired band and show posters. Anna Scatalina, obviously keeping an eye out, pushed the door with its tinkling bell wide.

"'Cella! Come into Café Scatalina!"

"Mama." She kissed her mother on both cheeks as she stepped into the dim interior. "You sure that's a good name?" Marcella's voice was hesitant.

"We not ashamed of our name," Papa Gio rumbled—an old argument—from across the room.

Marcella ignored this sally, instead putting hands on her hips and swiveling to survey. "Well, it's got a good location."

The black-and-white checkered floor was gritty with tiny gecko droppings, though none of the indoor-dwelling lizards ubiquitous to Hawaii were visible in daylight. Round tables were stacked in a corner, bent-backed café chairs towering in a stack beside them. A glass deli-style counter fronted the kitchen, separated from the dining room by an open pass-through window and swinging half doors.

"You know the economy, she no good," Papa Gio said. "So we get the café cheap."

"Was your offer accepted?"

"Yes. We the owners!" Anna gave a little hop and clapped her hands. "I can't wait to get to work on the kitchen. Come. I show you." She bustled through the swinging doors into a kitchen redolent of old grease, a crusty-looking gigantic steel stove its centerpiece. Piled dishware and pots and pans were stacked haphazardly on every surface. The smell of greasy, burnt things clung to Marcella's throat like a film.

"Mama, it's terrible in here. You need to have the cleaning included in the final price."

"I call the agent already." Papa Gio put his hands on his hips and drew down his brows. "Anna, she just want to get to work. We still need to decide what food we selling."

"I think we go with Italian theme," Anna said. "Like us."

"Are you going to do dinners? Or just breakfast and lunch? All three?" Marcella walked over to the floor mats, looked at them cautiously. They seemed downright sticky, and the heels of today's Jimmy Choos would sink right into the round holes that marked the thick rubber surface.

"Breakfast and lunch only. Perhaps little appetizers in afternoon," Anna said. "We old. We like go to bed early."

"Yes. And I'm worried—this is a big project, even after you get it cleaned. You have to decorate, set up a menu…"

"That's the fun part. And I already have employee coming—the Guatemalan boy you meet the other day. Eduardo. He come to work for us, help with the heavy work." Anna's brown eyes, so much like Marcella's, were wide with excitement. "I have new friend at college. She a photographer. She make big prints for walls. We paint, we buy new china and napkins, and we go!"

"So it's the Café Scatalina, eh?" Marcella pursed her lips. "Sure about that?"

"Yes, and we feature a brown turd as our logo," Papa Gio said.

Marcella spun around to her father, her mouth open. Both her parents burst into laughter.

"Oh, oh, oh," Anna gasped. "Oh, your face, 'Cella! The horror!"

"You got me good," Marcella said, succumbing to a chuckle. "Well, I'm glad we're finally joking about it."

"Your name Little Shit, you gotta laugh about it," Papa Gio said, pulling Marcella to him in a side hug. "We said on the way here how your hair would turn white if we named the café Scatalina and made a little turd for the sign."

"You were right. You guys know me too well. What can I help with?" Marcella sneaked her eyes to her watch. She was due for a briefing back at the Bureau in half an hour.

"Toasting." Papa Gio worked the cork on a bottle of champagne, while Anna produced plastic glasses from the pockets of her muumuu.

Marcella took hers reluctantly. It was ten thirty a.m. on a workday; it wouldn't do to arrive in front of Waxman with alcohol on her breath. But she couldn't turn her parents down either. She waved a halt to her father's pouring and cleared her throat.

"I'd like to toast. To the success of the Scatalinas in Waikiki—may everything we do prosper."

"Salute," her parents chimed, and they all drank. Papa Gio held his brimming cup high, flicked a few drops from the rim over the greasy stove.

"Everything this kitchen make taste *delizioso*," he said. "Thanks be to God for our good fortune, and for our daughter to live nearby."

"Salute," Marcella said, and they all took another swig—this could go on awhile. "Papa, darling. I have to run." She kissed him, set the plastic cup down on the counter. "Keep me posted on how I can help."

"Ciao, bella," her mother called as Marcella headed for the front door.

"Ciao. See you soon," Marcella called back.

She pushed out into the breezy sunshine, light sparkling off the moored boats of the marina. Tourists milled by en masse only a block away on Ala Moana Boulevard, but the area of the restaurant, while near major traffic, had a restful feel. She took a big deep breath of fresh salty air and blew it out. Her midsection sent back tingles, pummeled during last night's sparring.

The bistro was a good thing for her parents. And who knew? They might make a success of Café Scatalina, with a brown turd as a logo. Yep, they'd got her good that time. She laughed aloud as she got into the Honda.

Marcella took a minute in the women's room to comb her hair, disordered by the wind off the yacht harbor. She was stabbing bobby pins into the latest incarnation of FBI Twist when the door opened, admitting a petite blonde wearing a khaki skirt and purple polo shirt.

"Dr. Wilson!" She spat the last of the pins into her hand and turned with a big smile to greet the police psychologist. "I didn't know you came this far afield—thought you were based in Big Island."

"Got a new job—I'm consulting with the FBI now as well as state and local police," the psychologist said. "Great to see you, Marcella. You're looking amazing, as usual."

"It's a curse."

"I'm sure you find a way to make it work," Dr. Wilson said with a smile.

Marcella had met the psychologist on Maui at her friend Lei's police station, where the peripatetic consultant was doing a training for the island's detectives. Lei had worked with Dr. Wilson on several cases and personal business over the years, and through her glowing reports, Marcella felt like she knew the woman. She finished her touch-ups as Dr. Wilson used one of the stalls and then washed her hands.

"So are you here on a case?" Marcella asked, blotting lipstick off her lips. Waxman was bound to give her a hairy eyeball if she had much on, but she wanted to look her best for the briefing—not that she was hoping Kamuela would be there or anything.

"Possibly. SAC Waxman sent me over some information to review and come up with a 'profile' for one of the cases." Dr. Wilson's sharp blue eyes met hers in the mirror. "Guess we'll have to see what conference room we end up in."

"Well, I'm hoping it's my case. I could use a psych profile on our three main suspects. I was going to ask Waxman for a consult; maybe he beat me to it." The two women walked down the hall together toward the main conference room.

"Are you in touch with Lei?" Dr. Wilson asked. "I'm a little worried about her."

"We just talked the other day. What's going on?"

"She's stressed—big transitions. Wondered if she'd called you."

"Yeah. She's coming over in a few weeks."

"Well, get her to talk to you."

"Spoken as her therapist?" Marcella knew Dr. Wilson had been the one to help unlock Lei's memories on the Big Island.

"Speaking as a friend and colleague. There's always a lot at stake in your profession."

"For her and me both," Marcella said, as she opened the main conference room with its whiteboards and oval table. She turned to the psychologist with a grin. "Looks like you're on my case."

Waxman stood up from where he was holding court at the end of the table. "Dr. Wilson, so glad you could make it on such short notice."

"Yes." Dr. Wilson opened the leather valise she'd been carrying and distributed some printouts to the team gathered around the table: Waxman, Gundersohn, Ang, Rogers, and Detectives Ching and Hernandez from HPD. Kamuela was not in evidence, and Marcella felt a stab that felt suspiciously like pain.

"Where's Detective Kamuela?" she asked Ching as she helped hand out the papers. She knew he said he'd ask to be transferred, but she didn't want to believe it.

"He had some other cases come up," Ching said. His gaze was guileless; Marcella doubted Kamuela would have told his partner the real reason for his departure.

An unfamiliar feeling—rejection, loss—sank into the pit of her stomach and lay there like a lead ball. She'd known things couldn't end well; it didn't make it any easier to have been right.

Marcella sat next to Dr. Wilson, who smiled graciously as Waxman took them through the high points of the case to the current situation: three main suspects, surveillance teams on each, the lab being watched.

"We just released the lab back to Dr. Truman, and he's getting back to work today," Waxman finished. "We have some additional staff from HPD in the lookout room at the moment." Waxman liked to make up new phrases like "lookout room."

"Thank you." Dr. Wilson stood up, went to one of the whiteboards. "I worked up some patterns on each of your suspects. I haven't had much time to go in depth, but I wanted to give you some initial impressions and see if they assist in narrowing the field. Let's start with Kim."

Rogers put a blowup of Peter Kim's driver's license photo into a clip at the top of one of the whiteboards, the Korean scientist looking earnest and conservative in a brush cut and button-down. Dr. Wilson slid on a pair of tortoiseshell reading glasses and consulted her notes.

"According to comments from various other lab partners, Kim is the most standoffish of the interns. He came from Korea seven years ago. He has well connected family here in Hawaii, and two mysterious deposits to his account in the amount of nine thousand, nine hundred, and ninety-nine dollars. An e-mail trail connecting him with a lab in Korea has also been uncovered. He reputedly doesn't have a girlfriend; nor does he appear to be gay."

She took a sip of water from a glass Gundersohn poured for her, pulled the glasses off to dangle by a beaded chain, and looked up to address the group. "Kim strikes me as a classic first-generation immigrant from an Asian family. He's a loner, ambitious, hardworking, and focused. He doesn't have time for extraneous entanglements. He's focused on success and making his mark, adding to his family's established successful track record, and making money. He seems to evaluate others in terms of usefulness and will curry favor with those who can help him with his goals. He doesn't appear to have any sort of religious orientation, which will tend to make him someone who does the expedient thing. In other words, he'd have wanted to profit from BioGreen.

"His motivation for a murder would be something related to his goals. He fits a profile of someone who'd kill for profit or ambition, but not passion. Ergo, I could see him shooting Dr. Pettigrew to prevent her from giving away the BioGreen formula, but not strangling Cindy Moku—a very personal murder that was then dressed up to look like a hanging." She paused, looked around the table. "How seriously have you considered that there are two killers?"

No one answered immediately; then Marcella spoke up. "I've been thinking about that more and more, but the thing that brings us back is the blog entries. They point to one killer."

"The blogs could be faked, planted to point to someone— namely Fernandez, as they were uploaded from his work computer," Rogers said.

Waxman waved a hand. "We've thought of that. We're considering the blog entries as one aspect of this investigation, not definitive in themselves. Go on."

"Well, Kim does not have the markers of a psychopath or antisocial personality disorder—some early ones include cruelty to other children and animals, fire setting, crimes, and conduct problems. From everything I can tell, he's been a model citizen, if a little cold and detached." Dr. Wilson slid the glasses back on and picked up another folder. "Let's discuss Fernandez next. The blog's uplink location aside, he's a strong candidate for several reasons: He had a relationship with Cindy Moku. He openly disagreed with Dr. Pettigrew regarding BioGreen's distribution rights. He's known to have an abrasive manner, a diagnosis of Tourette's, and an early record of fire setting. He has engaged in some potentially suspicious behavior since being surveilled, though again, nothing that couldn't be explained by the pressures he's been under."

Rogers slipped an eight-by-ten photo of Fernandez's surly face under one of the clips at the top of the whiteboard as Dr. Wilson went on. "Apparently, he is also quite brilliant and contributed an essential piece of the BioGreen research that broke the formula through to the next level. Coworkers say he felt he had a proprietary interest in BioGreen and did not agree with any free distribution of the research."

"That's all information we already gave you, Dr. Wilson," Waxman said impatiently. "What we want is your take on it."

"I'm getting to that." Dr. Wilson gave the SAC a quelling look over her glasses. Her crystal-blue gaze was authoritative. "Fernandez is a complex individual with some definite mental health issues. He meets criteria for a schizotypal personality disorder, with additional markers for antisocial personality disorder and the accompanying Tourette's.

"In layman's terms, he has a twisted and egocentric outlook on the world and sees other people as lesser than himself. He despises women and yet worked under one and engaged in a relationship with one that may or may not have had an abusive element. In my professional opinion, he has the means and ability to be the killer of both victims, and for the reasons just stated: Dr. Pettigrew was not recognizing him as he felt he deserved, and Cindy confronted him about killing Pettigrew—and he strangled her for it."

Everyone digested this. Marcella gazed at the photo, thinking about the various behaviors Fernandez had demonstrated. His verbal abuse toward her—which may or may not be Tourette's—his apparent "breakdown" in the kitchen, bold body language when he thought he was unobserved, even his quick thinking in calling his uncle Bennie.

"Whether he killed these women or not, Fernandez is a very disturbed individual. That brings me to your third suspect, Zosar Abed." Dr. Wilson took another sip of water, adjusted her glasses, and opened another folder.

"Dr. Abed also has a 'love-hate' relationship with these two women. An Indian native, he is ambitious and driven to make a name for himself, but for reasons other than the first two. He apparently adores his mother and put Dr. Pettigrew on a pedestal as a replacement for her during his time in the lab. He is emotionally labile, demonstrating mood and behavior swings, and he was 'in love' with Cindy Moku, who had rejected him. He also felt an investment in the rights to BioGreen, as they all seem to. He could have killed Pettigrew because she failed him in some essential way, thus falling off her pedestal—and Cindy he could have killed out of jealousy."

Waxman looked at the notes in front of him. "So it sounds like you are saying all three of our suspects are capable of the murders, or even just one of them—but for different reasons."

"That's exactly what I'm saying. I have one last suspect bio— Dr. Ron Truman." She flipped open the next folder. "I know you said the first three were your main suspects, but I think Truman is a strong candidate for one reason—ambition." She took off her glasses and her vivid eyes passed across Marcella's face, leaving her feeling naked. "Truman is basically inheriting Dr. Pettigrew's position and will be next in line on the published papers—which I have on good authority may be submitted for a Nobel Prize— putting him as primary researcher in a very enviable position. And let's not forget he's having an affair with Natalie Pettigrew, niece and heiress to Pettigrew's fortune. This man has means, motive, and opportunity. A handsome face and charm have hidden any manner of monsters before; don't let them fool you this time, either."

A long pause followed this. Marcella wrote, *Truman?* on her notepad. She hoped it wasn't him—she liked him, and reminded herself it was dangerous to do so.

"So really, who is your best suspect, based on psychology alone, not including other physical evidence?" Waxman asked.

"I'm reluctant to say, as physical evidence is critical. The best profile in the world can be ruled out by a single hair."

"Give it a shot anyway." Waxman bit off his words, clearly impatient with such digression.

"Well then, I have to say Fernandez. I see him as the most antisocial. He'd be able to kill for his own reasons and remain relatively untroubled by it."

"Something's bothering me," Marcella said. "Cindy Moku. This is a girl who had it all—she was the hero of her family, bright, well liked, attractive. Why did she go for Fernandez rather than Abed? Or even someone a little out of her reach, like 'Dr. Handsome' Ron Truman?"

Dr. Wilson looked back at her notes. "I read all you gave me on Cindy Moku, and I think the answer to that lies in Cindy's mind. She might have been tired of being the good and perfect girl with all her family's hopes and dreams pinned to her. A part of her might have wanted to sabotage that, to be punished somehow. She sought out someone emotionally unavailable who was never going to do anything but use her."

Marcella's arched brows drew down in a frown. "I'm just not buying that. Cindy had every reason to choose someone who'd enhance her career. She wasn't promiscuous, didn't have any bad habits. Maybe Fernandez has a side we aren't seeing." Marcella went on to describe the changes in demeanor Fernandez had shown. "Maybe he was someone else with her in private, someone more intriguing than we've been able to see."

"Well, we'll have ample opportunity to study all of them," Waxman said, stacking the folders. "Thank you, Dr. Wilson. It doesn't narrow our suspect pool the way I was hoping it would, but we know more of what to look for and how to conceptualize our suspects' motives."

"Glad I could help," Dr. Wilson said. "I'll keep working on it, and I still have to review the tapes from your interviews with each of the interns. If something new emerges, I'll let you know."

Marcella followed Dr. Wilson to the doorway. "Thanks, Doc. I for one found this helpful, though I don't agree that Cindy somehow attracted an abusive relationship."

"I never said he was abusive," Dr. Wilson said. "Want to get a cup of coffee and discuss it?"

"Can't," Marcella said. "I have to get to the 'lookout room,' as they're calling it, and get eyes on our researchers firsthand. But here's my number. Maybe when I'm off work, we can get together." She handed her card to the psychologist with an inward sigh of relief that those sharp blue eyes wouldn't be seeing into her soul.

Marcella hurried to get down to the garage. She beeped open the "Bu-car" as Bureau-issued transport was nicknamed. Rogers got into the black Acura and shut the door. Marcella fired up the engine.

"Where's the fire?"

"I just want to get down to the lab, see what they're up to," Marcella said, tamping down the depression that rolled around her gut.

Kamuela was really gone. He'd done what he said he would and transferred off the case. There was a good chance it'd be years before they ran into each other again. Yes, she'd kicked him to the curb, and she missed him—missed the fizz of chemistry between them that woke her up when he was nearby. Missed his dark chocolate voice. Missed his presence on the case, his persistent but levelheaded approach. Missed his strong arms…

She hated that she missed him, hated that she hated it. Was mad that he'd listened to her and left. Mad at herself for caring, and mad that he'd got his hooks in her enough to feel like this.

Dammit all to hell.

She needed to keep moving—she needed action. Someone to take down, and soon. Preferably with a little police brutality involved.

Chapter 15

Marcella revved the engine and backed out of the stall. It wasn't long before the she and her partner stood in front of a keypad to the room directly above Dr. Pettigrew's lab, and Rogers punched in the code. The team from HPD, Ching and Hernandez, sat on a bank of video monitors with headphones on.

Ang, wearing a leather tool belt loaded with tech gear, was crouched on the floor doing something with wires. She looked up and acknowledged them with a brisk nod. Ching turned to greet them, lifting up one of the earphones.

"Hey, good to see you." He stood up from a folding metal chair set in front of the video screens. "Would love for you guys to give us a break so we could grab some food."

"Sure." Marcella surveyed the empty space, bare but for several steel tables set at right angles to form a bay for the equipment. Audio was on, and as she approached the surveillance area, she could hear the strains of classical music coming from the speakers. Each of what remained of Dr. Pettigrew's team was hard at work with pipettes, slides, microscopes, or computers.

Ang's cell beeped. She glanced down at it, and her curved black brows shot up over wide eyes as she looked up at Marcella. "Blog went live again!"

"Which computer?"

All heads swiveled to look at the lab below in the surveillance cameras. Only Truman was on a computer, the one in the back office that had been burgled for the formula.

"I have an IP address," Ang said. She hustled around to the monitors and slid into Ching's seat. "The entry is time stamped, so all we have to do is find out who was on at that time."

She pulled up a list of the IP addresses of the computers in the room. "It's the one over near the back. It's just out of video range. But we should still be able to see who goes back there." She glanced down at the phone again. "Unfortunately, my trip wire is about thirty minutes behind the time stamp. I'm going to have to roll back to half an hour ago." She turned to look at the detectives. "I got here fifteen minutes ago from our team meeting at the Bureau. Do you guys remember who was on this computer half an hour ago?"

Ching and Hernandez looked at each other. "No," Ching finally answered.

"Shit." Ang's fingers flew over one of the keyboards. "I set this up last night to go live this morning after you gave the go-ahead to open the lab to Pettigrew's team. Only reason I'm here now is that I'm checking all the feeds and the visibility angles, and a good thing too." She pointed a short, unpolished nail at one of the monitors. "See? That shelf blocks our view of that computer. I should have caught it earlier, but it's hard to make sure all the angles are right before we're live."

All eyes watched the rapid replay of the video, and as they approached the time stamp in question, she slowed the feed.

Abed, Kim, and Fernandez all stopped in at the computer during the thirty-minute window of the upload.

"Could someone be uploading the blog post and doing something else at the same time? Or have it on a time delay?" Marcella asked.

"Possible. But if he's that computer savvy, he wouldn't be uploading a personal incriminating blog on a work computer in the first place." Ang tapped the screen. "I wish my trap were closer to the time stamp, but the good news here is that we can rule out Truman. He never used that computer anywhere near the time the blog was uploaded."

"Can we get a copy of the text?" Rogers asked. Ang nodded and retrieved the content for their review.

Blog Entry

Back in my space where
Destinies
Are discovered
Back where my microscope
Measures blueprints of worldbits and splices
The ordinary into the supreme.
Smells a little musty in here
Like cops and suspicion—like that
Bitch agent with the shiny teeth, and shoes that go
Click-clack.
I'd like to stuff them
Somewhere the sun don't shine.
It's funny that Dr. P's
Paranoia was the thing
That brings my work back
To me.
Thanks Dr. P.
Finally
I almost feel sorry
That I killed you.
Posted: 2:05 p.m.

The bald words, with their poetic spacing, seared Marcella's eyes—especially the hostility aimed at herself. It creeped her out that one of those innocuous-looking scientists was a double murderer and had her shoes on his mind.

"We have to be able to narrow it down," she said. "Let's go through this footage more slowly."

Rogers and Marcella clustered next to Ang as they replayed the digital from within thirty minutes of the time stamp more slowly while the HPD detectives watched the current feed.

"Wonder what they're doing on there," Rogers said, as Abed, his small frame enveloped in a white lab coat, disappeared behind the shelf. They could see the hem of his white coat protruding off the seat of the chair. He was there for around five minutes, then got up and left. A few minutes later Kim came and occupied the chair, then Fernandez.

"I'm sorry, guys," Ang said, pushing a hand through her hair in frustration. "I put the trap on there, and it only beeps me when there's been an entry within thirty minutes. And with this bad angle, I can't see what they're doing on the computer. So just because the blog post is time stamped, doesn't mean the time is exactly when it was uploaded. We have to get in there and adjust the cameras. So—they don't know they're being surveilled, correct?"

"Correct," Marcella said. "The UH president knows. It was our condition for allowing them back into the lab, and our suspect pool is so narrow, we had compelling reason to get a judge to approve it. What we need to do is shake those guys up, see if something pops. How about Rogers and I go down, nose around, and adjust the camera while we're at it? You and the HPD guys can monitor from here. They know they're all still under suspicion. I don't think a visit from us is going to seem too out of line or tip them off to the surveillance."

"Sounds good."

A short time later Marcella pounded in the combination that opened the lab door. Rogers shot her a side glance.

"Where's the fire?" he hissed for the second time, as Marcella threw her shoulder against the steel door, depressing the handle. It flew inward, hitting the wall.

"Sorry," she said to the three startled faces that looked up from their tasks.

Truman came to the door of the inner office, hands fisted on hips. "Quite an entrance, Agent Scott," he said. "Got some news for us or something?"

"No. Just stopping by to see how things are going," Marcella said, striding in to stand too close to Abed. Rogers gave a slow-molasses chuckle, trying to smooth things over.

"We just thought we'd pop in, check if anyone had heard or seen anything new. As you know, we're still looking for whoever killed Dr. Pettigrew and Cindy."

"Everything working okay? Able to get going with Dr. Pettigrew's notes? I got those off a camera the killer threw in the Ala Wai Canal, you know. Bet he wouldn't have thrown it away if he knew what was on it." Marcella walked over to Kim's station, leaned over his shoulder to look at the hieroglyphic notes in his lab book.

Fernandez's tic was acting up. He'd turned away and was fiddling with a pipette, a series of croaks and whistles betraying agitation.

"No, nothing new," Abed said, blinking big chocolate eyes owlishly behind round magnifying lenses. "We'll call you right away."

Kim ignored the agents and continued to make notes in a lab book.

Marcella strolled to the back of the room, angling for the hidden camera. "Just wanted you to know a few facts from Cindy's case. She was trying to tell us something. I think she knew who

Dr. Pettigrew's murderer was, and she knew her killer. She called that person to confront them. The rest, they say, is history." She turned back to face the room at large in front of the camera, a wired nodule attached to the metal shelf. She pushed on it with her shoulder to move it to a wider angle.

Her earbud crackled. "No go. Camera's off the computer area now."

Rogers took over, smacking a table hard with his open palm so all eyes snapped to him. Marcella now had a chance to move the camera again.

"This investigation is far from over. You all are here until we find some hard evidence linking one of you to the bodies. We never give up until we close a case, and Dr. Pettigrew and Cindy deserve justice."

Fernandez croaked, and Truman frowned from the doorway, obviously confused by this turnaround in attitude from his cordial meeting with Marcella in the early morning. "You'll have our full cooperation, Agents. We want to find who did it as much as you do."

"I very much doubt that," Marcella said. Ang's voice in her ear confirmed the camera now had full visibility, so she strode to the door. "We'll be seeing you. Sooner rather than later."

Rogers elbowed her as they entered the stairs—they couldn't ride the elevator to the floor above in case someone looked from the lab and saw by the lights they weren't exiting the building. "Think we came on a little strong?"

"No. I want to stir those guys up, see what happens. Hopefully they'll turn on one another and let something slip." They rejoined the surveillance team. Ang's triangular grin met Marcella as she slipped in the door.

"Very aggro. That'll put the cat among the pigeons."

"That's the idea," Marcella said as she seated herself by the monitors, Rogers beside her.

Ang turned up the volume as Truman looked around the lab in the grainy feed.

"Well, which one of you did it?" he asked with a nervous chuckle. The laugh was met by another nervous chuckle from Abed, a grunt from Fernandez, and a head shake from Kim.

"They were fishing," Kim said, eyes still on his work. "They would bring us in if they had anything."

"Shee-it," Rogers said. "Kim's a cool customer."

Truman turned and went back into his office, cranking up the instrumental music, and each of the scientists went back to work.

"Dammit," Marcella said.

"Like watching paint dry," Ang said a few minutes later.

"Or grass grow," Ching added. "We're overdue for a lunch break. See you in half an hour." He and his partner left.

"Dammit," Marcella said again, and got up and paced. It was a very long afternoon. Her cell rang as she was heading down the hall for a bathroom break. She picked up for Waxman.

"Wanted you to know we had a call from the university president. Dr. Pettigrew's estate and the university have been served with a claim that AgroCon Ltd. owns the rights to BioGreen. They have the research and have served the university with a cease-and-desist order on any work on the project."

"Holy crap! Sir," Marcella exclaimed. "How'd they get the formula?"

"Claim it was sold to them by 'a partner' in the development of the formula. Probably whoever killed Dr. Pettigrew. We need to get eyes on that document. We could get one from UH, but I want to see what AgroCon says. Take Rogers and go get us a copy from the source."

"Of course, sir. What's the university doing?"

"They're filing a countersuit that they never agreed to the sale and they are the principal interest in the research. Natalie Pettigrew's lawyer handling the estate has signed on with the university in a countersuit that AgroCon needs to return the research immediately."

"This could be the break we've been looking for," Marcella said, breaking into a trot as she headed back to the lookout room. "I'll keep you posted on what we find, sir."

"You do that." Waxman hung up.

"Matt, we've gotta hit the road. New orders!" Marcella hooked her jacket off the folding chair. "See you guys later. I'll bring you up to speed on the way."

AgroCon vice president, Lance Smith, was not happy to see them. He sweated under a blond toupee he'd added to his ensemble since their last visit.

"I need Legal's okay before I release a copy to you." He depressed a button on the desk. "Janice, put a call into Legal regarding these agents' request for a copy of the BioGreen affidavit."

"It's a matter of public record, and this is an open homicide investigation being handled by the FBI. I guess I'll have to call the attorney general and see how he wants me to handle it." Marcella paced in front of his desk, hands in her pockets, letting her heels tap on the shiny bamboo floor. She hoped they left pockmarks.

The VP frowned, harrumphed, then yanked open a drawer on the desk. "Well, since it's a matter of public record, I guess it won't matter that much." He took out a file, flipped it open. Depressed the button on the desk again. "Janice, can you make a copy of this document? Immediately, please."

A tight-lipped receptionist came in, took the papers, and left.

"So let's chew this over a minute," Rogers said in his best down-home manner. "Two things: You have the research, which last we talked, was stolen from the university. This makes us naturally curious as to how you obtained it. Second thing—what possible basis of ownership do you have of said stolen research?"

"I'm not comfortable answering these questions without Legal present," Smith said, sitting down in his cushy leather chair with a whoosh of escaping air. "I'll give you a copy of our court document, because as you say, it's a matter of public record. But unless Legal sends someone up right now, we are done talking."

Janice returned and handed the papers to her boss, ignoring the agents.

"Janice, did Legal get back to you? These agents want to ask some questions I'm not comfortable answering without counsel present."

"I'm sorry, sir. They're all tied up."

"We'll have to do this down at the Bureau offices, then," Marcella said. She took out a card, wrote a time on the back of it, slapped it down on the polished desk. "Be there tomorrow morning at ten a.m. with whatever dog-and-pony show you want to bring."

She snatched the copies out of his hand, spun, and strode out without giving him a chance to engage in more power struggles.

"See you tomorrow. It won't be as friendly," Rogers said over his shoulder as he followed her out.

Marcella took the passenger seat, leaving Rogers to fire up the Acura and negotiate the guard gate as she scanned the document. "Says here they had a vested interest from the grant money, then paid additional compensation to a "full partner in the project" who has "ownership rights" due to "key research provided by this individual" who then signed over his rights to AgroCon. That individual isn't named. Dammit!"

"That document won't stand up," Rogers said, as they headed back to the Bureau to deliver the document to Waxman. "I'm sure Natalie and the university's lawyers are drawing up a rebuttal as we speak."

"Yeah, but as we all know, possession is nine-tenths of the law, and somehow they have the formula. One of those lab rats stole it, gotta be, and finally found the nuts to take it to AgroCon. He probably didn't want to implicate himself in Pettigrew's murder before now. Maybe he knows something that protects him now, or maybe he's getting ready to take the money and run."

As if on cue, Marcella's cell phone toned—Ang at the "lookout room."

"Looks like Kim is making a move." The tech agent's voice was tight with excitement. "He seems to be gathering all the photos of the lab book pages we retrieved from Dr. Pettigrew's camera into one folder. They were scattered around the lab with all the members of the team working on different portions of the research."

"Grab him if he makes a move to leave the lab with those photos," Marcella said, glancing at Rogers, whose sandy brows had climbed in inquiry. "We're on the way to HQ to drop off the AgroCon documents, but we'll be back shortly."

Rogers turned on the sirens and lights and stepped on the gas.

Chapter 16

Marcella was a little winded, Rogers not at all as they slipped back into the lookout room from hurrying across the campus and up several flights of stairs. Ang and Ching looked up from the monitors. "He's gathered all the photos together from the workstations. Check him out."

Kim kept his head down and his movements deliberate as he strolled to the back office. He had a fat folder under one arm.

"Those are the photos. All casual, he just walked around and picked them up from each work area," Ang said. "Truman still has some photos with him. I think Kim's deciding if he can get away with snatching those too."

Kim put his head into the back room where Truman was still in front of his computer.

"Hey, boss. Going out to grab something to eat," Kim said, voice tinny over the audio feed.

"Sure." Truman never looked up. They saw Kim's eyes resting hungrily on the stack of photos beside Truman's monitor, but he turned away and headed back across the lab.

"Move!" Rogers exclaimed, and he and Marcella darted for the door and the stairs.

"Sophie, stay with the HPD team and keep an eye on the lab!" Marcella called over her shoulder.

Once outside the lab, Kim walked rapidly down the linoleum hall with the folder under his arm, heading for the elevators. Marcella was right behind as Rogers burst out of the stairwell beside the elevators and cut Kim off.

"Stop right there."

Kim's face blanched, a tightening of the eyes and mouth, but he thrust out his chest, blustering. "What the hell is this about? Haven't you harassed us enough?"

"Hand over that folder," Marcella said. When he made no move to obey, she snatched it from him, flipping it open. "Aha. Looks familiar—the research the FBI retrieved from Dr. Pettigrew's camera."

"You're coming with us," Rogers said, pushing him against the wall. Kim fumbled a cell phone out of his pocket and Rogers took it, clicking cuffs on to his wrists.

"I'm calling for legal representation," Kim said through white lips.

"You aren't doing anything until we talk down at the Bureau office," Marcella said. They marched Kim out to the Acura and got on the road.

They put Kim in Conference Room B, used for hostile interrogations. It contained nothing but a bolted-down steel table, mirrored observation wall, and a few metal chairs. Rogers clipped Kim's cuffs to a ring on the table and met Marcella and Waxman in the observation room next door.

"He's asking for a lawyer," Marcella said, handing Kim's cell phone to Waxman. "I'm wanting to download the contents of this phone."

"Kid's savvy—there was never any doubt of that," Waxman said. "Can't touch the phone without probable cause, and I don't think we have enough yet. You have to let him make the call, then do what you can with him once his lawyer gets here. I've got a call in to the judge we've been working with on the surveillance tap to approve charging him with stealing the formula and the murder of Dr. Pettigrew."

"I know we can get him on the robbery and selling the formula to AgroCon, but are you sure we have enough to get him for murder?" Marcella frowned, hands in her pockets.

"I'm fast-tracking search warrants for his home, car, and work locker. We need to find that .22 used on Pettigrew or something tying him to the murders, so I'm going to try for that. We can hold him for twenty-four hours at least, perform the searches, and charge him with the robbery to start."

"Okay." Marcella and Rogers took the earbuds he handed them and Kim's cell phone.

"He'll probably get bail and his family will be able to pay it, so we've got a narrow window to tie this guy to the murders. Go get him. I know you can." Waxman's smile was distinctly wolfish, and Marcella felt herself warming to her boss for the first time.

She hurried to her office and picked up a pen and a yellow legal pad, tightened the FBI Twist, adjusted the ankle straps on her shoes, and rejoined Rogers at the door to Conference Room B.

Kim looked up as they came in, fixing on Rogers. "I'm timing this. So far now, I've been denied my rights for forty-three minutes."

"Relax." Rogers took one of the metal chairs, straddled it—all casual male bonhomie. He handed Kim's cell phone back to him. "Just wanted to check in with our boss first. Go ahead and make your call."

Marcella tossed her head and tapped her toes, feeling impatience well up as Kim scrolled through his contacts—but her heart sank as she heard him say, "Hello, is Bennie Fernandez available?"

She walked it off, back and forth, back and forth, as they listened to Kim arrange for one of Honolulu's best—because Bennie was already working with Fernandez, another partner was being dispatched. Bennie Fernandez, and his firm, meant it wasn't going to be easy. And they could have used some easy.

Kim hung up his phone with a definitive punch of the button. "Mr. Samson is on his way. He told me not to talk to you until he gets here and we've conferred."

"Bennie Fernandez's firm, eh? Guess Jarod put you onto him."

"Yeah. Bennie is his uncle. Jarod says he's been very helpful." A smirk at the corner of Kim's mouth snapped Marcella's brows together as she narrowed her eyes at him. Rogers gave a tug on her arm—she was supposed to leave him alone until the lawyer got there. She followed Rogers out reluctantly.

"I can't stand him."

"Keep a lid on it, Marcella. You're so grouchy lately. Get a cup of coffee, come back in a few." Rogers pulled his sandy brows down. "You know if he says anything after he's asked for his lawyer, it could be inadmissible. Save your breath."

"You're right. I'm doing a 'Lei' here," Marcella said, and they both smiled, remembering Marcella's hotheaded friend. "Okay. Coffee chill-out time." She headed down the hall and poured herself a cup of the perfect brew in the lounge, turned to the window and looked out at the ocean, sipping it. It wouldn't do any good to scare Kim off. Her good intentions lasted as long as talking with Samson the lawyer, who downplayed Kim's intentions with the photographed records.

Marcella felt frustration rising again as Rogers finished the Miranda catechism and Kim brushed his fingers through his bangs, clearly feeling secure with his lawyer, Archie Samson, beside him. Archie was Bennie Fernandez's longtime right hand, and his fake-friendly voice set Marcella's teeth on edge. She decided to go with direct.

"We caught you stealing the lab notes red-handed. You also never explained the big cash deposits to your accounts."

"I did tell you. A family member gave me the money."

"I've advised him not to say anything about the purpose for his retrieval of the notes," Archie Samson said.

"I think you want to tell us about it." Marcella lowered her voice to somewhere between throaty and phone sex. "I think you want to brag a little. I mean, you deserve to. You got away with stealing the formula, selling it to the highest bidder, and a couple of murders."

A tide of red rose up Kim's neck. "I never murdered anybody."

"Ah, so that means you admit you stole the research and sold it. Probably were feeding information to both Korea and Agro-Con all along. Then, when you heard Dr. Pettigrew wanted to go public with the formula, you killed her and took it. When you felt like there was another viable suspect, such as Fernandez, I'm thinking, or Abed—you went back to AgroCon and gave them what you'd stolen. Now you need to finish the job, make sure they don't have any competition on the market." Marcella leaned in close, whispering the last of this into Kim's ear.

If she'd read him right, he'd hate having her touch him, move into his personal space—she'd never seen him so much as brush the sleeve of any of the other interns.

She was right. He pushed away abruptly, brought up short by the handcuffs.

"I never killed anyone!"

"Agent Scott, my client says he has nothing to say about the notes, and he denies killing anyone," Samson said, clearly surprised by Marcella's aggressive tack with his client. "This is verging on harassment."

Marcella modified her tone but continued to ignore Samson, addressing Kim. "You keep denying murder, but you don't deny stealing for AgroCon and the Korean lab. Dr. Pettigrew knew you were communicating with them. So suppose we believe you, that one of the other guys killed Pettigrew and Cindy. Well then, you're a small fish. A little corporate stealing—you'll get nothing but a slap on the wrist, and we might be able to offer you something off that if you can give us something on who did the murders." Marcella settled herself in the metal chair next to Rogers, brushing imaginary lint off tailored gray slacks she'd chosen that morning.

Kim bent his head forward so they couldn't see his face. "I don't know anything. Not really."

Rogers pounced. "Not really?"

Samson leaned over and whispered in Kim's ear, and the intern nodded and spoke.

"I just know...I was the only one in the lab when Dr. Pettigrew got a phone call. It was kind of late, but we were still there working. She said she had to go out. She looked very upset and went out still wearing her lab coat, which she always hangs up. I figured it was time to make my move, before someone else made theirs. We'd all been hearing bits and pieces—Dr. Pettigrew had met with the brass at the university. She wasn't telling us anything, but I was afraid she was going to release the research for free on the Internet or something crazy like that."

Marcella and Rogers both stayed quiet—unwilling to break the spell of his disclosure. Marcella tried to arrange her face into sympathy.

"Anyway, she got the call and left. I ran and got the fire ax from the hallway extinguisher, banged on the safe with it. But I'd already watched Truman and Dr. Pettigrew open it and had the combination. I threw stuff around to make it look like an outside burglary and took the laptop and the cell stock."

He took a deep breath, blew it out, apparently relieved to be confessing. "I hid the research; then I gave it to AgroCon. Once we were all back in the lab, I knew I had to get the photos, make sure AgroCon was the only one with the formula. Personally, I think Fernandez killed Dr. Pettigrew and Abed killed Cindy."

"Why is that?" Rogers chanced a question.

"Abed was obsessed with Cindy. He was jealous of Fernandez. And he told me he couldn't see what Fernandez had that he didn't have...He was so insulted she'd chosen Fernandez over him. He seemed to think he was God's gift or something. And Fernandez—when he solved that RuBisCO problem, he really threw his weight around, kept trying to tell Dr. Pettigrew he had rights she couldn't take away."

"Got anything harder? Like, who it was on the phone that called Dr. Pettigrew?"

"No. I don't know who called her that night. But I know where Abed keeps some things of Cindy's. Maybe he took something away from the scene, from her body."

"Where is this stuff of Cindy's?" Marcella asked. Samson whispered again and Kim said, "Abed has some stuff at his house."

A few minutes later, Rogers unlocked the cuffs as much-reduced charges were discussed.

"Please assist us with any information regarding the murders," Marcella said to Kim, ignoring Samson. "We can reduce your charges further."

"You don't need to tell them anything about selling an interest you legitimately owned in a future product," Samson told Kim. "We'll sort out these burglary charges in court."

They left.

"Dammit." Marcella stood, tapped the legal pad on the steel

table. "I wanted to charge him, but we aren't even holding him on those burglary charges. What now?"

"Boss, where are we at on the search warrants for Abed, Fernandez, and Kim?" Rogers asked through the comm. "We need to search them ASAP. We have to find something tying one of them to the murders."

"Check the fax. Judge said they were signed," Waxman said.

"On our way." They headed for the central fax machine.

Marcella stood at Abed's door, the folded search warrant in hand. Her stomach growled loudly as she lifted her hand to knock on the sun-peeled laminate door, with its jute welcome mat spelling out ALOHA and several pairs of rubber slippers. All available agents had been dispatched to perform simultaneous searches at the suspects' three residences, and Waxman had requested a few more detectives from HPD. Marcella, Rogers, and Gundersohn each were leading one of the searches. Ang was her sidekick this time.

"That sounds like a hungry stomach. We could have stopped to grab something to eat," Ang said.

"I'll catch up with food later." Marcella banged on the door.

Abed lived in a stucco duplex off a drab residential street just off campus. A bike chained to the metal railing around the porch testified to his mode of transport, and a sagging gutter off the roof oozed dead leaves from a neighboring avocado tree.

The door opened. Abed's chocolate-brown eyes widened. "What can I do for you, Agent Scott?" He wore a pair of sweats and a green-and-white UH football jersey. "I just got home from the lab."

"I'm sorry to barge in like this, but we have a warrant to search the premises." Marcella handed him the warrant. She turned her head to look as a vehicle pulled up to the nearby curb. Kamuela got out of the Bronco, face foreboding as a Tiki god's, a crime kit in hand.

The rumble of her empty stomach turned to butterflies. Dammit.

"I've cooperated the whole time," Abed said, drawing her gaze back to him. He hoisted up his pants. "I don't know what you could want from me."

"Just routine at this point," Marcella fudged, the hairs on the back of her neck lifting with awareness of Kamuela's presence as he came to stand behind her, just a little too close. His bulk cast a shadow over Abed's sallow face. "Why don't you step out, grab a burger or something? We'll be done before you know it."

"Okay. I'm calling a lawyer though."

"That's always your right."

Abed slid his feet into a pair of slippers and pattered down the cement steps, phone to his ear.

"What do you bet he's calling Bennie Fernandez?" Ang said. "Hey, Marcus. Glad you could join us."

"I have other cases," he growled, and brushed past Marcella to go inside. "Let's get this over with."

"Think you should know we just got some intel that Abed has a cache of stuff related to Cindy," Marcella said to his back, determined to be polite and professional. "Keep an eye out for something like that, anything feminine-looking."

"I know how to do a search." Kamuela opened the closet near the front door.

Marcella knew she wouldn't like it if she were pulled off something she was working on to go work someone else's case. Someone she never wanted to see again.

"Hopefully this will be quick." Ang addressed the back of Kamuela's head as she snapped on gloves and opened her kit.

"I have other cases and they matter too. You Feds think your murders are the only ones that count."

"Sorry you got roped in," Marcella said, her voice soft. "I never meant for this to happen."

He turned to face her, and Marcella saw the hurt behind the bitterness in his dark eyes. A long moment passed as they looked at each other.

Ang cleared her throat behind them. "Guess I'll take the kitchen," she said, and walked off.

"I'm sorry," Marcella said. "I'm really damn sorry."

"I'm sorry too." He turned back to the closet, flicked on a light. "This isn't the place or the time."

"I know." Marcella walked to the back bedroom before she made a fool of herself any further.

Abed was tidy. She looked around his monastic bedroom, a single twin mattress on the floor, a small, low altar with a wooden statue of Ganesh, a Buddha and a photo of an orange-saried woman garlanded with marigolds—probably his mother. At the other end of the room was a student desk with a computer on it. Neatly stacked scientific texts lined the wall.

Marcella turned off the lights, lowered the blinds, flipped back the comforter, and turned on the special flash. Sure enough, various stains fluoresced but no blood. She lifted the mattress. A girlie mag, a box of condoms, and a tulsi bead necklace clustered near the edge. She left them for now, still moving.

The lacquered altar held sandalwood-smelling ash in a brass holder placed in front of the ornaments. It also had a small drawer. She pulled the tasseled knob.

A rubber hair tie, a toothbrush. A pen. A thin gold chain with a plaque hanging from it, embossed with a black Gothic letter "C." A key chain with a smiling Hawaiian child's face slotted into a clear plastic palm tree. A small black notebook.

"I found Cindy's stuff," she called, shining the light into the drawer.

Ang peered over Marcella's shoulder as she stirred the items with a gloved finger. She heard the heavier footsteps of Kamuela approach.

"Hard to tell what might have belonged to Cindy," Ang said.

"Black hairs in that rubber band, and that necklace has the look of one of those returned ex-girlfriend gifts. The initial's right." Marcella picked up the notebook, flipped the pages. It was filled with small, hieroglyphic-looking notes. "This could be interesting. And the child on the key chain is Cindy's cousin."

"Too bad there's no piece of rope with her blood on it in there, or the .22," Kamuela said. "All this shows is that he still had a thing for her."

"It shows he's a little obsessive, too," Marcella said, sliding the items into separate evidence bags. "The fact that he still had a thing for her is significant."

"Marcus is right. What we really need is the weapon and blood or trace from either of the victims." Ang moved away, opening the closet door. Kamuela returned to the front room, and Marcella felt that lead ball start rolling in her stomach again.

He couldn't stand to be in the same room with her. Oh well. It was her own fault. If she wanted him back, she was going to have to do something about it.

Trouble was, she didn't know if she wanted to.

No, these things never ended well.

Chapter 17

Marcella dragged her sweaty, exhausted body the last few feet from the elevator to her apartment door, stuck the key in, stumbled inside. Shut the door, turned the locks, put on the bar, slid down the door to sit on the floor.

Loverboy waggled his fins at her from his bowl on the table.

"Yeah, I know. Just resting a minute here. I got my ass kicked at the Fight Club, buddy." She pulled herself upright with the door handle. "Okay. Off to the shower."

Under the stream of hot water, she let her mind wander through the rest of the happenings of the day—the turning in of evidence back at the Bureau lab, the networked phone call with the rest of the team, discussing what had been recovered at each residence, the mandatory dismissal by Waxman as she began to droop for lack of food in the briefing. She'd downed a hot dog and a Big Gulp as she headed home only to have Ang invite her to the gym…and getting punched and flung about had taken her mind off the libido and angst generated by seeing Kamuela again.

Marcus Kamuela. Dark eyes under straight brows. Those shoulders. The big hands whose calluses she'd recognized as belonging to someone who handled a weapon. That classically cut mouth, set in a line as he looked at her without a trace of the tenderness they'd shared.

Damn the Club. Had she done the right thing dropping out? She still had a powerful itch that even exhaustion from grappling with Sophie Ang for two hours couldn't kill. It had always been her philosophy that the best way to get over a spill was to get back on the horse—a cliché that brought a smile as she bent her face forward.

Water dripped from it like tears as she mulled.

Well, that decision was done, and Marcella definitely didn't have the energy to go to a bar and pick up a random stranger, with time-wasting but necessary social games to get there. Well, she still had her vibrator. Cold company, but it would have to do. She sighed and turned off the water.

Marcella stood in the lab the next morning with Ang, Gundersohn, and Rogers, looking at collected evidence from the three residences. "So we got some artifacts of Cindy Moku's from Fernandez's place as well," Gundersohn said in his pedantic way. "Secret deodorant. A comb. A pair of panties from under the bed."

"Sure those are Cindy's?" Marcella asked.

"Fernandez identified them as belonging to the victim."

"But no weapon."

"We found some e-mails from AgroCon to Kim on his computer," Rogers said. "Nothing tying Kim to cither of the victims."

They looked at the small, inconclusive collection of items, and Marcella finally said, "I need more coffee."

She spun on a cream-colored heel and headed for the door. Ang was right behind her. "Feeling okay from last night? I felt kind of bad. You're picking it up so fast. I know I was a little hard on you."

Marcella smirked at the other agent. "I think I got you a good one. Check your collarbone."

"I know." A bruise darkened the other woman's golden-brown skin. "I saw it this morning. Sure you're good?"

"I'm fine. Just tired, is all. I think I went all out yesterday. I was sure something was going to break on the case, and when it didn't, I was so frustrated. Thanks for calling me. Fight Club took my mind off the day."

"Did it take your mind off Kamuela? What's going on between you?"

"Nothing." Marcella sped up.

"I saw you guys looking at each other—a lot of hot vibes for nothing."

"Okay, there was something. But not anymore. And it's— a bummer, is all." They reached the break room and Marcella hooked down her favorite mug, splashed coffee into it.

"Why? You guys seem perfect for each other." Ang took the pot from Marcella.

"I'm not the relationship type. I like a good shag, but nothing more. It would turn into something more with him." Marcella took a big swig. The coffee scalded her tongue, and she gulped it anyway, to smother the knot in her chest. "I don't want to talk about it."

"Okay. Just curious."

"How about you?"

"I'm divorced."

Marcella started. "Really? You don't look old enough to have that kind of baggage."

Ang made a harsh sound that might have been a laugh and poured some half-and-half from the fridge into her coffee. "I was a child bride."

"How'd you end up in the FBI?"

"Recruited. I actually grew up in Thailand. My mother was

Thai, and my father's an American diplomat—and yes, he's black. I saw you wondering about my background. Anyway, I was working at a firm in Hong Kong. I speak five languages, one of them computer, and one day I got a call from a headhunting firm that finds talent for the Bureau. I was looking to get away from the husband, so I took the offer."

"You speak American like a local."

"Dialects are a specialty."

"You're full of surprises. Thanks, Sophie, for inviting me to the gym. It's really a great outlet for me right now."

Rogers stuck his head in. "Coffee klatch is over, ladies. We have surveillance detail. Agent Ang, they have you working over the computers we brought in."

"No problem." Ang strode off. Marcella watched her go thoughtfully, taking another sip of black coffee. Ang was intriguing—and an exceptional agent. She found herself liking the woman more than ever. Maybe she did have more than one other woman friend.

Rogers stuck his head back in. "C'mon, Little Shit."

"Hey—my name is classified." She punched him in the shoulder, not lightly.

"Mean right hook, Marcie!" He recoiled in exaggerated pain.

"Not Marcie either, dammit." She socked him again. "Watch out. I'm training. Doing some MMA."

"Yikes! I apologize, Agent Scott, for my inappropriate whimsicality." They walked down the hall, bantering, and Marcella felt her world tipping back to normal.

Marcella sat in her Honda outside Fernandez's apartment. The day had passed in relative comfort and boredom in the lookout room into the lab, with various discussions about the AgroCon injunction, the scanty and inconclusive evidence recovered in the searches, the behavior of Kim, who had been fired from the lab.

That little scene had been entertaining to watch, as Kim walked back into the lab, casual as could be, to be confronted by his teammates and Dr. Truman with fire in his green eyes.

"You stole the research, sold it to AgroCon, and have the balls to walk back in here? Did you kill Dr. Pettigrew, too, you slimy little bastard?"

"I'll get my things and go," Kim muttered. Truman pushed him in the chest, so the Korean bounced back several feet.

"You'll just go. And count yourself lucky you can walk out of here."

Dr. Handsome in a snit had been enough to pucker up Marcella's nipples—not that it took much these days.

She lifted a small pair of binoculars as Fernandez came out of the apartment in the blue-purple evening with its scent of plumeria from the tree beside the building. He was moving with the bold ease she'd glimpsed a few other times. She frowned as he strode to the stairwell and clattered down the stairs. He had a backpack on.

After the lab team disbanded for the evening, Marcella had followed Fernandez home with a brief stop for a singularly unsatisfying McDonald's salad. Rogers was on Kim, and Gundersohn on Abed. Marcella lifted her radio.

"I have movement. Subject exiting the building."

"Ten-four," Rogers's voice said. "Nothing here. Subject looks buttoned up inside."

"Ten-four," Gundersohn said. "Subject inside. Keep us posted."

"Roger that." She set down the radio.

Fernandez unlocked a door on one of the garage storage units. She'd wondered how he got around—none of them seemed to have cars—and frowned as he backed up a motor scooter and put on a helmet. She radioed again as she pulled out a good distance behind the young man on his scooter. This time, the helmeted head swiveled often and she saw him checking his mirrors. Fernandez was paying attention to his surroundings—this couldn't be good.

"Subject is on the move in a scooter. I'm on him. He has a backpack."

"Direction? What's your location?" Rogers's voice was sharp.

"Don't know where he's going yet," Marcella said. "Heading into downtown." She braked as Fernandez took a corner. "I'll call for backup if needed."

"I'll let Dispatch know to have Agent Ang get ready—she's the only one from our case still at the building."

"Copy that, thanks." Marcella set the radio down. Her palms prickled with nervous sweat—knowing Ang was getting ready to back her up if needed was reassuring. She kept another car between them as Fernandez turned onto Ala Wai Boulevard, the one-way road fronting the widest part of the Ala Wai Canal.

"Uh-oh," Marcella said aloud.

Chapter 18

Marcella hung back a block as the scooter cut up onto the bike lane that ran along the edge of the canal. She lifted the radio to her lips. "Dispatch. Patch me through to Agent Ang."

"Roger that."

A *brr* of static later, "Agent Ang."

"Scott here. Following subject on scooter along bike path beside the Ala Wai. I need backup."

"Roger that. I'm on my way. What's your twenty?"

Marcella gave the cross street, Kapahulu Avenue, and put the radio down. Better safe than sorry, if Fernandez was up to something.

The scientist slowed the scooter, turning into the bumped-out area of a parklet. A bike rack under a tree, cast into shadow, obscured him as Marcella drove by at her careful pace. She radioed again.

"Subject parking scooter. Parking and pursuing on foot."

"I'm exiting the building," Ang replied. "Ten minutes out."

Marcella pulled into the nearest alley opposite the park and up onto the sidewalk. She exited the vehicle, thankful she'd put on dark sweats and running shoes in preparation for the surveillance shift. She pulled the hood of her sweatshirt up and, beeping the Honda locked, jogged back across busy Ala Wai Boulevard, even in the late evening a major artery of Waikiki.

Marcella ran with the purposeful stride of a jogger down the bike path toward the park, unobtrusively patting her pockets for her phone, checking that her weapon was unclipped in the shoulder holster under the sweatshirt, her FBI shield clipped to her waistband. She slowed as she reached the tree with the bike rack and almost cursed as she saw the scooter was chained to the rack and Fernandez nowhere in sight. She kept going, past the area, swiveling her head to see where he'd gone, oblivious to the mixed scents of plumeria and exhaust fumes.

Walking the opposite direction, head down and backpack a hunchbacked shape, was Fernandez. She jogged in a U-turn and angled across the grass, already wet with evening dew and scattered with a confetti of trash. A crazy quilt of colored light from the city scattered over the dark skin of the Ala Wai as she slowed her pace, following the cement walking path along the lip of the canal, tracking the dark figure ahead of her. She inserted her Bluetooth and speed-dialed Ang.

The other agent sounded out of breath. "Where's your radio?"

"Left it in the car. What's your twenty?"

"Just turning onto Ala Wai Boulevard."

"We're on the move, headed north on the walking path. I'll keep this open."

"Copy that."

Fernandez stopped, and Marcella slowed.

There was nowhere to go but past him, as he stood looking out at the canal. She kept her pace steady and her head down, hoping that with her hood up, he wouldn't recognize her. She passed by him, eyeballing the backpack—it looked empty but for something heavy at the bottom, forming a dip in the fabric.

She slowed once she'd passed him, moving up another fifty feet or so, then turning to face the canal. She lifted her foot against the parapet to tighten her shoelace, noticing a silver moon reflected in the water and high scudding clouds that contrasted with the yellow lights along the cement path. She slanted a glance back at Fernandez.

He had the backpack off and his arm was inside.

That couldn't be good.

She pulled her weapon, dropped into a shooting stance as he took out something that gleamed dull black in the amber light of the nearby streetlamp.

"Stop! FBI!"

Fernandez froze. The object was still in his hand, arm extended and turned to the side to toss it into the canal. He shifted, arm still out, and turned toward her. His face was white under the shock of floppy hair, his eyes shadowed holes.

"Drop the weapon on the ground. Get on your knees and put your hands on your head. Do it now!" Her voice cracked over him, a whip of authority. Fernandez belched suddenly and moved his arm—from extended over the canal to straight in front of him, the black bore of the pistol looking Marcella in the eye.

That's when she remembered she wasn't wearing a vest.

Chapter 19

Marcella's already amped-up heart rate took off to another level, and sweat burst out all over her body.

"Whore," he said, followed by a series of grunts.

"I'm going to chalk that up to stress." Marcella softened and lowered her voice, slowing down the words. Time to talk him off this ledge or they were both liable to end up dead. "Set the weapon down now and kneel and put your hands on your head and I won't shoot."

"Bitch," he said, and fired.

She felt something smack her shoulder as she pulled the trigger, the Glock's report muffled by the roar of blood in her ears. Fernandez toppled backward to land faceup on the cement.

"Report!" Ang's voice screamed in the Bluetooth in her ear. "Marcella! Are you all right? I'm on foot, almost there!"

"I'm fine," Marcella said, and then the pain hit, a feeling like a ten-ton wasp sting followed by numbness. Her arm fell to her side, and she felt the warm gush of blood, smelled its iron tang. Her head swam. "Oh. Dammit."

She dropped to her knees and set the Glock on the ground

in front of her with her good hand, then pressed her hand hard against her shoulder.

That's how they were when Ang ran up—Marcella on her knees, the Glock set neatly in front of her, blood oozing through her fingers. Fernandez on his back, the .22 pistol still in his hand—and a hole in his chest. The lights of the city reflected in his open eyes and in the black puddle spreading like a halo from beneath him.

Marcella smiled at her mother, who stopped at the door to blow a few more kisses and said for the third time, "'Cella, I can spend the night."

"No, Mama, really. I'll sleep better by myself. Thank you for everything." She waved her good arm at the balloons, flowers, and stack of baked goods beside her bed. "I'm only here until tomorrow. It's just a little nick. I told you."

"Come." Papa Gio waved at Marcella over her mother's worried frown. "We let her rest. She's going to be fine."

"Our baby was shot!" She heard her mother's wail moving away down the hall. "How can that be fine?"

Marcella closed her eyes. The pain meds were kicking in at last. The round had gone into the notch of her shoulder beneath her collarbone and stuck there, millimeters away from her shoulder joint, causing agony and near-paralysis in her left arm. Surgery to remove the bullet had taken an hour or so, and she still felt a little nauseated from the anesthesia.

After that, the stream of visitors and her frantic parents had whacked whatever stamina was left right out of her. She'd lucked out and the bed next to her was still empty. Blessed silence reigned. She pressed the button, lowered the back of the bed. Dimmed the lights.

Closed her eyes.

Strange designs in red floated across the backs of her eyelids.

Some sort of reaction to the meds? Exhaustion pulled at her, a heaviness in every limb, but she felt strangely disembodied—almost as if she could get lost in that red room.

She opened her eyes. Kamuela was standing next to the bed, looking down at her. His frown was enough to scare babies.

"You're awake," he said disapprovingly. Kamuela's hands were on his hips. His curling hair looked windblown, and his mouth was tight.

"Am I? I didn't expect to see you here. Thought there'd be a white light, angels—my dead grandma." She laughed, a dry bark. "Don't they have visiting hours? I just kicked my parents out."

He pulled a chair up next to the bed, ignoring this. "How bad is it?"

The pain meds were definitely kicking in because she blew a raspberry and her lips felt numb, which made her giggle. "Nothing big. Shoulder. Hurt like hell, but I'll be out tomorrow."

"You should have had a vest on." The line between his brows hadn't softened and neither had the hard set of his mouth.

She flipped her good hand. "It was just supposed to be surveillance. Guess I didn't really think anything as dramatic as Fernandez ditching the murder weapon would happen."

"You Feds are supposed to be all high tech and work in teams. Can't believe they let one of their best agents go out alone, no vest, no backup, after a suspect we knew was mentally disturbed."

"Hey. That was all on me. And who appointed you my big brother, anyway?" Marcella found her eyelids drooping, but she didn't want to go back into that red darkness.

"Big brother." He shook his head, a movement reminiscent of a bear shaking off a mosquito. "No way. Not that."

"Amen." She reached out with her good hand. "Come here. Kiss me." She fumbled, grasped the cotton sleeve of his shirt, tugged. Let her eyes fall shut and turned her mouth up, hungry for his.

Nothing happened. She opened her eyes. He was just looking at her.

"What's wrong?"

"I'm not going to take advantage of an injured woman addled on drugs." Kamuela reached over to grasp her good hand in his big warm one. "I want to kiss you. But when I do, it's going to be because you asked me to. In your right mind, not tanked to the eyeballs on morphine and having a postshoot urge to merge."

"Playing hard to get. It just might work." She couldn't keep her eyes open any longer. "Don't leave me. Please."

The red room behind her eyes claimed her, but before she fell into it, she thought she heard him say, "Don't you leave either."

A dull thumping of pain, a drumbeat in the darkness, dragged Marcella up from the depths. She opened her eyes, felt the cool fingertips of a nurse on her arm, the blood pressure cuff inflating.

"Hurts," she said, and coughed. Her throat was so dry.

"Here, a couple Percocet. We need to get you off the hard stuff," the overly cheerful nurse said with a smile as she handed Marcella a paper cup and a couple of tablets. Marcella took the pills, her eyes wandering until she found what she sought—Kamuela's bulk stretched out on the armchair in the corner that extended into a sleeper. His big feet, clad in athletic socks, hung at least a foot off the short "bed." A thin cotton blanket was tucked up under his chin.

"Yeah, your boyfriend's finally sleeping," the nurse said. "So cute, the way he held your hand for hours."

"Really?" Marcella felt her dry lips pulling into a smile. A ridiculous smile.

He hadn't left. He'd spent hours holding her hand.

When she fell asleep again, she was still smiling.

———————

A voice calling her name woke her up this time. Sunshine streamed in the window, insultingly bright, lighting her eyelids.

"Agent Scott." It was Waxman's voice calling her. Dammit. She'd been having a very nice dream and Waxman definitely wasn't in it.

Marcella opened her eyes, gaze going straight to the chair in the corner—empty. Waxman hove into her vision, pressed and neat, Gundersohn behind him like a barge behind a tugboat, and Rogers bringing up the rear, hidden behind an enormous bouquet of yellow roses.

"Hi, Chief," she said, wishing there were time for a few more pills before what was doubtless coming next.

"We sent your visitor out—need to do your postshooting debrief. What was Detective Kamuela doing here?"

"It's personal." Marcella felt her cheeks heat up. "We're friends."

"Uh-huh. Friends," Waxman said. "Anyway, we'll keep this short for now. So, begin at the beginning—what happened?" He set a small digital recorder on the movable bedside table. Rogers shoved the roses in among the other offerings and took up a chair beside her, lending moral support by aligning his body with hers, facing their superior.

Marcella told her version of events. Gundersohn took notes. Her throat gummed up at the end, the part where she shot Fernandez, and Rogers handed her a plastic cup of water.

"Did Fernandez make it?" He'd looked gone to her, but she wanted confirmation.

"He's lost a lot of blood, but it looks like he's going to pull through. The bullet they took out of you is a match for the one that killed Dr. Pettigrew," Rogers answered. "We can't interview him until he's out of intensive care."

"So it's over then. Fernandez was the guy."

"Looks like it," Waxman said. "We'll continue this later. I've set up your postshooting psych interview with Dr. Wilson. You two seemed to hit it off, and she's still in town. That's later today. You're on administrative leave until the investigation closes."

"Is that necessary? I'm sure I can do something for the case once I get out of here."

"You know the drill, Agent Scott." Waxman smoothed his tie, looking irritable.

"Any chance you could get that nurse in here for some more pain meds?" Marcella's face must have looked bad because Rogers hotfooted it into the hall. She was left with Waxman staring down his straight nose at her, with Gundersohn standing like a mountain behind him. The SAC clicked off the recorder, tucked it inside his immaculate jacket.

"You were out of bounds on this one." Waxman's ice-blue eyes swept over Marcella's blanched face, tumbled hair, and gapping hospital gown. "I've half a mind to write you up."

"I identified myself. I directed him to drop his weapon. I watched him decide to shoot me, and I wasn't about to die with him. As to 'going out of bounds'—I called for backup the minute he left his apartment. Not my fault Ang couldn't get there in time, and I wasn't about to let him ditch the weapon right in front of me."

"That's where you went wrong, Agent Scott. We could have retrieved the weapon from the canal and you could have taken him into custody safely when your backup arrived."

Rogers reappeared with the nurse in tow, and Waxman stood up. "We'll continue this later."

"Can't wait," Marcella said, trying for a little sass but feeling tears well up as the kindly nurse handed her the pills and a cup of water.

Gundersohn hung back for a minute. "He was upset you got shot," the big Swede said. "He doesn't like getting upset."

"I don't like getting shot either." The tears decided to spill.

She coughed to hide it, reaching for the napkin that had arrived with her lunch.

"Get well soon," Gundersohn said, making it sound like an order.

Marcella wiped her eyes with the napkin. The chopped hamburger steak swimming in brown liquid the nurse had set on the tray blurred.

"Sorry Waxman's such an ass," Rogers said. "Damn, that lunch looks bad."

"I can't do anything right for that man."

A long silence passed while Rogers got up, fussed with the flowers, turning them so they were more visible. "You like yellow roses? Beth picked them out for you, because we're from Texas and all. She and the girls are coming by later."

Marcella's heart sank. She just wanted to pull her blanket up over her head and cry, then sleep for several days—not be brave for Rogers's family. Kamuela chose that moment to return, followed by her parents. Marcella closed her eyes in misery.

"Marcella, what's the matter?" Her mother swooped in for a hug of her good shoulder, simultaneously removing the tray from in front of her. "Don't eat this terrible thing. I brought you some nice pasta." She opened one of the white cardboard containers she'd carried in and set to stirring and fluffing.

"I'm fine, just waiting for the pain meds to work." Kamuela moved to sit in one of the side chairs next to her bed with no trace of self-consciousness or explanation. He picked up her cold hand, balancing it gently on his palm because of the IV taped to the back. Rogers grinned at them from across the room, clearly pleased by this development. Papa Gio sat down on the sleeper, which had been refolded into a chair, fussing with the pleats in his pants as Anna fussed with the food, opening more containers.

"Did you guys meet each other? This is my friend Marcus

Kamuela. Marcus, Egidio and Anna Scatalina, my parents," Marcella said.

"We met," Kamuela said, smiling. He had a dimple in his left cheek. She hadn't noticed it before. "I heard some pretty interesting stories about when you were a kid."

"Marcella, she always getting herself into trouble," Anna said, tucking a napkin into Marcella's neckline and scooping up some of the pasta mixture with a fork. "Here, open up."

"I can feed myself," Marcella grumbled, but submitted. Sometimes it was easier to let her mother have her way. Besides, it felt kind of good to be waited on after her encounter with Waxman.

"So, Mr. Kamuela. How did you meet my daughter?" Papa Gio rumbled from across the room.

"I'm a detective. We met on the job. She's excellent at her work," Kamuela said, and then deliberately kissed her fingertips. "It's one of the many things I like about her."

The room went still. Marcella's mouth hung open for the next bite as her mother froze, goggling at Kamuela. Marcella closed her mouth and felt that now-familiar blush prickle across her chest and up her cheeks—she needed to say something. Rogers couldn't have grinned any wider from across the room.

"We're dating," she said to her flabbergasted parents.

"Oh," Anna said, and shoveled the bite into Marcella's mouth. "Oh! That's wonderful!" She set down the box of food. "You must be so special for our Marcella to date you!"

"Marcella, she too busy for a relationship," Papa Gio rumbled. "She not interested in babies, you know. She interested in guns."

"Mr. Scatalina, I'm too busy too. And I like guns too. As to babies…There's plenty of time for that." Kamuela winked at Marcella. She yanked her hand away, then groaned as that moved her shoulder wound.

"'Nuff already. Mama, no more food right now. I promise I'll eat more later. My stomach is upset, and I need a nap. Can you all come back in an hour or so? I hope they'll be letting me out of here soon."

"That's my cue," Rogers said. "I'll tell the family you're tuckered out. We'll come see you when you're home." He gave her a thumbs-up as he disappeared around the door.

"We'll take you home with us," Anna said, rubbing her hands together in anticipation.

"No, Mama. You know how I have trouble sleeping. I want to go home to my own house." Kamuela came back to her bedside after helping Anna set the food in the little fridge, fluff the pillows, and retuck Marcella's blankets—only then would her parents leave. By then the pills had begun to work, and she felt loose and dreamy.

"So we're dating," he said.

"Yeah. Because I could hardly tell my parents anything different. I'm in my right mind now, and I think you owe me a kiss."

He got up and went to close the door and then took the thin green curtain on its clattering rings and encircled the bed with it. Once privacy was ensured, he toed off his shoes. She giggled as he climbed up onto the bed, his thighs straddling hers under the thin blanket. She'd elevated the back of the bed to eat, and now he bracketed her body with his arms, and light bloomed in his golden-brown eyes as his lips descended to touch hers tenderly.

"There."

"More," Marcella said, and hooked her good arm around his neck to draw him down into a deep kiss. She felt his hand tunnel behind her back, lifting her into his arms as he knelt above her, and whatever pain it might have caused her shoulder was entirely drowned in the satisfaction of being so thoroughly tasted and touched.

He moved her gently over to one edge of the bed, lowered the raised back, and lay down beside her, one hand on her belly and the other one circling around the pillow at the back of her head.

She fell asleep.

Evening sunset streaked shadows across the gleaming windows of the high-rise across from hers as Marcella gingerly settled into a chair on the little deck of her apartment. The "entourage," as she called the collection of friends and parents had finally left, and only Dr. Wilson was left, bringing a bowl of the reheated pasta, plates, and a glass of water.

"Thanks for coming over to my place to talk," Marcella said. "I love my parents, but they wear me out."

"It was my pleasure." Dr. Wilson had arrived just as she was being discharged and had come along for the process. Breeze lifted the blond bell of her hair as the psychologist brushed some dust off her deck chair with a napkin and sat. "Finally have a moment to hear about the shoot."

"Thanks for hanging in there. Thought I'd never get out of that hospital."

"They're just making sure you're okay. No infections, or blood clots, or whatever."

"So did you hear anything about my shoot? What they're saying about it, whether it was justified or not?"

"Too early to know. Relax. Let the process do what it does." Dr. Wilson handed Marcella a glass of water and a plate of pasta.

"I know. I just—keep wondering if I should have handled it differently. Waxman said I should have let Fernandez ditch the weapon and brought him in alive. It just didn't occur to me. I wanted that gun."

"I'm interested in why you felt you had to retrieve the weapon right away."

"I don't know...I didn't want it to get lost. I mean, I'd just been diving in the Ala Wai, and I guess I realized how murky, muddy, and difficult it is to see in there…and that weapon is all we have tying him to the murders. The evidence would have been compromised."

"Sounds plausible, but I'm still not sold." Dr. Wilson brushed back the smooth bell of her hair with her fingertips. "There's a reason you confronted him. You wanted to take him down."

"I guess I did. But I truly didn't expect him to turn the weapon on me. Obviously, I wasn't planning for that, without a vest or anything on." Marcella sipped. "He really had two sides to him—the meek maladjusted scientist with the tics and this bold side that came out only occasionally. I guess it was the bold side that murdered."

"I'm still not sure why it had to be you who confronted him, you who tracked him even. Who was in charge of the surveillance assignments?"

"Waxman. But I volunteered to watch Fernandez. I'd surveilled him before, and honestly, of the three, he seemed the most guilty to me."

"So this was partly an intuitive feeling."

"Isn't a lot of police work? We have a feeling, we follow up on it. I bet you psychologists could say we are subliminally assessing all the time and know something we don't know consciously." Marcella dug into her pasta. Even reheated, it was delicious—she tasted fresh tomatoes and basil, and little pine nuts popped with flavor on her tongue.

"I couldn't have said it better myself." Dr. Wilson settled back. "So there was something off for you about Fernandez. The weapon ties him to Dr. Pettigrew's murder—but what about Cindy Moku?"

"There's so much that's still unanswered." Marcella looked at the sliver of indigo sea between the high-rises, the sunset twinkling in the reflective windows. "The blogs tie him to Cindy

Moku, but we'll have to see what he says when he wakes up. Still, we can probably close the case on her murder too."

"That seemed to be what your SAC was planning to do. Who else could have murdered Cindy?"

"She probably saw or heard something about Fernandez's communication with Dr. Pettigrew—and confronted him about it, thinking she could get him to come in or something. She was that kind of girl."

"A brave kind of girl." The setting sun gilded Dr. Wilson's skin with copper and gold, lit her bright blue eyes. "You two had a few things in common."

"Her death is a huge loss to her family, to the Hawaiian community. Dr. Pettigrew's death is a loss to the world, possibly. I don't know what I have in common with that."

"Your family values you tremendously. You are obviously the apple of your parents' eye. And the loss to the FBI would be tremendous if you died in the line of duty. So—why don't you value your own life a little more?"

Marcella felt her throat close. She coughed, drank a sip of water. Looked into the penetrating blue eyes of the psychologist. This was a chance to come clean a little, see if it helped her find her way forward with Kamuela—wherever that led.

"Confidentiality?"

"You got it. Nothing in my report but that you completed the interview."

"I have a problem. A sexual problem." Marcella stirred the leftover pasta for something to do with her hands. "I like sex. It's a tension reliever. And it's a bit of—a compulsion."

"So what makes this a problem? I agree this isn't the kind of lifestyle choice the Bureau would sanction, but it seems like you have been handling it in a way that makes sense for you."

"I had a boyfriend in college. He was older, one of the professors actually, and he sensed something in me, I guess. He taught me…so much." Images flashed across her brain, memories of every kind of sexual deviancy. "I tried it all. I did it all, whatever he wanted. Even the painful stuff. He got me to like it. When I finally broke away from him, I weighed ninety-seven pounds. I was battered and bruised, and I still have scars." Marcella touched the stitchery of silver threads on her breast.

"How long did that go on?"

"Almost two years."

"How did you get away from him?"

"I got my prelaw degree, and I applied for the Bureau. I told him he didn't belong in the rest of my life, and I left for Quantico. He couldn't reach me in the Bureau—I feel protected there. I've often wondered if the real reason I joined was to get away from him and from my parents."

"Seems like it filled the bill. So have you had any other long-term relationships? How long has it been?"

"No. I've dated here and there, and since I transferred to Honolulu, I've had some one-night stands. But no. I didn't want anyone getting their hooks into me."

Hooks. He'd used hooks on her one time…She shook her head briskly to clear it.

"I'm almost immediately bored by men once I go out with them. Until Marcus Kamuela. I met him at a singles club, of all things, and he…just seemed to know what I needed in bed. And even though the sex was hot, it wasn't ever degrading…I don't know how to explain it."

"I think you're explaining it just fine. Sex first, get to know you later—it's different, but you seem to be working it out."

"I don't know about that. I don't know where this is going, or if I want it to go anywhere—and yet I know I do." Marcella rocked back the cheap aluminum chair and stopped, brought up short by pain from her shoulder in its sling. "I can't trust myself. He's got to have something wrong with him. I mean, he was a member of the club too, for godsake. He's probably a sicko perv under the nice smile and cop badge. And he'll figure out I'm a sicko perv, too, and dump me."

"Aha. Well. Take it from a professional. I think he's already seen what kind of woman you are, and it isn't scaring him off." Dr. Wilson pointed to the scalloped edge of Marcella's bra peeking out from her plain white blouse. "What's that?"

"Oh." Marcella smiled, plucked the tiny white crane out. "He stuck that in my blouse when he left." She unfolded it, felt the dimple appear as she read aloud, "'I'm glad we're dating.'"

"Sounds like a real sicko perv," Dr. Wilson said.

Marcella laughed and tucked the crane back in. "I really liked waking up to him next to me in the hospital. He's something special, and I don't want to hurt him or lead him on."

"Why don't you just take it one day at a time, see where it goes?"

Marcella sighed. "Yeah. I guess I can try. That's just never been my style."

Chapter 20

Marcella woke too early and cried out as her shoulder was jarred—pain was what had woken her. She steeled herself to use her abs to lift herself into an upright position. It didn't go well because of the cushy bed.

Shaking, sweaty, and moaning, she swung her legs off the side, wondering why the hell she had sent her parents and Kamuela away. She staggered into the kitchen and ran a glass of water at the sink. At least her mother had shaken out a row of pain pills on the sill, anticipating she wouldn't be able to get the childproof cap off. Marcella scooped up two, glugged them down with the glass of water, and made her way over to her computer to check e-mail while she waited for them to work.

Her e-mail in-box was loaded, but she clicked on the red-flagged FBI notifications one first, a forward from Rogers's work e-mail: *Thought you'd want to know the BioGreen formula went live on the Internet as a free download. AgroCon is having a shit fit*. Attached was a link to a scientific blog with the formula, all Greek to Marcella. A footnote all in caps proclaimed, IN MEMORY OF DR. TRUDY PETTIGREW.

"Son of a bitch. Someone posted it. No wonder AgroCon is pissed." Marcella sat back, jarring her shoulder and emitting an inadvertent squeak.

Loverboy did a few laps around the bowl beside her computer, his version of agreement.

Marcella scrolled through the rest of her e-mail and finally felt the fuzziness of the medication. She barely made it back to bed before falling asleep.

Sunlight was a bright lance across her bed when she next woke, and this time her mother was in her room, lifting the box of tissues, the wooden bowl containing loose change and her cred wallet, and dusting the dresser. Marcella dimly remembered giving her a key to the apartment.

"Hi, Mama."

"Oh, Marcella." Her mother spun, set down the duster, came to feel Marcella's forehead with the back of her small, cool hand. "How are you today?"

"Better, I think. This is the first time I haven't woken up in pain."

"Oh good. The doctor, they say to taper off those strong pain medicines."

"I know. It's fine." Marcella's shoulder area was stiff with bandages. Her mother helped her sit up and put on the sling. Marcella shuffled to the bathroom and did her business, brushing her teeth and peering at her matted hair and puffy face in consternation. Marcus Kamuela had kissed her looking like this? Geez, the guy must have it bad.

She found herself smiling, a distinctly cat-with-canary grin— even as she felt butterflies of uncertainty. She tightened the belt of her robe and went out into the kitchen, where her mother was generating delicious smells.

Marcella took the glass of fresh-squeezed orange juice and the paper her mother handed her.

"Where's Papa?"

"At work." Anna cracked an egg into a bowl with flair. "He's at the bistro, overseeing the men working."

"Great. I'm so glad you guys found some hardy slaves to clean that kitchen." Marcella took a sip of the juice, feeling energy come back into her body with each swallow.

"Not only that. They painting, taking out the deli counter. We have another idea for that," Anna said. "So who is the family of the young man you dating?"

"Mama, I don't know. We—we just started." Marcella realized she was getting nervous over the whole thing and wondering if her reaction to Kamuela wasn't just what he'd called it, a "post-shoot urge to merge."

"Well, I want to get to know him. We have him over. I make something special."

"No, Mama. I'm not ready for that. Tell me more about the restaurant. Maybe he can come to the opening."

That got her mother going, and Anna chattered on as Marcella sank into one of the kitchen chairs. Her mind was chewing over the posting of the formula.

Who'd posted it? One of the researchers obviously—Natalie Pettigrew, while she might have access to the information, wouldn't necessarily have understood it enough to complete the abstract that described BioGreen.

So either Abed, Truman, or Kim had posted it. And she eliminated Kim because he was the one who'd sold it to AgroCon. Actually, she was betting on Truman. He'd want the formula to get the maximum exposure, and perhaps he'd done it with Natalie's blessing.

Anna had switched to Italian, describing the new decor in the bistro, a retro-chic contrast of turquoise and chocolate brown. They were doing the tables over and painting the chairs in the chocolate. They'd settled on a café-bar-type breakfast and lunch menu and planned to be open four days a week to start.

"Sounds wonderful." Marcella really was happy her parents had found a project to keep them busy and united.

Looking at the paper, with its update box on the Pettigrew murder and Fernandez shooting, a thought occurred—what if Peter Kim was in trouble now that the formula was public? He might try to flee and take the formula to Korea—though it was available free, he had experience with building the BioGreen algae and could probably get a Korean version up and growing before anyone else—and effectively dodge charges in the States.

She frowned. "Just a minute, Mama. I need to make a call. Where's my phone?" Anna pointed, and Marcella retrieved it and went out onto the little deck, closing the glass door behind her as she speed-dialed Rogers.

He didn't pick up. She left a message about her worries regarding Kim.

"Breakfast ready!" her mother fluted.

Marcella ate the omelet mechanically and was startled when Anna hung up her apron. "I have to go help your Papa. I come back and check on you later."

"Thanks, Mama." Marcella kissed her goodbye and felt surprisingly bereft when her mother slipped out the door. She headed back to the bedroom, but the worry about Kim wasn't going away. What if no one was watching him anymore and they all thought the investigation was over now that she'd taken out Fernandez?

Marcella couldn't settle to anything. It was too bad Rogers wasn't answering his phone—she had one more person she could try. She speed-dialed Sophie Ang. Still no answer. She didn't leave a message, just sat on the edge of the bed frowning. It wouldn't hurt to just go out, take a look. She just didn't feel confident about Kim. He could so easily be packing his bags, with the formula in them. She knew the building where Kim lived; it wasn't far.

She would just go and see what he was up to. She was on leave, and she didn't even have her gun and cred wallet, so this was purely a surveillance visit. Not that he needed to know that.

Marcella dressed awkwardly, brushing her hair and leaving it down, slipping on a button-up shirt, pulling up loose black rayon pants. Simple things like putting on her running shoes were impossible one-handed, so she slid on a pair of black leather mules, loaded her backup Glock into her purse, and headed for the door. Waxman held her Bureau-issued weapon and creds wallet until her shooting investigation cleared.

Loverboy charged the glass of his bowl, and for some reason that reminded her of Kamuela. She got her out phone and called him. Again, no answer.

"Hey, Marcus. I'm going by Kim's apartment. I'm worried he's going to try to run with the BioGreen formula out there in cyberspace, and I just have a feeling. Call me back."

Twinges with each step reminded her she'd been shot only a couple of days ago, so she went slowly, thinking of her mother having a fit about this little field trip. That gave her the juice to get on the elevator and take it down to the parking garage.

Driving the Honda was awkward but possible. She was thankful she had automatic shift as she had to do everything with her good right hand. She drove slowly and carefully out of the garage and up into the suburban sprawl outside the Manoa campus to Kim's apartment.

He lived in a low-rise on a side street, not far from the other interns' apartments. She pulled up into one of the stalls marked "Guest" and sat in the car, considering.

She could wait out here and surveil the building. That was what she'd thought she'd do, until someone called her back and took it further.

Or, she could go up there and see what Kim was doing. Get

an eyeball on his activities. See what he was up to, and if nothing, fine. If something, then good. She'd warn him not to leave, pretend she was on duty. After all, how would he know? And she was still armed, if awkward.

She tried Rogers again, left a message that she was outside Kim's building and planning to go up. What could be going on that he wasn't picking up? Well, she wasn't desperate enough to call Gundersohn or Waxman, so she slid the Glock into the loose pocket of the pants and got out and locked the car.

She looked up at the building. Of course Kim had to live on the third floor, and of course there was no elevator. She sighed and went up the battered aluminum stairs with their sandpaper-striped treads, stopping to pant and recover at each landing.

The shoulder didn't hurt so much as her energy was sapped.

She stood in front of Kim's door, which was weathered in sun-streaked patterns, pausing on the frayed jute WELCOME mat and thought twice. Kim was represented by the pestilential Bennie Fernandez's firm. He was bound to have it in for her after she shot his nephew, and here she was on his client's doorstep with nothing more to go on than a hunch.

She lived to piss Bennie off. Marcella stuck her finger on the bell.

Nothing happened.

She pushed it again.

Nothing happened again.

She knocked.

She heard quick footsteps, and she stepped to the side out of view of the peephole.

"Who is it?" Kim's light tenor voice. Well, good, at least he was here.

"Kelly," Marcella improvised. "I live on the floor below. I wanted to borrow some…laundry detergent."

"Don't have any," Kim snapped.

"Hey, you don't do laundry? C'mon, man," she wheedled. "I know you do."

"Okay, whatever. Just a minute." She heard the footsteps retreat. He sure was touchy for a guy being approached by a young female in his building.

Abruptly the door opened and Kim's hand protruded, holding a box of Sun laundry detergent. "Keep it."

Marcella moved forward, shoved the door in with her good shoulder. "Hello, Mr. Kim."

"Oh, it's you. Get out of my house." With surprising strength, Kim shoved on the door, knocking her back.

Marcella rallied and heaved back, groaning as her bad shoulder took some pressure. He let go abruptly, and she staggered forward into the gloom, stumbling.

Stars exploded into blackness as he hit her with something.

Chapter 21

Marcella came around slowly, to discover she was immobilized on the floor, lying on her side—unfortunately on her bad shoulder. It throbbed to the beat of her heart. Her head added more painful thumping. She took inventory with her eyes shut: Her hands were taped—she could tell by the way her palms and legs were pressed together. A slight flexing yielded no results—she was securely bound. There was tape over her mouth too.

Dammit.

She kept her breathing slow and even and cracked her eyes open.

Kim was in the final stages of packing. She must have interrupted him, because he was muttering as he threw a few more items into a bag. All she could see were his jeans-clad legs directly ahead through the bedroom door. He disappeared out of view.

She wasn't able to do anything but delay him—perhaps one of her messages would be picked up and Kamuela or Rogers would show up. It would probably be smart not to agitate him further—he'd already assaulted a Federal officer; it might not seem like much more to add murder to the list of charges. But she'd never come down on the side of cautious.

As if on cue, Kim hefted the black duffel bag and headed back toward her. She shut her eyes, staying limp as he grabbed her feet and hauled her out of the doorway.

She snapped her legs out of his hands abruptly and lashed out with all she had, getting him in the groin with a lucky kick. He doubled up with a strangled cry, backing away from her. Wriggling like a worm, she tried to move back toward the door. Delaying him. That was all that was needed; that was all she could do.

He straightened slowly, hands over his pelvic area. He narrowed his eyes with an intentness that she wished Dr. Wilson could see. His normally impassive face twisted, teeth bared, and a flush rose in his cheeks, darkening them, as his hands pulled into fists. Rage was in his face—rage and contempt. And some strange kind of dark hunger.

She saw the second he made up his mind what would come next.

Dammit. Oh shit.

It's never a good idea to kick a man in the nuts, especially when tied up. Come to think of it—she never should have come. What an idiot. Just the kind of thing her reckless friend Lei would have done. Waxman was going to have a conniption; she'd have proved him right that she was a loose cannon. Well and truly out of bounds this time. Funny, the stupid little thoughts you have before dying. "Oh shit" was the most common response to imminent death. Was that really all she could come up with?

All these thoughts and more flitted through her mind as she watched him go to his utility drawer and open it. Her breath puffed rapidly through her nose, and her eyes skittered around looking for an escape.

There wasn't one. She wriggled into the doorway anyway,

pressed up against the door as if by sheer will she could wish herself through it.

"I would have let you live, you know," he said conversationally, digging around in there. "But I feel like killing somebody for the way this ended, and it might as well be you. Handy how you got rid of Fernandez—he made such a good patsy. You get to die, knowing you shot an innocent man who didn't know what to do when he found a murder weapon in his bag." He extracted a length of half-inch white laundry cord, cut it, doubled it, snapped it between his hands before her wide, hypnotized eyes.

"Cindy couldn't believe I'd kill her either. Stupid girl called me over to tell me she knew I was spying for AgroCon. I couldn't have that. I was ready to give them the formula. It was sad actually. I hated doing it. But I won't hate doing it to you, nasty, nosy FBI bitch."

He stepped over to straddle her, and Marcella rolled and whipped her legs to the side, knocking one leg out from under him with a move she remembered from grappling with Ang. He went down with a grunt, but threw his weight on her torso, pressing down on her wound. Agony had her expelling precious air through the tape on her mouth in a high-pitched scream, the sound of a muffled teakettle. He followed up this advantage, climbing astride her and throwing the rope over her head. She bucked, and he lurched but got the rope around her neck and tightened it.

She couldn't breathe, couldn't make even a peep as the loop dug into her throat. She kept trying to buck him off. The last thing she saw was his face above her, grimly intent, before gray turned to blackness and closed in around her vision.

Chapter 22

The blackness retreated the same way it had come—slowly, peeling back to gray, forming into shapes that her brain eventually interpreted. Someone leaned down to blow into her mouth. She wanted them to stop, but her arms wouldn't move, nothing on her body was responding. The face descended again, and she saw it was Marcus Kamuela, and there were tears on his cheeks. One hit her in the eye. She blinked.

He paused, yelling, "She's awake! Rogers, she's awake!"

Matt Rogers, a knife in his hand from cutting her restraints, sat abruptly back on his ass. He dropped the knife, mashing the heels of his hands into his eyes. "Thank you, God."

Kamuela hauled her up into his arms. "Marcella. Damn you, woman."

She couldn't speak. She coughed feebly. Rogers jumped up and ran to the sink, ran a glass of water, handed it to Kamuela, who held it to her lips.

Sip, sip, sip. The water felt like ambrosia on her bruised throat. She realized her arms were free, and now pain competed—her head, her shoulder, her neck.

The door burst open for EMTs and a gurney. Marcella waved her hands impatiently, anxious to ask about Kim, but when she tried to speak, nothing came out but a croak.

"Just rest," Kamuela said. "We got him." He pointed to the couch, where Kim sat, handcuffed and bound, eyes still darkly murderous. She tried to speak again to no avail, and mimed pen and paper. Rogers went to the utility drawer and dug around, bringing a small spiral notebook and pen over even as the EMTs continued to check her over, redoing the shoulder dressing that had broken into bleeding and poking at the bump on the back of her head.

He did Cindy, Marcella wrote. *He set up Fernandez.*

"Thanks," Rogers said. "I'll talk with you later about your cowboy antics in coming here. Let's go." He hoisted Kim by the arm and hauled him to the door, where Ching had just arrived. "Got one for your holding cell."

NO HOSPITAL, Marcella printed on the notebook. *I just want to go home.*

"I can do that," Marcus Kamuela said, and hoisted her up into his arms and out of the paramedics' protesting clutches. "Let's go home."

Marcella lay without moving as she woke in the dark, checking in with her body. The aches and pains of yesterday were still there, pulse points of complaint, but minor compared to being overheated. She was downright hot, and that's what had woken her up.

A rumbling snore made her smile even as she tried to wriggle away from Kamuela's bulk. The man was so large, her cushy mattress was sagging in his direction, dragging her into his heat. She thought she'd succeeded in sidling away when a hand slid around her waist and he pulled her in beside him, the length of her bare body touching his.

Apparently he'd taken her clothes off after she'd fallen asleep under the influence of more pain medication. She sighed a little. At least she was lying on her good side. Her bare behind was tucked against his side, and by the change of his breathing, she could tell he was awake.

Something else was awake too. It was long and hard and even hotter than the rest of him, and it was just the thing to take her mind off her aches and pains.

He lay still, probably trying to be a gentleman, and in the dark she smiled as she wriggled her tush against his groin and let out a little moan as if asleep. She heard the hiss of breath past his teeth as he eased away from her, and this time she followed, arching her back to settle her rounded ass against him, stretching in mock sleep.

The hand that had pulled her in began to wander. It circled around her full breast, pinching her nipple into a puckering point, trailing down her belly, making her shudder and twitch. Gently, so gently, the hand teased at the curls over her mound, a finger sliding down into her slick warmth.

She gave up the pretense and gasped, pressing her ass back against him, lifting her knee to give him access.

"I didn't bring a condom," he said.

"It's okay. I take something," she whispered. He needed no further invitation. His fullness entered her from behind even as he worked her from in front, and she was moving against him and he into her, the early dawn filling with tiny kitten cries that seemed to be all her damaged throat could emit.

He pulled her fully against him, his powerful arm a steel band, and she held back to feel the shudder of him coming from the top of her head to the bottom of her feet. And then she let herself go, joining him in breathless oblivion.

Thank God she was on birth control, because that one would have started the next generation for sure. And man, she felt better.

She sighed, and stretched, and decided Advil was all she'd need that day—that and maybe a few more orgasms. Way better than physical therapy.

He got up first, fetching a towel from the bathroom, sliding back into bed with her and cleaning them both without words or fuss. She fell asleep again in the notch of his shoulder, and this time the warmth of his body was profound comfort.

Marcella sat on her tiny deck. Wind off the ocean fluttered her cotton robe. There was coffee, lots of it, in a hefty mug at her good hand, and Marcus was combing out her hair.

Life was good, even recovering from being strangled and shot—definitely sweeter because of it. She took a sip of coffee, closed her eyes, and let her head fall against the metal chair back, feeling the warmth of the sun on her face.

"Don't tell anybody I did this," he muttered, spritzing detangler on the damp brown tresses and working the comb gently through. They'd just got done washing her hair in the bathtub with the flexible shower head to avoid wetting her bandage, an ordeal that had left her white-faced and trembling, rethinking just Advil. Kim had hit her on the back of the head with a brass Buddha statue, leaving a goose egg.

"Ow," Marcella said as the comb tugged on the tender spot. He dropped it and backed away.

"Shit. I can't do this."

"If you don't do it now, it's going to be worse later," she said, her heart swelling at his tenderness. He would never hurt her; in fact, she knew, all the way to her bones, that somehow he'd fallen in love with her.

Tears, falling off his face into her eyes, had told her that.

He picked up the comb and continued as she relaxed, checking in with herself about this new revelation. It didn't seem like such a bad thing. Her usual phobia didn't seem to be rearing its ugly runaway reflex. In fact, she wondered if she might be a little in love too. How had that snuck up on her?

"I got the tangles out." He sounded triumphant. "Now I'm going to switch to the brush. It helps it dry nice without getting frizzy. My sisters used to do it that way."

"You have sisters?"

"Two. Older than me. They'd be laughing their asses off to see me now." The brush slid effortlessly through her hair. Swish, swish. She closed her eyes in pleasure.

"No, they wouldn't. They might tease you a little, that's all." She felt confident of this—she pictured his sisters, tall, sturdy, competent women with dimples and big smiles. She wanted to meet them someday.

"All done." He sat in the other chair beside her, picked up his mug. He took his coffee loaded with sugar and cream.

"Thanks for helping with my hair." She took a breath. "I'm dying to know. What's going on with Kim?"

"He refused to listen to Bennie Fernandez. Wanted to tell us all about how he shot Dr. Pettigrew when she realized someone was stealing information from the project—then set Fernandez up with the gun, figuring he was a good stool pigeon who'd crumble under pressure and do something stupid—which is exactly what he did. Cindy was going to blow the whistle on him, so he killed her and tried to make it look like a suicide—but planted some of Fernandez's hairs and trace on her for insurance, and he knew Abed had a thing for her, so he pointed the finger at him too."

Marcella frowned. "What about the blogs?"

"He did those to frame Fernandez," Kamuela said. "He posted them from Fernandez's usual workstation as part of the frame-up. He did that again while we were surveilling but then decided to go around and pick up all the notes and get busted. He was such a bumbling criminal, he actually threw us off."

"Yeah, I just chalked him up as a thief. He didn't really cover his tracks. I mean, those deposits, trying to steal the lab books and letting us catch him at that?" Marcella shook her head. "Amateur hour."

"It appears he's studied our system. He thought we'd write him off as a thief, which is exactly what we did, and he wouldn't get more than a slap on the wrist, and that after AgroCon paid him. He chose well when he set up Fernandez."

Marcella's hand shook as she sipped her coffee. "Jarod Fernandez was innocent and I shot him."

"But he shot you first. You didn't have a choice." He wouldn't let her look away. It was time to find out a little more.

"Listen, I've been meaning to ask you—do you still belong to the Club?" She took a sip of her coffee to disguise her nervousness.

"No. I quit after you dumped me."

"I quit then too." Their eyes met. The wind ruffled her clean, shiny, soft, well-brushed hair.

"So why'd you belong?"

"You first," he said, eyes on his mug.

"Okay. I had a bad relationship in college. He kind of—burned me for other men. Then I was busy with the Bureau, and sometimes I just wanted to get laid, without all the hassles and games, you know?"

"I do." He nodded. "And that's exactly why I went. Between my mama and my sisters, it's been nothing but setups and 'oh you'd like my friend Kelly's cousin' for years now. I wasn't ready to settle down, and I was sick of fending off all the family matchmaking. I just wanted to go somewhere and not be me. Just be some guy, any guy, and get laid. My family is such a big deal. You haven't met them yet—but it's going to be interesting." His voice went heavy with dread.

"You've met my parents. How much worse could it be?" Marcella turned to smile over her shoulder at him. "I'm Italian. I'm from Jersey. I can handle a few Hawaiians."

"There are more than a few," Marcus said darkly. He set his mug down, got up to stand in front of her. "Let's go inside."

He was wearing her other robe, a plain white terry cloth that barely covered his knees, and the belt looked like it was going to come undone any minute, an intriguing prospect.

"Why? I like it out here," she whispered, and reached out to give the belt a tweak. Sure enough, it came undone. She gave another tug, and he took another step forward to stand between her knees.

His hands in her hair weren't as gentle this time as she took him in her mouth, or when he knelt between her thighs and grasped her knees, or when they finally rolled onto the carpet in the living room and he looked into her eyes from above.

No masks or games or scars separated them, and Marcella was surprised at how good it all was.

Marcella looked around the gaily decorated, newly repainted interior of Café Italiano. Through the half window she could see her mother, a tiny figure dwarfed by a chef's hat, manning the great gleaming steel stove, surrounded by several minions. Her father, dapper in a tuxedo shirt, bow tie in Hawaiian print, and black trousers, gestured Marcella and Kamuela in.

"Welcome to the grand opening celebration of Café Italiano." He escorted them through the tables to one directly in front of the kitchen window. "Your mama, she want to see you while she cooking."

"Of course, Papa. I feel bad we're taking up space on this special day."

"You the guests of honor!" Anna Scatalina darted through the swinging doors, and she hugged Marcella, careful to avoid her bad shoulder, though a week after the hospital, Marcella was no longer wearing the sling. "Welcome, 'Cella! Welcome, Marcus!"

"Aloha, Mrs. Scatalina." Kamuela reached down to give her

mother a hug, lifting her off the ground and knocking her chef's hat back. "So glad to be here on this special day."

"So, Papa. I see we're at a six-top. Don't you need this table for more people?" Marcella settled herself in one of the newly repainted curve-back chairs. She'd benefited from lots of bed rest, "physical therapy" and a lemon-honey throat concoction Dr. Wilson had dropped by.

"They coming now, I see," Papa said, and cut a swath through the restaurant to lead Waxman, Gundersohn, Rogers, and Ang back to their table. "On the house today," he said magnanimously, handing around menus.

"Hey." Marcella grinned. "Welcome to Café Italiano."

"Wouldn't have missed it, Little Shit," Rogers said with a wink. She narrowed her eyes at him as Waxman took his seat two over from her, smoothing his tie with his usual dignity.

"The mystery of Marcella's last name is cleared up," he said, opening his menu. "I for one support her decision to shorten that colorful moniker."

"Thank you, sir," Marcella said. "I thought Scott was just easier."

"On that we agree." They ordered, and Waxman was the first to raise his water glass. "To Agent Scott. Good health and good hunting."

"Hear, hear!" the rest chimed in, and they all sipped their beverages.

Papa Gio, newly wreathed in a ginger lei, escorted another party, five large Hawaiians, to the six-top next to them.

Kamuela stood up in shock. "Mama! What you doing here?"

"Your friend, she invited us." Marcus's mother, majestic in a purple muumuu trimmed in velvet, took Marcella's hand in hers. "My son speaks highly of you." Mrs. Kamuela's smile was wide and white, just as Marcella had imagined.

"As he does of you," Marcella said. "Thanks so much for joining us on our opening day. It's a big deal to come over from Maui."

Marcus's mouth still hung ajar in surprise to see his relatives as Marcella greeted, hugged, and "talked story" with his sisters and their husbands. The Kamuelas eventually got settled next to the FBI table.

"How'd you do this?" Marcus hissed, when his relatives were occupied with their menus.

"I looked through your cell for the most-called number. Next down from mine, it was hers." Marcella gestured toward his mother. "She's lovely."

"She's just all impressed with your parents owning a restaurant," he muttered, but the red on his neck and the dimple in the wall of his cheek told her how tickled he was that she'd invited them.

"Anyway, I'm told there's something even more exciting we're here for," Waxman said. Their food arrived, and in the general hubbub of tasting and commenting, Marcella almost forgot what he'd said until her father wheeled a large TV mounted on a rolling cart over to their table, getting Ang involved with checking the feeds to a VCR underneath. With a flourish, Papa Gio turned it on.

The grainy picture showed a ceremony of some kind. A draped stage, a podium, a row of brightly colored international flags in the background, red and green tones overly bright on the old TV. A man with a white beard said something. Ang turned up the volume on the dial:

"We are very excited this year to announce the nominees for the Nobel Prize for chemistry."

Marcella frowned, turned to Waxman. "What's this about?"

"Watch and see."

She turned back, taking a bite of the delicious gnocchi her mother had whipped up, refocusing on the aged screen.

The narrator droned on with names and obscure titles of projects. "Nominated for the discovery of the structural and mechanistic studies of ion channels." After each name and project title, he shook the hand of whichever scientist toddled up to the podium and handed them a scroll documenting the nomination.

Marcella took another bite and then paused, mouth ajar, as the narrator said, "And a nomination goes to Dr. Ron Truman of the University of Hawaii for work in the discovery of protein binding in photosynthesis." Stepping up to the podium were a couple this time—Dr. Handsome Truman and beside him, slim as a whippet and just as nervous-looking, Natalie Pettigrew.

They solemnly shook hands with the announcer, and Truman leaned in to the microphone. "This nomination really belongs to Dr. Trudy Pettigrew." He shook his scroll toward the ceiling. "You deserved this, Dr. P."

Natalie threw her arms around him in a hug, and the room burst into a little stronger applause. Apparently the gift of BioGreen was not going unnoticed by the world.

"Just thought you'd enjoy seeing that," Waxman said, busying himself with a salad decorated with strips of marinated flank steak. Marcella looked at her plate of pasta and blinked rapidly.

"Thanks. I did. Not much left of that lab team—but at least it looks like Truman and Natalie are having a happy ending."

"And so are we," Marcus Kamuela said, and in full view of her coworkers, his family, and her parents, he tipped her chin up and kissed her.

Acknowledgements

From the time she appeared in Torch Ginger, Marcella Scott demanded her own book. I wrote *Stolen in Paradise* in a four month blaze beginning in November 2011, a particularly tough time personally with my husband having a major operation. I distinctly remember the hospital staff wheeling him away to surgery, and opening my laptop. . . and disappearing into Marcella's Honolulu for the rest of the day, moving from waiting room to waiting room, ending up beside his bed still writing. We stayed in Waikiki in a condo right above where I set the Scatalinas' restaurant. I enjoyed the dragon boats, the fireworks at the Hilton, and walked in Ala Moana Park each morning. I fell a little in love with downtown in spite of the circumstances that brought us there.

I also wrote this book to enter my daughter's world and understand it better. She's a scientist at Stanford, and I found myself fascinated with the "world of the lab." Insular, hierarchical, yet often functioning like a family of oddball brilliant people, I saw a hotbed of intrigue waiting to happen! I trailed my daughter around her lab with my camera and notebook, taking notes and learning about fascinating new things like "lab books" where everything on a project is hand-recorded. (Who knew?)

Marcella's got some scars, but she's not as damaged as her friend Lei and it doesn't take her as long to recognize a good thing when it smooches her on those perfect lips. Marcella is the kind of woman you love to hate— effortlessly gorgeous, fashionable, funny, sexy and confident. I wrote her as a foil for Lei, and she continues to fulfill that function—while showing herself to be her own unique, badass heroine with a tender side. (A sort of female James Bond, to my mind.)

I want to thank my circle of amazing beta readers: Noelle Pierce, Greta Van Der Rol, Holly Robinson, Bonny Ponting, Ilima Loomis. Thanks also to my editor, Kristen Weber, and my new writer friend Shannon Wianecki, who listened to my freakout the morning the manuscript came back, finished, from the copyeditor and the GMO demonstrations were all over the news in Hawaii. I realized the timing was going to be interesting on the release of the book and I needed to do some revisions, and I was nervous as heck. (I'm not going to tell you what those revisions were!)

Thanks to my amazing family, especially my daughter Tawny Neal whose world of the lab is a fascinating subculture I was privileged to briefly share. Thanks also to retired Captain David Spicer, who read the manuscript for "cop accuracy" and saved Marcella from warrants vs. subpoenas and nonregulation gold sandals. My FBI world is fictional, including the goofy Conference Room A, so please bear with my mistakes—which would have been worse without David's important feedback.

I hope you end up rooting for Marcella and Marcus and their ongoing role in the Lei Crime Novels. As always, your reviews on Amazon and elsewhere matter a LOT—so let me know what you think. I read them. Every one.

Much aloha!
Toby Neal, April 2013

Watch For These Titles

The Lei Crime Series

Blood Orchids (book 1)

Torch Ginger (book 2)

Black Jasmine (book 3)

Broken Ferns (book 4)

Twisted Vines (book 5)

Companion Series

Stolen in Paradise: a Lei Crime Companion Novel

Unsound: a Lei Crime Companion Novel

Middle Grade/Young Adult

Path of Island Fire

Sign up for email updates on new releases at

TobyNeal.net

CPSIA information can be obtained at www.ICGtesting.com
Printed in the USA
BVOW08s0240220716

456451BV00003B/44/P